STORIES MY GRANDFATHER TOLD ME

Memorable tales arranged
according to the weekly *Sidrah*

(BEREISHIS / בראשית)

by
Zev Greenwald

Translated from the Hebrew *Maasei Avoseinu* by
Libby Lazewnik

Illustrations by
Tova Katz

question: The entire *perek,* both before and after this verse, deals with Hashem's greatness. Why, then, did David *Hamelech* pause to insert the words, "How wondrous are Your creations, Hashem," in the midst of all the praise?

With clear emotion and tremendous enthusiasm, the teacher offered his own explanation. "David *Hamelech,*" he said, "was so overcome with emotion as he listed Hashem's praises that he reached a point where he could not contain himself a moment longer. With fullness of his heart, he exclaimed, 'How wondrous are Your creations, Hashem!' Only after this heartfelt outburst was David *Hamelech* able to continue with his list of praises."

Hearing this, the eavesdroppers at last saw the teacher's greatness and began to understand their Rebbe's high opinion of him.

Drafted for the Shabbos

וַיְכַל אֱלֹקִים בַּיּוֹם הַשְּׁבִיעִי מְלַאכְתּוֹ אֲשֶׁר עָשָׂה

And He abstained on the seventh day from all His work which He had done.

(Bereishis 2:2)

In the year 5620 (1860), a vast army of soldiers camped in and around the city of Horodna, and established a large military camp. Among the soldiers were many Jews who were forced to work on Shabbos and the Jewish holidays.

When the *tzaddik,* R' Nachum of Horodna, heard about the plight of these Jewish soldiers, he was greatly saddened. He decided to ask his friend, R' Alexander Moshe Lapidus, who was then serving as Rav of a nearby town, to join him in seeking an audience with the company commander. They would ask the commander to let the Jewish soldiers desist from all work on Shabbos and the holidays.

R' Alexander Moshe agreed to accompany R' Nachum and together, the two went to see the military leader.

As Rabbi Lapidus spoke, he pointed to R' Nachum. "Sir, you see beside me a holy and righteous man. He has come here to ask a favor of you: Allow the Jews among your troops to rest on the Sabbath and our holy days."

Bereishis / 15

Upon hearing R' Alexander Moshe's words, the commander grew visibly excited. "I am fortunate that you have brought a holy man here. Perhaps he can find a way to cure my only daughter, who has lain sick for many days now. The doctors can not heal her. If you are successful, I will do as you ask. You have my word!"

"This we cannot do!" Rabbi Lapidus burst out. "Are we to take G-d's place?"

But R' Nachum whispered in his ear, "*Hakadosh Baruch Hu* can do it!" And before the commander could react to Rabbi Lapidus' words, R' Nachum asked to see the sick girl.

The girl lay in bed, very ill indeed. R' Nachum gazed at her for a moment, then went to stand in a corner of the room. Lifting his eyes heavenward, he prayed, "Master of the Universe! In the merit of your holy Shabbos and Your holy festivals, heal this girl, so that all the nations may know that you are the L-rd of all the world — and that life and death are in Your Hands!"

The two righteous men then turned to the commander. "We have done what we can. Hashem, in His mercy, will send a complete cure to your daughter."

That same day, the girl opened her eyes and asked for something to eat. A few days later, she had recovered completely from her long illness.

A week had passed when an elegant coach pulled up outside R' Alexander Moshe's home.

A messenger descended from the coach, entered the house, and asked the Rabbi to return with him to see the company commander. The Rabbi sent for R' Nachum, and together the two returned to the army base.

The commander greeted them with joy and honor. He led them into his daughter's room. The little girl was playing with her toys as though she had never had a day's illness in her life.

"Welcome, Rabbis of Israel!" the commander cried. "As you can see, your prayers have been answered, and my daughter is fully recovered. Every doctor who treated her despaired of finding a cure, yet you did it. You have given life to the person dearest to me in the world!

"And now," he continued, "I will keep my end of the bargain. I will do as you have asked. From this day on, the Jewish soldiers will be exempt from all duties on the Sabbath and the Jewish holidays!"

Shabbos in the Chofetz Chaim's Home

וַיְבָרֶךְ אֱלֹקִים אֶת יוֹם הַשְּׁבִיעִי וַיְקַדֵּשׁ אֹתוֹ
G-d blessed the seventh day and sanctified it
(Bereishis 2:3)

Leib, a 14-year-old boy, studied in a small yeshivah in Russia. On one occasion, he was due to return home for a visit. The train was scheduled to reach his station on Thursday afternoon. He would board there and travel to his home in Stuchin, Poland. Even if the train ran exactly on schedule, Leib knew that he would arrive home just hours before Shabbos.

As it turned out, the train did not arrive at the station until Thursday evening. By the time Leib had boarded, darkness had fallen. By Friday morning he knew he would never reach Stuchin before Shabbos. He would have to find another place in which to spend the holy day.

Leib asked a conductor for a list of the stations where the train was due to stop. He had decided that if he recognized one of the stops as a place where Jews lived, he would get off the train, in the hopes that someone would invite him home for Shabbos. To his joy, the conductor informed him that one of the cities was very close to Radin. Leib was quite excited at this news, because his aged great-uncle, the Chofetz Chaim, lived in Radin. Leib's grandfather was the Chofetz Chaim's brother. It looked as though he would be able to spend Shabbos at the home of his illustrious relative.

When the train came to his stop, Leib gathered his belongings and got off the train. He asked passersby the way to Radin, and quickly made his way to his great-uncle's house. His arrival was greeted with joy by the Rebbetzin. She explained that her husband had already left for shul, adding that, as a rule, the Chofetz Chaim, as the Rav, went to shul early in order to learn with some of the congregants before *davening*. She advised Leib to rest a bit before going to shul.

Having spent the entire previous night awake on the swaying train, Leib was exhausted. He fell asleep immediately.

Upon awakening, the first thing he saw was the Chofetz Chaim seated at his Shabbos table, learning from a *sefer*. His uncle welcomed

Bereishis / 17

him warmly, then suggested that the boy wash his hands and *daven* *Kabbalas Shabbos* and *Ma'ariv,* after which they would eat the Shabbos meal together.

When Leib had finished *davening,* the Chofetz Chaim summoned his wife to join them at the table. The Chofetz Chaim made *Kiddush,* and the three of them — the aged rabbi, his wife, and the 14-year-old youth — sat down to their Shabbos feast.

When the meal was over, the Chofetz Chaim excused himself and went to his room to sleep.

Leib prepared himself for bed as well. He tried to fall asleep again but to no avail. At last, he rose and went into the kitchen, where a clock stood on a shelf. Leib looked at it to check the time, then rubbed his eyes in disbelief. The clock appeared to be functioning and yet it showed 4 o'clock! How could it be 4 in the morning already? Shaking his head in bewilderment, Leib returned to his bed.

When he awoke in the morning, he again went into the kitchen, where this time, he found the Rebbetzin.

"Good Shabbos," he began. Then he asked her the question that had been troubling him. "Last night, after the meal, I couldn't fall asleep right away. I went into the kitchen, and saw that the clock showed that it was 4 in the morning! Does the clock work properly? What time did we finish the meal last night?"

"It was very late when we finished," she answered.

"But the meal didn't last that long! What time did we sit down to eat? Did I sleep so long when I first came?"

"I'll tell you what happened," replied the Rebbetzin. "When the Rav returned from shul, you were in a very deep sleep. I wanted to wake you so that you could hear *Kiddush,* but my husband stopped me. He said that you were tired from your long journey, and advised me to let you sleep. He said that he would wait, and make *Kiddush* when you woke up.

"When some time had passed, not wanting to make me wait any longer, he asked our son Aharon to make *Kiddush* so that my son and I could eat our meal. Meanwhile, my husband sat and learned, waiting for you to wake up. We agreed that he'd call me when you did, and that we would sit down together to the Shabbos meal, in your honor."

The Rebbetzin added, "You slept for hours, but the Rav was determined not to start the Shabbos meal without you!"

Had Leib not asked his question, neither the Chofetz Chaim nor his wife had planned to say a word about their extraordinary behavior that Shabbos night!

In the Merit of Welcoming Shabbos Early

וַיְבָרֶךְ אֱלֹקִים אֶת יוֹם הַשְּׁבִיעִי וַיְקַדֵּשׁ אתו

"G-d blessed the seventh day and sanctified it"

(Bereishis 2:3)

R' Simchah Kaplan, Chief Rabbi of Tzefas, related the following story:

When I was learning in the yeshivah in Mir, I lived with a couple who had only one son. One Friday, as I was leaving for the yeshivah, I saw the man of the house preparing to leave for the city's marketplace to transact some business. As the man was on his way out, I heard his wife say, "It's *erev Shabbos;* come home early!"

When I returned from the yeshivah that afternoon, I came upon the woman standing at the window, looking out for her husband's return. She kept repeating over and over in an anxious tone, "It's almost Shabbos, it's almost Shabbos…"

Surprised, I exclaimed, "But there's still plenty of time. Shabbos won't be here for hours!"

Hesitantly, she replied, "Let me tell you a little about our life, and you will understand my worry.

"For many years after we were married," she continued, "we were childless. Then, *Baruch Hashem,* after years of suffering, we were finally blessed with a son. But to our sorrow, he was not developing properly. We suffered a great deal as we struggled to find out what was wrong with our son. The city's physician told us that the child had a defect in his heart. He advised us to travel to Vilna, to a prestigious doctor who lived there.

"After examining the boy and performing various tests, the great doctor told us that our son would not survive more than a few years. 'There is no medicine for his illness,' the doctor said. 'Go home, and make peace with this reality.'

"Shattered and brokenhearted, we left the doctor's home. Our stumbling footsteps brought us to an inn, where I burst into bitter tears and could not be consoled. The other residents of the inn heard our trouble and told us that on the way home to Mir, it would be worth our while to stop at Radin, home of the Chofetz Chaim. 'Go to him,' they advised, 'and you will surely be helped!'

"We traveled immediately to Radin, only to lose hope once again as we learned that the Chofetz Chaim was very weak and unable to see anyone! As we stood there, dispirited, Heaven helped us: We met a young man, a husband of one of the Chofetz Chaim's granddaughters. This man had studied at the Mirrer Yeshivah and had lived for a time at our house. Here was a clear case of 'Cast your bread upon the waters, for most days you will find it...' He took us into his grandfather's room. The Chofetz Chaim was sitting in his chair, a *sefer* in hand.

"We sat down and related the story of our son's illness. The Chofetz Chaim asked, 'How can I help? I have no money; how else can I be of help to you?'

"I burst into inconsolable tears as I related my story. His grandson added, 'And this is an only child!'

"In a warm voice, the Chofetz Chaim said to me, 'My daughter, undertake to greet the Shabbos Queen early.' When I asked what he meant, he replied, 'By noon on Friday, let the Shabbos tablecloth be spread on the table, the candlesticks arranged on it, and from candlelighting time do not do any work, come what may!'

"As the words left the Chofetz Chaim's mouth, the resolution formed in my heart to follow his instructions to the letter.

"As soon as we returned to Mir. we saw an improvement in our son. Little by little, he began to eat. He started to develop and look like other boys his age. We visited our doctor and he was astonished by what he saw. Unable to conceal his amazement, he asked us to return to Vilna, and even financed the trip to the doctor in Vilna.

"Upon our arrival in Vilna, the doctor examined our son once again.

"'Are you trying to pull a fast one on me?' he demanded. 'This is a different child; not the one I examined just a short time ago!'

"We told him: 'He is our only child!'

"The doctor asked, 'Have you been to Vienna?' (Vienna was then a world-class center of medicine.)

"'No,' we answered.

"'Then where?'

"'We went to see the Chofetz Chaim,' we told him, 'and he gave us his advice...'

"The doctor was very moved, and he said, 'We physicians have the power to fix what exists. We see a defective heart, we try to repair it. But the Chofetz Chaim is able to heal without any material to work with!' He shook his head, and added to the parents, 'Now I can tell you that your son's heart was completely deteriorated. It was essentially gone...'"

The good woman of the house concluded softly, "From that day to this, we complete all of our Shabbos preparations very early. That is why I'm worried about my husband's lateness in returning home."

A Taste of Gan Eden

וַיִּטַּע ד' אֱלֹקִים גַּן בְּעֵדֶן מִקֶּדֶם וַיָּשֶׂם שָׁם אֶת הָאָדָם אֲשֶׁר יָצָר

"Hashem G-d planted a garden in Eden, to the east, and placed there the man whom He had formed."

(Bereishis 2:8)

It was the custom of R' David of Lelov to travel to his friend's home in a nearby village, so that the two might travel together to see the Chozeh of Lublin. R' David's friend lived in great poverty. When R' David arrived, the friend hurried to inform his wife, and bade her to hurry to prepare a meal in honor of their special guest.

The good woman was very distressed. There was nothing in the house, not even wood with which to make a cooking fire. All she had on hand was a little flour. How in the world was she to prepare a meal?

She did what she could. Running out into the nearby forest, she gathered a few wood chips and twigs for a fire. Then she rolled the flour with just water, having no oil or spices. Then she cooked it. This was the meager meal that she served the two *tzaddikim*. After they had eaten, the two men departed for Lublin.

When R' David returned to his own home, he told his wife, "At my friend's house in the village, I was served something that truly had the taste of *Gan Eden*!"

The Rebbetzin, knowing how far her husband was from reveling in the pleasures of this world, was so struck by this remark that she hurried to the village to ask the woman how she had prepared the meal that R' David had so lavishly praised.

The woman told her how little she had had to work with — just a bit of flour. She had had nothing in the house to lend flavor to the dish, but as she had prepared it, she had prayed: "Master of the Universe, you know that I would not hold back any delicacy in honor of this *tzaddik*. But what shall I do? I have nothing in the house — but You, Master of the Universe, have *Gan Eden*. Please, put some flavor of *Gan Eden* into the meal I am preparing, so that the *tzaddik* will enjoy it." She had enjoined Hashem's help in this way, all through her task.

"Apparently," the woman ended, smiling, "Hashem heard my prayer. That's why the *tzaddik* tasted the flavor of *Gan Eden* in the simple food that I served him!"

Bread for the Hungry Scholar

וְעֵץ הַחַיִּים בְּתוֹךְ הַגָּן

Also the Tree of Life in the midst of the garden

(Bereishis 2:9*)*

During World War I, the Chofetz Chaim moved his yeshivah from Radin to a small town in the Chernigov region. With the outbreak of the Bolshevik Revolution, the town became desolate. There was no food to be found. The yeshivah students became the first ones to suffer.

One Shabbos afternoon, the Chofetz Chaim was returning from shul after *Minchah* when he encountered the local commissar, Archik. Archik was a known Bolshevik, who had once studied in yeshivah. Archik recognized the Chofetz Chaim.

"Good Shabbos!" the Chofetz Chaim greeted him.

"For me, Shabbos is a day like any other," the commissar replied.

"*Nu, nu*, so be it," the Chofetz Chaim said. "All days belong to *Hakadosh Baruch Hu*.

The two went on to chat about different matters. Finally, the

Chofetz Chaim asked, "Would you like to hear a few words of Torah?"

"No!" Archik answered vehemently. "Torah and me? I am very far removed from all of that!"

The Chofetz Chaim calmed him down, but did not give up. "But perhaps, in spite of this, you'll be so kind as to listen?"

Archik reluctantly agreed.

"The Torah says that when *Hakadosh Baruch Hu* planted *Gan Eden*, He placed the Tree of Life in the center of the garden. Why did He place it in the center? Why not in a corner of the garden? He did this so that everyone would have access to the Tree of Life, each according to his abilities; one in Torah, another in piety, and a good-hearted fellow, like you, in good deeds. Know, Archik, that yeshivah students are dying of hunger. Tell *your world* it is their job to come and buy them a little food!"

With those words, the two parted ways.

A short time later, as the Chofetz Chaim was singing "*Hamavdil*" at the close of the Shabbos, a wagon pulled up in front of the yeshivah. It was loaded with sacks of flour for the yeshivah boys.

The Eternal Question

וַיִּקְרָא ד׳ אֱלֹקִים אֶל הָאָדָם וַיֹּאמֶר לוֹ אַיֶּכָּה

Hashem G-d called out to the man and said to him, "Where are you?"

(Bereishis 3:9)

When R' Shneur Zalman of Liadi was arrested by the Russian authorities, one of his interrogators visited his cell, interested in discussing Judaism with R' Shneur Zalman.

"Tell me," the interrogator questioned, "what is the meaning of the question, 'Where are you?' that G-d asked the first man? Didn't G-d know where Adam was?"

R' Shneur Zalman answered with a question of his own: "Do you believe that our Torah is eternal?"

"Yes," answered the interrogator.

The Rebbe went on to explain, "Hashem asks every person, 'Where are you?' What is your place in your world? Every person is created with a specific purpose. You are already this many years old (and R' Shneur Zalman specified the interrogator's exact age). What have *you* done in those years? Have you fulfilled the purpose that was given to you?"

The man was deeply moved by the depths of this idea, and stunned at the uncanny accuracy with which the Rebbe had quoted his age. This, surely, was a genuine man of G-d. From that moment on, the interrogator struggled valiantly to ensure the Rebbe's release from prison.

A Good Deed for a Bad

וַיֹּאמֶר הָאָדָם הָאִשָּׁה אֲשֶׁר נָתַתָּה עִמָּדִי הִוא נָתְנָה לִי מִן הָעֵץ וָאֹכֵל

The man said, "The woman whom You gave to be with me —
she gave me of the tree, and I ate."

(Bereishis 3:12)

Here he was ungrateful.

(Rashi)

One day, R' Nachum of Horodna paid a visit to the home of a Jewish attorney who had distanced himself from other Jews and from Judaism. R' Nachum had come seeking donations for the needy, but the man's heart was as hard as stone.

When the attorney saw R' Nachum, he began reviling and cursing him. He screamed, "Who asked you to go wandering from door to door seeking donations? I won't give you a thing!"

Shamed, R' Nachum turned and left the house without a word.

Not long afterward, trouble fell upon the attorney. He was accused of antigovernment activity, arrested, and sentenced to two years' imprisonment. His wife tried in every way she could to win her husband's freedom. She hired well-known lawyers to prove her husband's innocence, but their efforts were in vain. The attorney's conviction was confirmed by the highest court, and he was sent to prison to serve his sentence.

While her husband languished in jail, the wife lost all their possessions and was left with nothing. She lacked even bread to give

Bereishis / 25

her children. Word of the family's plight reached R' Nachum's ears, and he hurried immediately to see the woman.

"Can I help you?" he asked.

Seeing him, the woman burst into bitter tears. "How can you help me? My husband is condemned to sit in prison for two years, while my children and I are starving. I gave all our savings to the lawyers. We don't even have enough food for one more day!"

R' Nachum offered words of encouragement. "Do not worry. Hashem, Blessed is He, will send help. How much do you need in order to feed your family for a week?"

"T-twenty-five rubles," the woman stammered in astonishment.

"Here are twenty-five rubles for now, as a loan. Go buy what you need for yourself and your children!" R' Nachum strongly advised her not to sell her apartment or her furniture, nor to neglect the children's education. She was to conduct her affairs bravely and vigorously, as she had done up until then.

From that day on, R' Nachum visited the woman each and every week, always bringing twenty-five rubles with him. He entered the house quickly and quietly, and left the same way, so that no one would catch a glimpse of him. He continued in this way to support the family for two whole years.

When his two-year prison term was over, the attorney was released from prison and he returned home. He found his family well, carrying on their lives as usual. The same attractive apartment, children who appeared healthy and well fed — as though nothing had happened to change their lives at all!

Incredulous, the man asked, "How have you managed to maintain our home? Who has been supporting you?"

"The same man who goes from door to door collecting donations for charity — he is the one who has supported me in my distress," his wife answered. "Each week, he has brought me twenty-five rubles. Without him, who knows what our end might have been!"

Hearing this, the attorney's eyes began to stream with tears. He ran out of his house and dashed directly over to R' Nachum's house. He fell at the *tzaddik's* feet, imploring forgiveness for the misery and pain he had caused him when he had come asking for a donation. He expressed his heartfelt gratitude to R' Nachum for all that he had done for his family, and promised to repay the debt out of the very first income he made.

From that day on, the attorney was a changed man. He returned to his people with all his heart, and always remained open and available for everything that was good.

In Hot Pursuit

בְּזֵעַת אַפֶּיךָ תֹּאכַל לֶחֶם
By the sweat of your brow shall you eat bread
(Bereishis 3:19)

R' Levi Yitzchak of Berditchev saw a Jew rushing through the marketplace. The *tzaddik* asked him, "Why are you running so fast?"

"I am running after my livelihood," the man replied.

"But how do you know," R' Levi Yitzchak asked, "that your livelihood is in front of you, so that you must run after it? Perhaps it is located behind you, and you are actually running away from it all ..."

Hashem's Business

בְּזֵעַת אַפֶּיךָ תֹּאכַל לֶחֶם
By the sweat of your brow shall you eat bread
(Bereishis 3:19)

R' Levi Yitzchak of Berditchev once saw a man walking quickly, seemingly very preoccupied with his affairs. The *tzaddik* stopped him and asked, "What is your business, Reb Yid?"

"I have no time to talk now," the man answered breathlessly.

R' Levi Yitzchak persisted, "Just tell me, what is your business?"

"Please, honored Rebbe, do not delay me now! I am very pressed for time because of my various business affairs."

Still the *tzaddik* held him back. "I understand, your affairs are pressing upon you. You have many business matters on your mind. But I am not asking about all those things. I ask only one question: What is your business?"

The other man looked at him in astonishment — utterly bewildered.

R' Levi Yitzchak explained, "The affairs you are so busy with are all for Hashem's sake. Your purpose, after all, is to sustain the life which Hashem has given you. But your income is Hashem's business. Your business is only to fear and serve Him!

"In that case," R' Levi Yitzchak concluded, "why are you abandoning your sole business to run after Hashem's?"

Why Are You Running?

בְּזֵעַת אַפֶּיךָ תֹּאכַל לֶחֶם
By the sweat of your brow shall you eat bread

(Bereishis 3:19)

R' Levi Yitzchak of Berditchev once climbed up on the roof of his house, which was located in the center of the marketplace, and called aloud: "Jews! Seeds of a holy nation. Remember why you are running and where you are running to. You remember everything... except your Creator. *He* is forgotten!"

The Favor

הֲלוֹא אִם תֵּיטִיב שְׂאֵת וְאִם לֹא תֵיטִיב לַפֶּתַח חַטָּאת רֹבֵץ וְאֵלֶיךָ תְּשׁוּקָתוֹ וְאַתָּה תִּמְשָׁל בּוֹ

Surely, if you improve yourself, you will be forgiven. But if you do not improve yourself, sin rests at the door. Its desire is toward you, yet you can conquer it.

(Bereishis 4:7)

Its desire is toward you, the desire of sin; this is the drive toward evil. It constantly longs and desires to trip you up. Yet you will conquer it; If you want to, you will overcome it.

(Rashi)

Late one night, as R' Yisrael Salanter sat learning in the *beis midrash,* he happened to overhear a conversation between two young men who were spending the night in the deserted women's section. One of the youths, who was terribly thirsty, asked his friend to accompany him to the town's only well so that he could draw a drink of water. He was afraid to walk there alone so late at night. The second young man stubbornly refused him this favor.

As his thirst grew, the first youth pleaded with the second once again. "Please walk me to the well! I'll even pay you ten kopeks for your trouble." This was a large sum for a young man in those times. But once again, the other refused, turning a deaf ear to his friend's pleas.

This conversation galvanized R' Yisrael Salanter into action. He got up and ran out into the night. When he reached the well, he drew out a bucket of water and carried it back to the *beis midrash* for the thirsty young man.

Then he summoned the youth who had refused to accompany his friend, and gave him long and earnest *mussar* about being uncaring and unresponsive to a friend in distress.

The Wily Yetzer

הֲלוֹא אִם תֵּיטִיב שְׂאֵת וְאִם לֹא תֵיטִיב לַפֶּתַח חַטָּאת רֹבֵץ וְאֵלֶיךָ תְּשׁוּקָתוֹ וְאַתָּה תִּמְשָׁל בּוֹ

Surely, if you improve yourself, you will be forgiven. But if you do not improve yourself, sin rests at the door. Its desire is toward you, yet you can conquer it.
(Bereishis 4:7)

Its desire is toward you, the desire of sin; this is the drive toward evil. It constantly longs and desires to trip you up. Yet you will conquer it; If you want to, you will overcome it.
(Rashi)

A Jew came to complain to R' Yechiel Meir of Ostrovtza. "My shop does not afford me a livelihood. In my father's lifetime, it supplied a very nice income — but today, I am in dire straits!"

The Rebbe asked him, "Tell me, what do you do all day?"

"What does the Rebbe mean? I stand in my shop."

"And when there are no customers, what do you do?"

"Well, I read a newspaper."

"In that case," the Rebbe said, "the matter becomes clear to me. Your father took a holy *sefer* with him to the shop every day, in order to learn every spare minute he had. This angered the *yetzer hara*, who sent him a steady stream of customers in order to distract him from his learning. You, on other hand, are busy reading your newspaper. Why should the *yetzer hara* bother with you?"

The Broken Letter

זֶה סֵפֶר תּוֹלְדֹת אָדָם

This is the account of the descendants of Adam
(Bereishis 5:1)

A certain rabbi in Russia owned a pair of *tefillin* that had been written by R' Moshe of Peshevarsk, author of the *Ohr P'nei Moshe*. R'

Moshe wrote every word of his *tefillin* in holiness and purity, and they were therefore considered extremely valuable.

One day, as a *sofer* was inspecting the rabbi's *tefillin*, he noticed a letter that seemed to be broken off, as though unfinished. The rabbi asked the *sofer* to complete the letter so that the *tefillin* would not be *pasul*, but the *sofer* refused to pass his quill over *tefillin* written by the Rebbe of Peshevarsk. The rabbi then brought the *tefillin* to another *sofer* with the same request. This *sofer*, too, declined.

In desperation, the owner of the *tefillin* finally took them to a *sofer* without telling him who had written them. When the *sofer* dipped his quill in ink and extended his hand to repair the letter, a book suddenly dropped out of the nearby bookcase, landing on the *parashah* of *tefillin* that lay spread out before him.

Those present were startled. But this was nothing compared to the amazement they felt when they picked up the book. After brushing away all the dust from the *parashah*, they saw that the seemingly broken letter was actually complete!

But even that astonishment paled beside the emotion they felt when, about to replace the book that had fallen, they discovered that the *sefer* was none other than the *Ohr P'nei Moshe*, written by R' Moshe of Peshevarsk himself.

Everyone Is Like a Holy Book

זֶה סֵפֶר תּוֹלְדֹת אָדָם
This is the account of the descendants of Adam
(Bereishis 5:1)

People jostled for place around R' Yitzchak of Worka's table. The Rebbe announced, "Every Jew is like a holy *sefer*, and must be treated with honor and holiness. It is inappropriate, therefore, to lean on him or push him."

One of the men present asked, "Doesn't the halachah state that it is permissible to lay one holy book on top of another?"

The Rebbe answered: "Every person is required to think of *himself* as though he were not a holy *sefer* at all. In that case, how dare he push aside his friend and climb on top of him?"

֎

The Burnt Document

זֶה סֵפֶר תּוֹלְדֹת אָדָם
This is the account of the descendants of Adam
(Bereishis 5:1)

The great *maggid*, R' Dov of Mezritch, could trace his illustrious *yichus* back to R' Yehudah *Hanasi*, and even further back to David, king of Israel.

When he was a young boy of 8, a fire broke out in his parents' home. The flames spread rapidly, and soon consumed the entire house. In Hashem's mercy, the lives of everyone in the house were spared but the house itself, and everything in it, were gone.

The person who felt the loss most keenly was the *maggid's* mother. She could not be comforted, and spent many days sighing and weeping over the tragedy that had befallen them. One day, her young son found his mother crying again over the house that had been burnt to the ground. He turned to her and said, "Mother, you are mourning the fire so much. We have to trust in Hashem to give us everything we lack!"

"My darling son," his mother answered with a heavy sigh, "I am not crying over the house, nor over all the valuable things in it that were destroyed by the fire. *Hakadosh Baruch Hu* is able to restore all those things, in one way or another. But among the things the fire swallowed up was one item whose value cannot be measured... and that is our family tree, describing our *yichus* going all the way back to David Hamelech. That was more precious to me than all the treasures of the earth — and that is one thing that I cannot get back."

Now the son understood the depths of his mother's grief. In his desire to comfort her, he cried out emotionally, "Don't worry, Mother. We'll write a new *yichus*! And the new *yichus* will start with me."

# פרשת נח

Parashas Noach

Clean Hands

וַתִּמָּלֵא הָאָרֶץ חָמָס
And the earth had become filled with robbery.
(Bereishis 6:11)

About 200 years ago, there lived a great *tzaddik* in Fez, Morocco. His name was R' Yehudah ben Attar. He was considered one of the foremost *poskim* of his time. From every corner of the land halachic questions came for him to answer — and his rulings were accepted by one and all. Faithfully though he served his community, R' Yehudah ben Attar refused to accept payment for his rabbinical work, earning his livelihood instead as a silversmith.

He was known everywhere as "Rabi Elkabir," the great rabbi. Wondrous things were associated with his name. Miracles seemed to abound for this great man, both during his lifetime and after his death.

The holy rabbi was once thrown into a pit of lions but the lions did not come near him or harm him in any way! For a full day and night he remained in that pit, and emerged whole and unscathed. This incident aroused the wonder of the gentiles, and made for an impressive *kiddush Hashem*.

Even after his death, miraculous things occurred to those who prayed at his grave. To this very day, people come to R' Yehudah ben Attar's final resting place if they are involved in litigation and wish to swear to their innocence. There is a solemn belief that he who swears falsely on the grave of R' Yehudah ben Attar will not live out his days.

Once, R' Raphael Baruch Toledano discovered a manuscript written by R' Yehudah ben Attar. Its pages were yellowed and crumbling. R' Raphael Baruch established an organization whose purpose was to publish such holy writings, and this manuscript became his first project.

36 / STORIES MY GRANDFATHER TOLD ME

It was no easy task. R' Raphael Baruch labored long and hard before the old manuscript was ready for publication. The project also required a large sum of money, because in those days printing was a very expensive business. R' Raphael Baruch spared no effort to raise the money, until he finally had the sum he needed. At long last, the book was printed. R' Raphael Baruch had made R' Yehudah ben Attar's work available to the general public, and many came and bought it.

The profits from the sale of the book were good. Most people would have been happy to keep them after all the work they had invested in printing the book. Not R' Raphael Baruch. He felt that the money was not his. He searched and searched until he found a descendant of R' Yehudah ben Attar: the grandson of a grandson, a pious Torah scholar who lived in poverty. R' Baruch handed over every penny to him.

So great was R' Raphael Baruch's integrity that he did not leave himself even a penny of profit from the sale of the book he had worked on so long and so devotedly. He wished his hands to be perfectly clean, untainted by even the shadow of a suggestion of taking something that did not belong to him.

May we learn from his example!

Honest Business

וַתִּשָּׁחֵת הָאָרֶץ לִפְנֵי הָאֱלֹקִים וַתִּמָּלֵא הָאָרֶץ חָמָס

And the earth had become corrupt before G-d; and the earth had become filled with robbery.

(Bereishis 6:11*)*

A *chassid* walked through the bustling Warsaw marketplace, seeking a very special *esrog* for his Rebbe, R' Avraham of Chechnov. The price of the *esrog* was immaterial to him, as long as his Rebbe would be able to take pleasure in having the best of the best.

Aware of this *chassid*, the merchants showed him their very best *esrogim,* each one more beautiful than the one before. The *chassid* examined each one carefully and then returned it to its owner. In every *esrog* he found some sort of flaw: This one was pointy, that one had a spot, the third sported a bump.

There was just one *esrog* that caught the *chassid's* eye. It was an extremely beautiful *esrog*, clean and shining. The *chassid* wanted to buy it, but the merchant refused to sell it. This particular *esrog* had been designated for the saintly Rebbe, the "Toras Emes" of Lublin. The "Toras Emes" was known for spending a princely sum on his *esrog* each year, and would surely wish to purchase this one.

The *chassid* would not give up. He begged. He pleaded. He raised his offer considerably, and was finally rewarded with the beautiful *esrog*. Joyously, he carried it back to his Rebbe.

The *tzaddik* of Chechnov accepted the *esrog* with joy. It was truly an outstanding *esrog* and had no equal.

On the first day of Sukkos, the Rebbe picked up his *arba minim* and was about to recite the blessing over them when he suddenly put them down again. He picked up the *esrog* and studied it from every angle. Finally, he summoned the *chassid* who had brought it to him.

The *chassid* came running. The Rebbe turned to him and asked, "Tell me please, how did you acquire this *esrog*?"

The *chassid* retold the whole tale to his Rebbe: how he had traveled to Warsaw to search for a special *esrog*, how all the merchants had clustered around him with *esrogim* that he had refused, and how, at last, he had spied the beautiful *esrog* whose owner declined to sell to him. The *chassid* had been forced to raise the price of his offer in order to buy it, but any price was worthwhile if it meant that he could bring his Rebbe such a perfect *esrog*.

"That's it!" the Rebbe exclaimed. "This *esrog* was intended for the Rebbe of Lublin! It is his. I have no permission to recite a blessing over it."

The Rebbe said the *berachah* over a different *esrog* — and the *chassid* learned an important lesson in the proper way to conduct business.

A Timely Rescue

וַיֹּאמֶר ד' לְנֹחַ בֹּא אַתָּה וְכָל בֵּיתְךָ אֶל הַתֵּבָה
כִּי אֹתְךָ רָאִיתִי צַדִּיק לְפָנַי בַּדּוֹר הַזֶּה

Then Hashem said to Noach, "Come to the ark, you and all your household, for it is you that I have seen to be righteous before Me in this generation."

(Bereishis 7:1)

One Friday morning, as the Chofetz Chaim was immersing himself in the *mikveh*, he noticed thick smoke. Fearing some catastrophe, he tried to leave the area, but he was overcome by the smoke fumes and fainted. There was no one else present in the *mikveh* at that time. When the bath attendant arrived, he was shocked to find the Chofetz Chaim lying unconscious on the floor.

Quickly, the attendant removed the Chofetz Chaim from the source of the danger. Every attempt to revive him, however, was to no avail. The Chofetz Chaim had sunk into a coma, his life signs were very feeble. A great uproar swept through the town; everyone prayed, recited *Tehillim,* and wept copious tears.

About an hour before the onset of Shabbos, the Chofetz Chaim suddenly opened his eyes — his spirit totally restored. The very first words out of his mouth were an urgent question: "Is it still possible to put on *tefillin?*"

To his joy, there was still time. He donned his *tefillin*.

It was only afterwards that the Chofetz Chaim learned how long he had lain unconscious. He grew very emotional.

"There is only one explanation. During those hours that I lay in a coma, my deeds were being weighed on the Heavenly scales. In Heaven, they were judging whether or not I deserved to have my soul returned to me. Apparently, I am a great sinner."

From that day on, the Chofetz Chaim constantly thanked Hashem for restoring his life. Every Simchas Torah, he would invite the bath attendant to his home to drink a *"l'chayim"* with him. At the same time, he would take the opportunity to wish the man a long life.

Indeed, the bath attendant lived a long time, passing away only weeks after the Chofetz Chaim. In fact, he left this world on the exact day that he had rescued the Chofetz Chaim from the *mikveh* floor, twenty-three years before.

No Cruelty to Animals

גַּם מֵעוֹף הַשָּׁמַיִם שִׁבְעָה שִׁבְעָה זָכָר וּנְקֵבָה לְחַיּוֹת זֶרַע עַל פְּנֵי כָל הָאָרֶץ

Of the birds of the heavens also, seven by seven, male and female, to keep seed alive upon the face of all the earth.

(Bereishis 7:3)

There was a pious man who lived in Tzefas. All his life, he busied himself atoning for his sins. He once visited the Ari *Hakadosh,* and begged the great *tzaddik* to reveal the sins that were hidden from him and how he might atone for them.

The Arizal gazed at the man's forehead and said, "You are a righteous man, without sin. But there is one thing that requires fixing in your home. I see on your forehead a sign that you have transgressed in the area of *tza'ar ba'alei chaim* (causing suffering to animals). You must atone for this."

Hearing these words, the man grew extremely distressed. He strained his mind to remember when and how he had caused suffering to an animal. But for all his efforts, he was unable to find a single shred of evidence of such a sin.

The man went home to question the members of his household. At last, it came to light that the maid was neglectful about feeding his chickens, so that they were forced to seek food in the neighbors' yards. The good man instructed his wife to personally see to the feeding of the chickens from then on — and not only his own, but those of his neighbors as well.

Upon his return to the Arizal, the holy *tzaddik* took another look at the man's forehead and gave him the good news: The sign had been removed and his sin erased.

The Keys to Rain

וַיְהִי הַגֶּשֶׁם עַל הָאָרֶץ

And the rain was upon the earth
(Bereishis 7:12)

In the city where R' Yisrael Abuchatzeira lived, it once happened that the natural spring dried up during the summer — and with it the attached *mikveh*. Because it was untenable that the city be left with no kosher *mikveh* until the rainy season began, the city fathers approached R' Yisrael for advice.

R' Yisrael suggested that they begin to dig a *mikveh* at once, and that they construct it in accordance with all the halachic refinements he had taught them. Promptly, the men of the city began to do as he said. Still, they wondered: What was the use of building a *mikveh* when there was no water? And where in the world would they find water in the middle of the summer?

When the work was completed, the men returned to R' Yisrael to report that the *mikveh* was ready. They waited only for water with which to fill it.

Soberly, R' Yisrael went out to the *mikveh*. He raised his eyes Heavenward and called out, "Master of the Universe, You have commanded us to behave in holiness and purity, and that is how we endeavor to live. We have done what we can, and built a *mikveh*. Now, do Your part for the glory of Your Name!"

Hardly were the words out of his mouth when bountiful rain began to pour from the sky, filling the *mikveh*.

R' Yisrael returned home and continued his study of Torah. Presently, someone came to inform him that the gutter that was used to fill the *mikveh* had not been built according to the opinion of all the *poskim*. R' Yisrael, who always tried in his actions to satisfy all halachic opinions, felt that something was lacking in the *mikveh's kashrus*. Immediately, he returned to the *mikveh* and ordered that the water be removed so that the mistake could be rectified.

The rabbis who had followed R' Yisrael to the *mikveh* were stunned by his command. "But the *mikveh* is kosher according to a majority of opinions. Why should we empty the *mikveh*? Where are we going to get more water to fill it again? After all, miracles don't happen every day!"

But R' Yisrael stood firm. In short order, the workers had followed his instructions. The *mikveh* was empty once again.

When the necessary repairs had been made, R' Yisrael again went out to the *mikveh* and spread his hands in prayer.

"Master of the Universe, You know that I did nothing for my own honor or for my family's honor. I did it only to increase purity in Israel!"

And again, the sky darkened, the rain fell, and the *mikveh* was filled with water.

A Prayer for Rain

וַיְהִי הַגֶּשֶׁם עַל הָאָרֶץ

And the rain was upon the earth

(Bereishis 7:12)

R' Nachman of Hordenka arrived in Eretz Yisrael during a difficult year of drought. The Turkish ruler of the city of Teveryah, who was always scheming against the Jewish residents, issued an appalling declaration. If rain did not fall within three days of his decree, he would expel every last Jew from his city.

R' Nachman did not panic. He assured those close to him that, in Hashem's goodness, they were going to have the opportunity to sanctify His Name.

According to the account written in *Tabor Ha'aretz* by the Chief Rabbi of Teveryah, R' Moshe Klieres, R' Nachman ordered his fellow Jews to go to the cave where R' Chiya and his sons were buried and to pray there for rain. He went with them. Though the day was sunny and dry, he advised them to bring along rain gear.

They left the city and made their way to the cave, protective clothing slung over their arms. A government official caught a glimpse of them at the city gates, and laughed heartily at the raincoats the Jews carried. Spitting in their faces, he declared that if they returned to the city without rain having fallen, he would grind

42 / STORIES MY GRANDFATHER TOLD ME

the Rabbi beneath his heels. The Jews, led by R' Nachman, did not answer him, but continued quietly to the cave of R' Chiya and his sons. There, they poured out their hearts in prayer.

Hashem heard them. Dark clouds filled the sky, and then a heavy rain began to fall — so heavy that, had the men not carried rain gear, they would not have been able to return to town at all that day.

Upon their return to Teveryah, the government official was waiting for them at the city gates. He placed R' Nachman on his shoulders and carried him into the heart of the city, where the people were overcome with joy at the blessed rains that were falling at last. Hashem's great Name was sanctified, with the non-Jews proclaiming, "Who is like You among the gods, and who is like Your people, Israel?"

This episode raised the Jews' esteem greatly in the eyes of the populace, and when, some twelve years later, a large influx of Jews arrived in Teveryah under the leadership of R' Menachem Mendel of Witovsk, author of *Pri Ha'aretz*, and R' Avraham Hakohen of Kalisk, they were received with the greatest respect and welcomed with open arms.

Chickens in Distress!

וְלֹא מָצְאָה הַיּוֹנָה מָנוֹחַ לְכַף רַגְלָה

But the dove could not find a resting place for the sole of its foot

(Bereishis 8:9)

The Arizal once stayed at the home of a pious and G-d-fearing man, who welcomed him with great honor and fulfilled the mitzvah of *hachnasas orchim* with a lavish hand. The Arizal remained in his home for several days, and his host's devotion moved him deeply.

As he prepared to leave, the Arizal said to his host: "How can I repay you for the abundant kindness and affection you have showered on me while I was your guest? Ask me what you will, and I will bless you!"

The man sighed. After a short silence, he said brokenly, "What can I ask for, Rebbe? I have everything, *baruch Hashem*. I have money and do not have to worry about my livelihood, and I am also healthy. There is only one thing I need.

"My wife, may she live long, has borne several children. But many years have past and she has not been able to bear any more children. We have asked doctors what the problem is, but they have not found anything wrong."

His holy guest thought for a moment, then said, "I see the reason. Know this, my friend: The trait of compassion, which is a mark of the children of Avraham *Avinu*, is very important. A person must be extremely careful not to cause suffering to his friends, to other people, or to any living creature.

"On your property is a chicken coop. In the past, a small ladder was fixed at its entrance, so that the chicks might go down to find bowls of food and water for their nourishment. When your wife noticed that the ladder and the ground beneath it were becoming dirty, she instructed the maid to place the food and water directly into the coop and to remove the ladder. From that day on, the chicks have been greatly distressed: Being young and small, they find it hard to fly, and now the pleasure of going up and down the ladder has been taken away from them.

"In their distress, the chicks have cheeped and chirped, and the sounds of their pain have risen to the Throne of Glory, where they stand as an accusation against your wife. Since then, she has been prevented from bearing children."

The host listened to this revelation with amazement. At once, he ran to find the ladder that had stood by the chicken coop. He quickly picked it up and returned it to its original place, at the entrance to the coop.

It was not long before Hashem blessed the man's wife, and she began to bear children as before.

Throw Your Burden Onto Hashem

וַתָּבֹא אֵלָיו הַיּוֹנָה לְעֵת עֶרֶב וְהִנֵּה עֲלֵה זַיִת טָרָף בְּפִיהָ

The dove came back to him in the evening and behold! an olive leaf it had plucked with its mouth.

(Bereishis 8:11)

In Jerusalem, R' Yosef Zundel of Salant opened a business selling vinegar. This business, which was managed by his good wife, barely provided a living for them.

Despite his poverty, however, when the time came for his daughter to marry, R' Yosef Zundel promised to support his son-in-law, R' Nosson Nota.

"How can you promise such a thing," his wife asked him, "when we are barely managing to support ourselves and hardly have any food in the house?"

R' Yosef Zundel replied, "You have a large earthenware jug. Fill it with water, and let He who ordered wine to turn to vinegar, order water to turn to vinegar."

The woman did as her righteous husband bade her, and a miracle occurred before her very eyes. The water in the jug turned into vinegar, supplying enough extra money to support their new son-in-law.

As time went by, R' Nosson Nota noticed that, all during the week, his wife never partook of the good dishes she served him, but ate only bread and dairy products. When he begged her to explain the reason for this, she answered that she was acting on orders from her father, R' Yosef Zundel.

The young man then went to his father-in-law and asked for an explanation.

"A good question," R' Yosef Zundel said. "And the answer is a simple one. You see, it's hard for me to expect my earthenware jug to supply enough good food for your wife as well."

All From Hashem

וַתָּבֹא אֵלָיו הַיּוֹנָה לְעֵת עֶרֶב וְהִנֵּה עֲלֵה זַיִת טָרָף בְּפִיהָ

The dove came back to him in the evening — and behold! an olive leaf it had plucked with its mouth.

(Bereishis 8:11)

It said: "Let my food be bitter as an olive [and provided] by the hand of the Holy One, Blessed is He — and not as sweet as honey [but provided] by the hand of flesh and blood."

(Rashi)

Every morning, after *Shacharis,* R' Zusha of Anipoli would announce, "Master of the Universe, Zusha is very hungry and wants to eat. Please, order him some food!"

Upon hearing these words, his *shamash* would enter and serve R' Zusha his breakfast of cake with a little something to drink.

One day, the *shamash* thought, "Why doesn't the Rav just ask me to bring his breakfast? Why does he always ask Hashem?" He decided not to bring in the meal until R' Zusha expressly asked *him* to do so!

That morning, R' Zusha went to immerse himself in the *mikveh* before *davening,* as was his custom. It was a rainy day and the streets of Anipoli were filled with mud. In order to cross the street, one had to step carefully over a narrow wooden board. R' Zusha was halfway across this board when a stranger in town, also a Jew, came walking in his direction. Seeing the poorly dressed and humble man hurrying along, the stranger thought it would be a great joke to topple R' Zusha into the mud.

R' Zusha fell. Covered in mud, he slowly rose and continued on his way without a word. Behind him, the stranger laughed and laughed.

He was still laughing as he returned to the inn where he was staying and told the innkeeper about the good joke he had played on the indigent passerby. The innkeeper asked him to describe the man he had pushed. Hearing the description, he paled. "Oh, no, what have you done? That was R' Zusha you shoved into the mud!"

The stranger began to tremble. R' Zusha was known far and wide as a holy and awesome man of G-d. "*Oy, vey,* what am I to do?" he wailed.

The innkeeper answered, "Take my advice. It is R' Zusha's custom to spend a long time *davening Shacharis* and then to eat something. I will prepare a tray of tasty cakes and fine wine. Give this gift to him and beg his forgiveness. A *tzaddik* such as he will surely forgive you with a full heart!"

Later that morning, R' Zusha completed his prayers. He removed his *tefillin* and said, "Master of the Universe, Zusha is very hungry and wants to eat. Please, order him some food!"

The *shamash* heard, but did not budge. Suddenly, the door opened and a stranger entered. In his arms he bore a tray laden with tasty cakes and fine wine. He walked over to R' Zusha and set the tray down before him.

Only now did the *shamash* understand that it was not *he* who provided the *tzaddik* with food — but Hashem!

A Most Unusual Gartel

וּמוֹרַאֲכֶם וְחִתְּכֶם יִהְיֶה עַל כָּל חַיַּת הָאָרֶץ

The fear of you and the dread of you shall be upon every beast of the earth

(Bereishis 9:2)

R' Eliyahu Hakohen of Izmir, author of *Shevet Mussar*, was once searching for his *gartel*, so that he could wear it for *davening*. Unable to locate it, he finally spied a black rope on the floor. He stooped down, picked up the rope, and tied it around his waist.

After he had completed his prayers, R' Eliyahu began to untie the rope, when it suddenly uncoiled itself and slithered away! It turned out that the "rope" he had worn was actually a poisonous snake!

In memory of this miracle, R' Eliyahu entitled his next book, *Eizer Eliyahu*.

When R' Moshe of Kobrin would recount this story, he would always add the following postscript: "It is really not so wondrous to find that the snake neither bit nor choked R' Eliyahu. No living creature can harm a person who has not damaged his *tzelem Elokim* — his G-dly image. As it is written, 'The fear of you and the dread of you shall be upon every beast of the earth.' And the fact that the snake did not try to flee while R' Eliyahu *davened* is also not astonishing; the snake was afraid of the *tzaddik*.

"The only really special point about this story is R' Eliyahu's greatness. In his tremendous devotion to Hashem even before he began to *daven*, he never noticed that the 'rope' he was picking up was actually a living snake."

Saved From the Pit

וּמוֹרַאֲכֶם וְחִתְּכֶם יִהְיֶה עַל כָּל חַיַּת הָאָרֶץ

The fear of you and the dread of you shall be upon every beast of the earth

(Bereishis 9:2)

When R' Moshe Leib of Sassov was to begin his journey back to his home town, he took leave of his Rebbe, R' Shmelke of Nikolsburg. His Rebbe gave him three gifts: a loaf of bread, a coin, and his own white silk robe. "You will understand soon enough what to do with them," his Rebbe said, as he saw R' Moshe Leib off with his blessing.

On the road, R' Moshe Leib passed the large estate of a wealthy gentile landowner, or *poretz*. From a pit that had been hollowed out near the entrance, he heard bitter wailing. R' Moshe Leib peered inside and found a Jew from the village there, a tenant who leased the landowner's inn. The Jew was crying with hunger: He had neither eaten nor drunk for three days. Unable to pay his debts to the landowner, the man had been hurled into the pit by the furious *poretz*, with the warning that if he did not pay what he owed, he would be left there to die of starvation and cold.

R' Moshe Leib's heart nearly burst with pity. He threw in the loaf of bread for the man to eat. Then he approached the entrance to the mansion and asked the guards standing there for permission to speak with their master. The guards described R' Moshe Leib to the *poretz* as a man of tall stature with a handsome face that radiated light and goodwill. Curious as to what business such a man might have with him, the *poretz* granted him an audience.

R' Moshe Leib came to the point at once, asking that the poor Jew be released. The *poretz* raised his voice in wrath: "And do you really think I will overlook what is owed to me?"

With no other option, R' Moshe Leib offered the single coin he possessed — his Rebbe's gift. The *poretz* grew even more furious, and hit R' Moshe Leib with his stick. This was a signal to the poretz's servants to seize R' Moshe Leib and throw him out. To add insult to injury, they set their master's dogs on him. They were large ferocious dogs that patrolled the courtyard and attacked unwanted visitors.

To the servants' wonder, the dogs circled R' Moshe Leib but did not touch him. They ran to tell their master, and the gentile came out to see for himself. Still, he remained unmoved. "It's obvious that this is no ordinary Jew. Let's give him one more test. If he passes it, I will set him free — and also the Jew in the pit whose liberty he requested."

The *poretz* ordered his servants to throw R' Moshe Leib into a cage containing a pack of snarling, meat-eating wolves. R' Moshe saw that the danger was very great; the wolves would tear apart and devour anything that came near them. Suddenly, he remembered something his Rebbe had told him. R' Shmelke had once explained that all wild creatures fear and dread a Jew who has not damaged his *tzelem Elokim,* his G-dly image. Even ferocious wolves will not harm such a man.

Calmly, R' Moshe Leib put on the white silk robe that his Rebbe had given him before they parted. The wolves backed away from him and cringed at the back of the cage. And there they stayed.

When the *poretz's* servants saw this, they were truly shocked and amazed. They ran to fetch their master, so that he might witness this miracle with his own eyes. Seeing R' Moshe Leib and the wolves in the cage, the *poretz* immediately issued an order that he be freed. He bowed deeply to the *tzaddik,* saying, "Now I know that you are truly a man of G-d. I will fulfill your every wish."

The Jewish tenant was helped out of the pit where he had languished for three days. Moreover, at R' Moshe Leib's request the *poretz* vowed never to punish any Jewish tenant again in this cruel manner.

The Rosh Yeshivah's Humility

וּמוֹרַאֲכֶם וְחִתְּכֶם יִהְיֶה עַל כָּל חַיַּת הָאָרֶץ

The fear of you and the dread of you shall be upon every beast of the earth

(Bereishis 9:2)

In a certain store in Jerusalem, chaos ruled.

"Excuse me! Make way, make way!" called a worker carrying a large pile of trays heaped with eggs. R' Ezra Attia, *Rosh Yeshivah* of Porat Yosef, was shoved to the side to make room for the worker to pass.

Gathering up his heavy baskets, the Rabbi went to stand at the end of a long line of customers. The hands of the clock moved very slowly as the line inched forward. A young and impatient yeshivah man began to push his way to the front of the line.

Another customer turned upon him angrily. "Don't push. Wait your turn!"

"I have only three things to buy, no more," the young man protested. "Why should I have to wait on such a long line?"

"And I'm buying only one thing!" someone else shouted.

A number of people began to push toward the cashier, who was at a loss about what to do. How to impose order on this chaos? Suddenly, his eye fell on one of the customers — and lit up.

"If the *Rosh Yeshivah* of Porat Yosef can stand quietly in line, how much more so should the rest of you!"

Instant silence descended on the store. Everyone turned to study the person next to him. Who was the *Rosh Yeshivah* who was carrying his own baskets and doing his own shopping?

At last, at the end of the line, they spotted a man quietly standing with one laden basket to his right and another to his left, absorbed in the text of a small Gemara in his hands.

"R' Ezra!" called a young yeshivah man at the front of the line, moving quickly out of his place. "Please, come stand in front of me. And afterwards, I can help you carry your baskets home!"

"Thank you," the *Rosh Yeshivah* smiled, "but that won't be necessary. How am I any different from all the other customers waiting here? Everyone's time is precious. Why should everyone wait any longer because of me? I will wait patiently — certain that, with Hashem's help, my turn will come at last!"

The Humble Villager

וְשֵׁם אָחִיו יָקְטָן
And the name of his brother was Yoktan.
(Bereishis 10:25)
Because he was humble and would make himself small.
(Rashi)

Near the city of Vilkomir there lived a Jew whose nickname was "Lowly Leib." Outwardly, he bore the appearance of an earthy ignorant boor.

The Rabbi of Vilkomir at that time was R' Shlomo, a student of the Vilna Gaon. Once, as R' Shlomo tried to return home on a cold Friday afternoon, the wheels of his wagon became mired in mud and refused to turn. The horses, exhausted from trying to pull the wagon free, stopped altogether. Shabbos was fast approaching. R' Shlomo had no choice but to request help from "Lowly Leib," the only Jew in the area that was otherwise wholly gentile, and spend Shabbos at his house.

When the Rabbi reached Leib's house and asked to stay with him for Shabbos, Leib at first tried to convince R' Shlomo to travel a short distance to an inn that would be much more suitable for him. But the hour was already too late for another trip. The Rabbi pleaded with Leib to extend his hospitality, and Leib consented.

Shabbos came and spread her beautiful wings over the little house. Leib greeted the Shabbos Queen with meticulous attention to every halachah — not behaving at all the way a simple, uneducated person would behave. R' Shlomo quickly discerned that his host was a *gaon*, a secret *tzaddik*, and posed various questions in halachah to him. R' Leib's answers were wonderful. R' Leib, however, had one request to make of the Rabbi: R' Shlomo was not to tell anyone what he had witnessed and what he now knew about R' Leib.

Years passed. One day, R' Shlomo came out of the shul and encountered a funeral procession. It was a meager procession, with only a small number of people accompanying the deceased. The Rabbi inquired after the identity of the deceased — and learned that it was none other than R' Leib.

Immediately, R' Shlomo tore his clothes and commanded the

52 / STORIES MY GRANDFATHER TOLD ME

chevrah kaddisha to carry the body into the shul. He told them to announce, in his name, that every Jew in town must attend the funeral of this man.

It was at the funeral that R' Shlomo revealed his secret at last. To his astonished townspeople, he let it be known that "Lowly Leib" had, in reality, lived the life of a hidden *gaon* and *tzaddik* all his days.

A Case of Mistaken Identity

וְשֵׁם אָחִיו יָקְטָן

And the name of his brother was Yoktan.

(Bereishis 10:25)

"Because he was humble and would make himself small."

(Rashi)

As the Chofetz Chaim was traveling by train one day, a fellow passenger started a conversation with him. "Where are you coming from, Reb Yid?", he asked the Chofetz Chaim.

"From the Pelech region, in Vilna," the Chofetz Chaim replied.

"But which town?"

"A small town by the name of Radin."

The questioner moved closer to the Chofetz Chaim and said, "They say that the Chofetz Chaim, who lives in your town, is a total *tzaddik!*"

"It's a lie," the Chofetz Chaim replied. "He is a simple Jew, just like the others in his town."

The passenger grew enraged at the chutzpah of this man, who dared belittle the honor of the Chofetz Chaim. The whole world was convinced that the Chofetz Chaim was the greatest man of his generation, while this old Jew dared to say otherwise!

But the Chofetz Chaim continued calmly. "No, no, I am acquainted with the Chofetz Chaim. He is not a *tzaddik,* he is a simple Jew."

Now his fellow passenger was really furious. He began to heap scorn on the Jew from Radin who dared belittle the Chofetz Chaim's honor. The Chofetz Chaim just sat and accepted this abuse.

The train pulled into the next station. More passengers boarded the train, among them several who recognized the Chofetz Chaim. At once, they approached him to request his blessing.

The other passenger realized his mistake. Greatly abashed, he turned in tears to the Chofetz Chaim and begged his forgiveness. "Please pardon me, Rebbe, I didn't know — "

The Chofetz Chaim looked at him in astonishment. "And why should you need forgiveness? How did you sin, and how did you insult me? You thought that I was a *tzaddik*, but you didn't know any better, so there is no fault on your side. Now that you know that I am no *tzaddik*, what is there to forgive?"

Witness to a Crime

וַיֵּרֶד ד' לִרְאֹת אֶת הָעִיר

Hashem descended to look at the city

(Bereishis 11:5)

R' Levi Yitzchak of Berditchev was once traveling in a wagon, when the wagon driver spied a bale of hay lying at the side of the road. As there was no one standing near, the driver decided to steal the hay.

He was about to lay his hands on the bale, when R' Levi Yitzchak, realizing what was about to happen, suddenly screamed, "Someone sees you! Someone sees you!"

Panicked, the wagon driver left the hay, leaped back into his seat, and slapped the horses with the reins to make them gallop away. It was only then that he threw a glance over his shoulder. He saw no one standing there at all.

Surprised, he asked, "Who saw me?"

R' Levi Yitzchak answered tranquilly, "Why, *Hakadosh Baruch Hu*, of course!"

פרשת לך לך
Parashas Lech Lecha

A Personal Lesson

לֶךְ לְךָ מֵאַרְצְךָ וּמִמּוֹלַדְתְּךָ וּמִבֵּית אָבִיךָ

"*Go for yourself from your land, from your birthplace, and from your father's house*"

(*Bereishis* 12:1)

R' Nachum of Chernobyl labored all his life to redeem Jewish prisoners. He would visit the homes of rich men in order to collect money for this important mitzvah. This money would find its way into the pockets of noblemen and authority figures, for the purpose of setting free the Jews they had imprisoned.

One day, R' Nachum himself became the target of an unfounded accusation and was thrown into prison. Another *tzaddik* came to see him in jail. Sitting with his friend, the visitor explained the verse at the beginning of *Parashas Lech Lecha* as follows:

"Avraham *Avinu* was an outstanding host. He worked very hard at the mitzvah of *hachnasas orchim*, welcoming guests into his home. He always looked for better ways to serve their needs. Hashem said to him, 'Go from your land' — become a traveler yourself and a guest in other people's homes. Then you will be able to sense very well what a guest needs and how better to serve him. In this way, you will be able to perfect this mitzvah in every detail."

The *tzaddik* added, "You, R' Nachum, have worked hard to free prisoners. Now Heaven has offered you the chance to experience firsthand what it's like to be thrown into jail, and how urgent it is to free Jews who are imprisoned. In this way, you will be able to understand this mitzvah to its very depths, and become even better in its practice!"

Who Is a Relative?

לֶךְ לְךָ מֵאַרְצְךָ וּמִמּוֹלַדְתְּךָ וּמִבֵּית אָבִיךָ ... וְאֶעֶשְׂךָ לְגוֹי גָּדוֹל וכו'

*"Go for yourself from your land...
And I will make of you a great nation"*
(*Bereishis* 12:1-2)

R' Yaakov David of Amshinov once visited a wealthy man to ask him to support the latter's own poor relative. The rich man tried to avoid his responsibility by claiming that the poor man was only a distant relative and one whom he hardly knew.

The Rabbi turned to him with a question. "Do you *daven* every day?"

In astonishment, the rich man asked, "Does the Rav suspect me, Heaven forbid, of not *davening?*"

"In that case, tell me how the first *berachah* of *Shemoneh Esrei* begins."

"As you know," the wealthy man answered with a trace of impatience, "it starts, "G–d of Avraham, G–d of Yitzchak, and G–d of Yaakov—"

"And who were these men, Avraham, Yitzchak, and Yaakov?"

"What do you mean? They were the *Avos,* our forefathers!"

"And when did these forefathers live? How much time has passed since then?" asked the Rabbi.

"Several thousand years, of course."

"Very true," R' Yaakov David agreed. "Several thousand years. Nevertheless, you mention their names three times a day, and in the merit of these 'distant relatives' who lived thousands of years ago, you ask to be saved from harm. But when I come to you to ask you to help your own relative, a man who is living this very day, in your own generation, you regard him as too distant?"

A Simple Man's Sacrifice

וְחָיְתָה נַפְשִׁי בִּגְלָלֵךְ
"And that I may live on account of you."
(*Bereishis* 12:13)

The Rabbi of the city of Zelotchov suffered greatly at the hands of a certain butcher, and often pleaded with Hashem to make the butcher leave the city. Hashem did help him and, eventually, the butcher departed for the city of Brody. The Rabbi was a *chassid* of R' Moshe Leib of Sassov, and would visit his rebbe faithfully on specific occasions.

On one such visit, he noticed that his "friend," the butcher was there, and that R' Moshe Leib treated the man very affectionately. The Rabbi was astounded, but said nothing. Later, he heard the butcher tell the Rebbe that living in Brody was too difficult for him and that he wished to return to Zelotchov. R' Moshe Leib blessed him with success in Zelotchov.

The Rabbi could not understand why R' Moshe Leib liked that butcher so much when he, the Rabbi, had suffered so much at his hands — or why R' Moshe Leib had blessed him with success in Zelotchov. Unable to keep silent any longer, he waited until the butcher had left and then related to his Rebbe all the troubles the butcher had caused him. "Why do you like him so much, Rebbe?" he asked. "Is he a great and important man?"

R' Moshe Leib replied, "In my eyes, all Jews are important."

Some time later, on a Yom Kippur night, troops surrounded the shul in Zelotchov. They had come to round up some men for military service. The Jews, outraged, rose up against them and killed six soldiers. This caused a great uproar. The Rabbi of Zelotchov was arrested at once, along with the *shochet* and all the community's leaders. A severe punishment was expected for them all.

When the butcher heard the news, he went to the governor of the city and said, "What do you want with those old men? Do you think they are capable of killing anyone? Set them free. I am the one who killed those six soldiers!"

The governor released the others and had the butcher executed.

Only then did the Rabbi of Zelotchov understand R' Moshe Leib's claim that every single Jew is important.

Extreme Caution

וַיְהִי רִיב בֵּין רֹעֵי מִקְנֵה אַבְרָם וּבֵין רֹעֵי מִקְנֵה לוֹט

And there was quarreling between the herdsmen of Avram's livestock and the herdsmen of Lot's livestock

(*Bereishis* 13:7)

And there was quarreling, because Lot's shepherds were wicked and would graze their cattle in the fields of others, and Avram's shepherds would rebuke them over the theft [they committed by grazing their cattle on other people's land]

(*Rashi*)

The Chofetz Chaim stood by the train, ready to send his parcel of books. An acquaintance of his came running up with a sheaf of tickets in his hand. Each passenger on the train was permitted a certain amount of baggage weight for free, and this man had collected baggage tickets from a number of passengers who did not need them — hoping thereby to free the Chofetz Chaim from paying anything at all for the parcel he was sending.

The Chofetz Chaim rejected the plan in no uncertain terms, and insisted on paying the full amount at once.

This method of delivering *sefarim* was one the Chofetz Chaim used often. Once, he arrived too late. The train was about to depart, and he had not yet handed in his parcel to the baggage compartment. Out of respect for the Chofetz Chaim, the station manager granted him permission to place it in a passenger compartment instead — at no cost.

Imagine the station manager's astonishment when R' Yisrael Meyer objected, saying that the manager only worked for the railroad company and had no right to waive any payments. The manager was forced to put the parcel of books officially, for pay, into the baggage compartment.

On another occasion, the Chofetz Chaim wanted to send some books through the mail. He wrapped them in paper, weighed them, and wrote the weight on the front of the package. Then he gave the parcel to a messenger to bring to the post office.

The Polish postal worker glanced at the package and saw the sender's name. Then he saw the weight written there. Immediately, he quoted a price.

The messenger was surprised. "Aren't you going to check that the weight is accurate?"

"No need," the clerk replied. "This rabbi has sent many packages with me, and every time I've checked the weight, it was always exactly what was written on the package. He is an honest man. Why should I check up on him?"

No Effort Spared

וַיִּשְׁמַע אַבְרָם כִּי נִשְׁבָּה אָחִיו ... וְגַם אֶת לוֹט אָחִיו וּרְכֻשׁוֹ הֵשִׁיב

And Avram heard that his kinsman was taken captive... He also brought back his kinsman, Lot, with his possessions.

(*Bereishis* 14:14-16)

At the outbreak of World War I, the war raged between Russia and Germany. A young man named Efrayim Leibowitz was a student at the Chofetz Chaim's yeshivah. A certain spy desired to demonstrate his success at his profession. He befriended some of the yeshivah students. Learning that Efrayim Leibowitz was a German citizen, he found an opportunity to slip a military plan of the Kovno siege into Efrayim's pocket.

That night, military personnel surrounded the house where the student boarded — and found the plans in his pocket. They immediately arrested both the student and his landlord.

The entire yeshivah administration, with the Chofetz Chaim at its head, fell under a cloud of suspicion. The secret police visited the yeshivah a number of times, to interrogate personnel and institute searches. As for Efrayim Leibowitz, the expected punishment for his "crime" was execution.

Through tremendous efforts on his behalf, he was not put to death at once. For two years he remained imprisoned, though no one knew where. Finally, in the year 5676 (1916), a message was gotten to the Chofetz Chaim. Efrayim Leibowitz was in a jail in a distant city.

With no regard for his own safety — for any attempt to intervene in Leibowitz's case would throw serious suspicion on himself by the Russian authorities — the Chofetz Chaim threw himself into the task of rescuing his student. He traveled in person to the capital city, St. Petersburg, to try to convince an attorney named Gruzenberg to take on the case, a case which no other lawyer would touch. The Chofetz Chaim also announced his intention of testifying in court on the boy's behalf.

In Teves of the year 5677 (1917), three illustrious witnesses took the stand in the military court at Vitebsk. They were the Chofetz Chaim, his son-in-law R' Tzvi Levinson, and R' Elchonon Wasserman. All three declared their certainty that Efrayim Leibowitz was innocent.

The accused was sentenced to ten years' hard labor.

Hearing the sentence, the Chofetz Chaim thanked Hashem for saving Leibowitz's life. As for the ten years of labor, he laughed.

"What fools! Do these regimes know if they'll be around even ten *months* from now? Are they sure they'll be here in ten *weeks*?"

Indeed, just two months later, on 22 Adar 5677 (1917), the Bolshevik revolution erupted in Russia. The czar was toppled from his throne. Prisoners were released, and Efrayim Leibowitz was set free.

To Free a Prisoner

וַיִּשְׁמַע אַבְרָם כִּי נִשְׁבָּה אָחִיו וַיָּרֶק אֶת חֲנִיכָיו יְלִידֵי בֵיתוֹ ... וַיָּשֶׁב אֵת כָּל הָרְכֻשׁ וְגַם אֶת לוֹט אָחִיו וּרְכֻשׁוֹ הֵשִׁיב וְגַם אֶת הַנָּשִׁים וְאֶת הָעָם

And Avram heard that his kinsman was taken captive, and he armed his disciples who had been born in his house... He brought back all the possessions; he also brought back his kinsman, Lot, with his possessions, as well as the women and the people.
(*Bereishis* 14:14-16)

During World War I, the Slobodka Yeshivah was relocated to the city of Kremenzburg, in Russia. From time to time, bands of wild ruffians would rampage through the city, murdering Jews or holding them for ransom. On one such rampage they captured an outstanding student of the yeshivah, who would later become one of America's foremost *gedolim*. His name was R' Yaakov Yitzchak Ruderman.

The captors demanded the sum of 10,000 rubles. If the sum was not paid, the student would be killed. R' Yaakov Yitzchak brought them to the home of his *Rosh Yeshivah,* R' Moshe Mordechai Epstein. But the *Rosh Yeshivah* did not have anywhere near that amount of money.

The kidnappers stormed out of the house, dragging the Jewish youth with them. They were just minutes away from carrying out their threat, when the *Rosh Yeshivah's* door suddenly flung open and R' Moshe Mordechai Epstein rushed out. Ignoring the danger to himself, he raised his voice and began shouting loudly.

Soon, a large crowd had gathered around them. The wild men, who had been brandishing their pistols at the *Rosh Yeshivah* and his student, grew alarmed. In a panic, they fled.

R' Yaakov Yitzchak was free.

Panic!

וַיֵּחָלֵק עֲלֵיהֶם לַיְלָה הוּא וַעֲבָדָיו וַיַּכֵּם

And he with his servants deployed against them at night,
and he struck them
(*Bereishis* 14:15)

A troop of soldiers entered the town where R' Zusha of Anipoli lived. They went into a Jewish wine shop, where they drank up every bottle they could find. It is the nature of wine that one sip leads to another; but when all the bottles and barrels were empty, the soldiers still were not satisfied. They demanded that the shopkeeper produce more wine. Trembling, he explained that there was nothing left. The soldiers had drunk it all.

In a rage, the soldiers began breaking bottles and equipment, shattering the furniture and slashing the walls with their sabers. The Jew and the members of his household stood stunned as their possessions and livelihood were laid to waste. Then the fury turned upon them. The soldiers began to beat them with great cruelty and force.

One member of the household managed to secretly slip out of the house and to escape. He made his way to R' Zusha's home and poured out the terrible story.

R' Zusha did not hesitate at all. He stood up at once and hurried to the wine shop. Looking through a window, he took in the scene. He

Lech Lecha / 63

64 / STORIES MY GRANDFATHER TOLD ME

saw the rampaging soldiers, the broken bottles, the destruction of walls and furniture. In a mighty voice, he called out the words we use on the High Holy Days: "And so, cast Your fear, Hashem our G-d, on all Your handiwork and Your dread on everything You have created."

Three times R' Zusha called out those words so that inside they could be heard. Suddenly, pandemonium broke out among the soldiers. Throwing down their packs and weapons, they ran for the doors and the windows. Panic stricken, they fled into the city's streets, filling them with terrified screams.

The captain of the troops was hastily summoned. With great effort, he managed at last to restore some sort of order among his men.

"What happened to you?" he demanded sternly. "What are you so afraid of? Are you soldiers — or a pack of frightened rabbits?"

"Captain!" one of the soldiers cried out from between his chattering teeth. "A man came to us and called out, 'Cast Your Fear—' And all at once, a deathly fear came over all of us; a terror such as we have never known on the battlefield. We are still trembling from head to toe!"

The captain wanted to meet the man who had thrown his troops into such terror and confusion. He ordered his men to take him to the place where the incident had occurred. Upon arriving, he gazed upon the wreck of the wine shop. He also found R' Zusha, who was still standing at the window, eyes glowing like torches.

The captain ordered his soldiers to pay for all the damage they had done. Then, with a word of apology to R' Zusha, he gathered up his troops and departed.

A Measure of Trust

וַיֹּאמֶר אַבְרָם אֶל מֶלֶךְ סְדֹם ... אִם מִחוּט וְעַד שְׂרוֹךְ נַעַל וְאִם אֶקַּח מִכָּל אֲשֶׁר לָךְ

Avram said to the king of Sodom, "...if so much as a thread to a shoestrap; or if I shall take from anything of yours!"
(*Bereishis* 14:22-23)

There was a special group of students in the Volozhin Yeshivah that spent time learning about the trait of *bitachon* — trust in Hashem. One night, R' Chaim, the *Rosh Yeshivah,* addressed the group. It was nearly

2 o'clock in the morning when he paused to ask the time. Nobody knew what time it was (this was before the days when yeshivah boys routinely wore wristwatches). R' Chaim resumed his talk.

"My dear students, it seems that we have not yet acquired true trust. If we had, Heaven would provide us with a watch — even one made entirely of gold..."

And he continued to discourse on the topic of *bitachon*.

As he was speaking, the door burst open and a Russian soldier ran into the room. He looked around quickly, and then approached R' Chaim.

"I am a Jew," he said. "I was living in the forest near the large city of Lodz when I was drafted into military service. My father, a very wealthy man, gave me a sum of money to bribe the military doctor, so that he would disqualify me from service. Trusting in the doctor's promise, I came for my release papers. So certain was I that I would be released that I did not hurry to change my expensive clothes for simpler ones.

"But bitter disappointment awaited me. The doctor made a mistake and mixed up my name with someone else's. Another man was freed in my place, and I was taken to a military base. I have been living at the base for several weeks, a lone Jew among many gentiles, and I've been afraid that they'll rob me of my expensive gold watch. I managed to obtain a short leave and left for the city."

Breathlessly, the soldier continued, "It's very late, and pitch dark outside. Luckily, as though Heaven itself pointed it out, I noticed one lighted building — this *beis midrash*. Would the Rav be willing to guard my watch for me?"

R' Chaim, taken aback by the soldier's unexpected appearance in the middle of the night, had listened attentively to his story. He agreed to the request, but added, "You should be aware that my home is like a *reshus harabim* — a public domain. I cannot accept responsibility that your watch will be well guarded!"

The soldier stopped to consider for a moment, then said, "Rebbe, I am hereby giving you this watch as a gift! Better a gift to a Jewish rabbi than stolen by gentiles."

From his tunic pocket he quickly removed the watch, placed it on the table in front of R' Chaim, and left the *beis midrash* at a rapid clip. R' Chaim ran after him to return the watch, but the man had vanished into the night.

Returning to his students, the *Rosh Yeshivah* concluded his talk: "We now see that if we have genuine and complete trust in Him,

Hashem will send us a watch — even a gold watch! Right before our eyes we have a concrete example of *bitachon*!"

R' Yitzchak Elchanan Refuses a Gift

וַיֹּאמֶר אַבְרָם אֶל מֶלֶךְ סְדֹם ... אִם מִחוּט וְעַד שְׂרוֹךְ נַעַל וְאִם אֶקַּח מִכָּל אֲשֶׁר לָךְ

Avram said to the king of Sodom, "...if so much as a thread to a shoestrap; or if I shall take from anything of yours!"

(*Bereishis* 14:22-23)

As a youth, R' Yitzchak Elchanan Spektor of Kovno lived in dire poverty. Money was so scarce during a certain period in his life that there was not even enough to buy himself a pair of shoes. Unable to walk over to the *beis midrash* to learn, he was forced to remain at home.

In his distress, he turned one day to a young man his own age from a wealthy family. "See my terrible financial situation," he began. "It is not even in my power to buy myself a pair of new shoes! Seeing as you are soon to be married, I assume you have bought new clothes for the wedding. Please be kind enough to give me your old shoes, which you most likely will not need after your marriage. Then I'll be able to return to the *beis midrash* to learn!"

The wealthy young man looked at him with contempt. "If you'd go out to work and earn some money, you wouldn't need any man's gift. You'd be able to buy shoes with your own money!"

Years went by. R' Yitzchak Elchanan became renowned as an outstanding Torah scholar and the leading halachic authority of his time. One day, he arrived in the city of Vilna, carrying a manuscript in his suitcase which he hoped to publish. A very large crowd came out to welcome him, and they received him with the respect usually reserved for kings. A staggering 20,000 people were on hand to greet R' Yitzchak Elchanan — leaving such a profound impression on the city that its local ruler forbade the *tzaddik* from returning. He was annoyed that the honor demonstrated to R' Yitzchak Elchanan on his arrival in Vilna was greater than the honor the people had shown when the czar came to visit. This would not do!

Among the throng that collected to meet R' Yitzchak Elchanan was the same rich man who had once scoffed at him so scornfully.

Knowing that R' Yitzchak Elchanan wished to publish his manuscript, and aware of the honor that would be heaped on the person who supported its publication, the wealthy man offered to pay for the entire project.

R' Yitzchak Elchanan looked at the man and recognized him as the very person who had refused him an old pair of shoes in his hour of greatest need.

"You are too late," he said quietly.

The Rav's sons, standing nearby, were stunned. When the visitor had departed, they turned to their father with the burning question, "Why," they asked, "did you reject the rich man's offer?"

R' Yitzchak Elchanan explained. "Do not be shocked, my sons. Listen, and I will tell you the story.

"In my youth, I was an orphan and very poor. It was a harsh winter, and my shoes were torn. I needed a pair of shoes in order to walk in the rain and the snow. I went to that man and asked for his help, but he turned me down.

"Know this, my sons: If only I had had a pair of shoes, I might have grown stronger in Torah. I might have achieved greater things — and that man would have had a share in my Torah. But because he refused to support a young boy, he is not worthy now of supporting the publication of this manuscript!"

The Price Is Right

וַיֹּאמֶר אַבְרָם אֶל מֶלֶךְ סְדֹם ... אִם מִחוּט וְעַד שְׂרוֹךְ נַעַל וְאִם אֶקַּח מִכָּל אֲשֶׁר לָךְ

Avram said to the king of Sodom, "...if so much as a thread to a shoestrap; or if I shall take from anything of yours!"

(*Bereishis* 14:22-23)

A story is told of R' Benzion of Bobov. He once entered a bookstore in Cracow and asked for a certain *sefer*. The bookseller stated its price as fifty gold coins; the Rebbe offered forty. The bookseller protested that the book had cost him a great deal. At once, the Rebbe paid the full price.

Those who had accompanied him into the store were astounded. Why had the Rebbe not negotiated further?

R' Benzion explained: "Had I agreed at once to the price of fifty coins, the bookseller would have been distressed afterwards and regretted not having asked me for sixty or seventy coins. He would have ended up feeling that he had lost. But now that I tried to bargain down the price, he took pleasure from the profit he made, and is not feeling bad at all!"

※

One Thursday night, R' Eliyahu Chaim Meisel, the Rav of Lodz, sat learning Torah with his grandson, Eliezer Yitzchak. Suddenly, a man entered the room and placed a *sefer* that he wished to sell on the table. R' Eliyahu Chaim asked its price, and the bookseller told it to him.

R' Eliyahu Chaim took twice the sum from his drawer and handed it to the man. "You can tell everyone that I bought the *sefer* from you at its full price."

After the man had left, Eliezer Yitzchak asked his grandfather, "Your library already has several copies of that *sefer*. Why did you decide to buy another copy?"

"Tomorrow is *erev Shabbos*," R' Eliyahu Chaim replied. "If that man came to me so late at night, it must mean that he does not have enough money in his house to cover his Shabbos expenses. He is ashamed to go begging for handouts, and so he tried to sell me a *sefer*. Knowing how much money he really needs to prepare for Shabbos, I gave him the appropriate sum, without paying attention to the book's actual market price."

※

One Who Despises Gifts Shall Live

וַיֹּאמֶר אַבְרָם אֶל מֶלֶךְ סְדֹם ... אִם מִחוּט וְעַד שְׂרוֹךְ נַעַל וְאִם אֶקַּח מִכָּל אֲשֶׁר לָךְ

Avram said to the king of Sodom, "...if so much as a thread to a shoestrap; or if I shall take from anything of yours!"
(Bereishis 14:22-23)

The Chofetz Chaim once appeared in the town of Novo-Alexandrovski with his bundle of *sefarim*. Entering a shul one morning, he found the *minyan* about to begin *Shacharis*. Quickly, he opened his bundle and left it on the table near the door. He wrapped himself in his *tallis* and *tefillin,* went to stand in a corner of the shul, and *davened* along with the others.

He was still immersed in his prayers when someone handed the shul's rabbi one of the *sefarim* from the stack by the door. Thumbing through it, the rabbi found it fascinating, and read portions of the *sefer* with great interest.

After the guest had finished *davening,* the rabbi approached the Chofetz Chaim with a friendly greeting. As was his custom on his travels, the Chofetz Chaim introduced himself as the author's representative, giving no name. The rabbi informed him that he had discovered a contradiction between the author's conclusion in explaining a "*Mekor Chaim*" and a response of an authority cited at the end of the *sefer*. The "representative" immediately explained the two sections succinctly and removed all confusion. The rabbi was astonished by the stranger's sharpness and the depth of his knowledge, highly unusual in a traveling salesman — especially that he had had the explanation at his fingertips, as though he had prepared it in advance. A suspicion arose in the rabbi's heart: Were the author and his "representative" one and the same?

He confronted the Chofetz Chaim directly with this question, and the Chofetz Chaim was forced to acknowledge the truth.

The rabbi purchased the *sefer* at once, and the rest of the worshipers followed suit. One of them offered a princely sum for the *sefer,* but the Chofetz Chaim refused to take more than its stated price. The man thought of a ploy. He took two *sefarim,* but did not pay for them until he saw the author climb onto his wagon in order

70 / STORIES MY GRANDFATHER TOLD ME

to leave town. As the wagon wheels began to turn, the man thrust a note of money into the Chofetz Chaim's hand. The Chofetz Chaim, believing it to be a one-ruble note — the price of two copies of his *sefer* — did not even glance at it, but put it in his pocket along with the rest of the money he had earned.

Upon his arrival in another town where he had planned to stop, the Chofetz Chaim counted his money. He discovered a one hundred-ruble note which he could not account for. He assumed that one of his customers must have mistakenly paid him with a hundred-ruble note instead of a one-ruble note. At once, he turned around and made his way back to Novo-Alexandrovski to return the money to its owner.

The Chofetz Chaim approached all his customers there — in vain. Finally, he made an announcement in the shul. This, too, brought no results.

After a fruitless search that lasted several days, the Chofetz Chaim realized that time was pressing and he must move on. He ascended the *bimah* in the shul between *Minchah* and *Ma'ariv*, where — in a trembling voice and with tears in his eyes — he pleaded with the congregation to have pity on him. Whoever had given him, mistakenly or on purpose, the hundred-ruble note, must take it back. The Chofetz Chaim assured them that he had no intention of using it in any case and would derive no pleasure from the money. His words made an impression on the man who had slipped him the large note, and he confessed at last to what he had done.

"But I gave the money to you with a full heart," he protested. "I do not wish to take it back."

The Chofetz Chaim, however, stood firm in his refusal to take pleasure from an undeserved gift, and the other man was reluctantly forced to take back the money. In place of the one hundred-ruble note, he gave the Chofetz Chaim the sum of one ruble, to pay for the two *sefarim* he had bought.

72 / STORIES MY GRANDFATHER TOLD ME

The Ba'al Shem Tov Learns to Trust

וַיֹּאמֶר אַבְרָם אֶל מֶלֶךְ סְדֹם הֲרִמֹתִי יָדִי אֶל ד'... אִם מִחוּט וְעַד שְׂרוֹךְ נַעַל וְאִם אֶקַּח מִכָּל אֲשֶׁר לָךְ וְלֹא תֹאמַר אֲנִי הֶעֱשַׁרְתִּי אֶת אַבְרָם

Avram said to the king of Sodom: "I have raised my hand to Hashem... if so much as a thread of a shoestrap; or if I shall take from anything that is yours! So you shall not say, 'It is I who made Avram rich."

(Bereishis 14:22-23)

"For the Holy One, Blessed is He, promised to make me rich, as it says, 'I will bless you, etc.'"

(Rashi)

The Ba'al Shem Tov was once sent to learn the trait of *bitachon,* trust in Hashem, from an old man who worked as a tax collector in a village.

Late one night, a police officer entered the house, rapped on the table three times with his stick, and departed. The Ba'al Shem Tov and his disciples did not understand the meaning of this incident, but a glance at the old man's face showed them that he was unconcerned. About half an hour later, after they had *davened,* the policeman came again, rapped on the table as before, and disappeared.

The Ba'al Shem Tov asked his host for an explanation. The tax collector answered, "That was a warning that today is the day I must bring in the village's taxes. If, after three warnings, the money is not handed over, the lord of the village will imprison the tax collector and his family."

"From your calm manner," the Ba'al Shem Tov remarked, "it's clear that you have the money. In that case, go ahead, before we partake of the meal, and pay it. We will wait for you."

His host answered, "At the moment, I don't even have a penny! But I'm sure Hashem will give me everything I need. Let us sit down and eat in peace. After all, I still have three hours."

At the conclusion of the meal, the police officer entered for the third time and banged on the table. The old man remained tranquil. He recited the *Birkas Hamazon* and then put on his Shabbos coat, saying, "Now I will go pay."

Lech Lecha / 73

"Do you have the required sum already?" the Ba'al Shem Tov inquired.

"I still don't have a penny. But Hashem will surely provide." And the man went on his way.

The Ba'al Shem Tov and his disciples went out onto the balcony to watch. Suddenly, they saw a wagon pull up next to the tax collector. The driver exchanged a few words with him, and then drove on. But a short time later, the driver stopped the wagon and waved at the other man to come near. He handed the old tax collector a sum of money.

When the wagon drew close to where the Ba'al Shem Tov and his disciples stood, they questioned the driver: "What did you say to our host just now?"

He answered, "I made him a business proposal in which I'd agree to purchase the liquor that he'll make next winter. At first, we couldn't come to terms. Only after I saw that he persisted in his terms and continued on his way did I realize that I'd have to pay what he asked. I know him as an honest and trustworthy man. I wanted to talk further, but he said he's hurrying to the lord to pay the taxes."

The Ba'al Shem Tov turned to his disciples. "See how great is the power of *bitachon*!"

Thirteen Covenants in One

וְהָיָה לְאוֹת בְּרִית בֵּינִי וּבֵינֵיכֶם
"And that shall be the sign of the covenant between Me and you."
(*Bereishis* 17:11)

A *bris milah* for a newborn grandson was held at the home of the Brisker Rav, R' Yitzchak Ze'ev Soloveitchik. At the conclusion of the ceremony, the *mohel* approached the Rav and said, "*Baruch Hashem* we have merited to attend a *bris* — and what a *bris*!" By this comment, he was trying to express his admiration for the Brisker Rav.

Surprised, the Rav asked, "What do you mean by saying, 'and what a *bris*'? What could be more important than a *bris* on which thirteen covenants are inscribed (the word '*bris*' appears thirteen times in the *parashah*)? What difference is there between one *bris* and another?"

The Rav continued with a parable. "It's like a poor schoolteacher who says, 'If only I had Rothschild's wealth, I'd be richer than he is! How? If I had Rothschild's money — plus my salary as a schoolteacher — I'd be even richer than he!'

"People would consider that teacher a fool.

"There is no overestimating the significance of any *bris milah*," the Rav concluded. "This bris is no more 'richer' than any other. How is it possible to say that, in addition to the wealth of this mitzvah, there is also an added 'bonus' because it took place at the home of a 'schoolteacher' like the Brisker Rav?"

פרשת וירא
Parashas Vayeira

An Open-Door Policy

אִם נָא מָצָאתִי חֵן בְּעֵינֶיךָ אַל נָא תַעֲבֹר מֵעַל עַבְדֶּךָ

"If it pleases you that I find favor in your eyes, please pass not from before your servant."

(*Bereishis* 18:3)

R' Chaim of Kosov's holy teachings focused on reminding his fellow Jews to love one another, to open their homes to guests, and to give charity with a full heart. When friends came to see him, he would question them: "Where did you sleep on your journey? Where did you eat?" And if it came to light that one of his own followers had behaved stingily or lazily in the matter of *hachnasas orchim,* R' Chaim would rebuke that man strongly.

In a certain peaceful village there lived a tax collector. A group of men were once passing through the village on their way to see the Kosover Rebbe when the night turned cold and rainy. They went to the tax collector's home, knocked on the door, and asked for permission to stay there for the night. He refused to let them in. With a steady rain falling on their heads, the men were forced to continue on their way.

In the morning, they arrived in Kosov and were brought into the Rebbe's presence. As was his habit, he questioned them about their journey. They told him about the cruel tax collector who had refused them shelter on a stormy night.

"In the end, he will need a *Kohen,*" the Rebbe said. He was referring to a Rashi that says, "If you withhold a *Kohen*'s gift, be assured that you will need to come to him" (*Rashi, Bamidbar* 5:12).

Not long afterward, that same tax collector came to R' Chaim in great distress. It seemed that the lord of his village had ordered him to leave in three months. All the man's efforts to change the decree had not helped a bit.

Vayeira / 79

"Actually," said R' Chaim, "it has always bothered me to see a tax collector like yourself living in a village far from any Jews, *davening* without a *minyan*, unable to answer 'Amen' or say '*Kedushah*' or '*Barchu*,' not hearing the Torah reading. How are you fulfilling your obligations as a Jew?"

R' Chaim continued, "The primary reason you were permitted to live there was the concept that '*hachnasas orchim* is greater than receiving the *Shechinah*.' By fulfilling the mitzvah of welcoming travelers into your home, many lacks were compensated for. As long as you observed the mitzvah of *hachnasas orchim* properly, its merit stood to your advantage and you could not be harmed.

"Now, however, people came to you, but you were cruel to them and did not let them in. In that case, what business have you living in that village? Live in a city together with your fellow Jews, *daven* in a shul morning and night, and raise your children to learn Torah!"

The tax collector burst into tears. "But how will I earn a living?"

"From this day forward," R' Chaim said, "resolve that your home will be open wide to all. Then Hashem will return you to your former position without any damage done."

The tax collector accepted this resolution immediately. Hashem softened the village lord's heart and the man was allowed to remain in his home and keep his job.

Royal Treatment

וְאֶקְחָה פַת לֶחֶם וְסַעֲדוּ לִבְּכֶם אַחַר תַּעֲבֹרוּ כִּי עַל כֵּן עֲבַרְתֶּם עַל עַבְדְּכֶם

"I will fetch a morsel of bread that you may nourish your heart. After, you shall pass, inasmuch as you have passed your servant's way."

(*Bereishis* 18:5)

Hachnasas orchim was bred into R' Isser Zalman Meltzer, *Rosh Yeshivah* of Yeshivas Eitz Chaim, from birth. Whenever he heard a knock on the door, he would hurry to answer it himself.

Members of his household asked, "Why do you trouble yourself so?"

"A poor man may be standing in the doorway," he would answer.

"I must hasten to supply what he lacks!"

Once, after midnight, there was a knock on the door. R' Isser Zalman got up to answer it, as usual, but someone else in the house got there before him and called out, "Who's there?"

R' Isser Zalman grew angry. "So late at night, you ask, 'Who's there?' It may be a case of *pikuach nefesh,* a life in danger, and there's not a moment to lose."

Another time, a member of the household ran into the house gasping, "The Brisker Rav is coming!"

R' Isser Zalman jumped up, put on his Shabbos coat in honor of the special guest, and ran at full speed to the outer stairs to welcome his visitor.

A few minutes later, his family was astounded to see the *Rosh Yeshivah* bring a simple Jew into the house! There was a resemblance to the Brisker Rav, but it was clearly not the great Rav at all!

R' Isser Zalman seated the man at the head of his table with unusual honor and asked in a warm, humble voice, "How may I honor my important guest? Would you like a cup of tea, or perhaps a pastry? Or maybe you would like to wash your hands and enjoy a full meal?"

The stranger blushed and apologized for troubling the *Rosh Yeshivah*. He explained that he was about to travel overseas. His daughter had reached marriageable age, and he needed to collect funds for her wedding. He had come to request a letter of support for his cause.

At once, R' Isser Zalman took paper and pen in hand and composed a glowing recommendation, and immediately handed it to the man. He blessed the man with many heartfelt wishes for his success. Then he rose to accompany his visitor out, descending the stairs to the street and watching the man continue on his way.

Upon his reentry into the house, his students and family surrounded R' Isser Zalman, all asking the same question: "Why give all that honor to a simple Jew?"

R' Isser Zalman explained. "In truth, *hachnasas orchim* is a great mitzvah and so is the mitzvah of treating others with respect. Really one should treat every Jewish person, whoever he is, the way one would treat an outstanding *talmid chacham*. Avraham *Avinu* treated his guests royally when he thought they were Arabs. But we, for our sins, are careless of this mitzvah. We make distinctions between one Jew and the next.

"Today, I intended to welcome and honor an important figure. Was

I to refrain from doing that good deed just because my visitor turned out to be a simple Jew? Is there even such a thing as a 'simple Jew'?"

A moment later, he added, "If Heaven has decreed that this Jew receive special honor — honor worthy of the Brisker Rav — then in the end that honor must come to him!"

The Uninvited Guest

וְהוּא עֹמֵד עֲלֵיהֶם תַּחַת הָעֵץ וַיֹּאכֵלוּ
He stood over them beneath the tree and they ate.
(*Bereishis* 18:8)

R' Eliyahu Chaim Meisel, the rabbi of Lodz, was well known for the way he welcomed visitors to his home. Another rabbi, who spent two months under R' Eliyahu Chaim's roof, told this story:

"The whole time I was privileged to be in R' Eliyahu Chaim's house, we never said *Birkas Hamazon* after a Shabbos meal without a quorum of ten men at the table. There were always about twenty people for each meal.

"One Friday night, we were seated at the table enjoying the meal when, just as the soup was being served, the door opened and an uninvited guest walked in. He took off his coat and began to sing '*Shalom Aleichem*' out loud. While he sang he paced the room, hands tucked into his belt, like a man making himself at home.

"The Rebbetzin went over to him and asked him to hurry and make *Kiddush,* as the soup had already been served and his portion was getting cold. The man made *Kiddush,* but at the first sip of wine he began coughing dreadfully, until he nearly choked. He kept up this coughing throughout the meal.

"At the end of the meal, the Rav stood up to graciously thank the man for coming, despite the fact that he had come without an invitation. The man revealed that he was a visitor in town and that he suffered from some sort of ailment. Nobody else had agreed to host him — so he had come to the Rav's house.

"'In that case,' R' Eliyahu Chaim said, 'Come eat with us again tomorrow!'"

A New Twist

וְהוּא עֹמֵד עֲלֵיהֶם תַּחַת הָעֵץ וַיֹּאכֵלוּ
He stood over them beneath the tree and they ate.
(*Bereishis* 18:8)

One winter day, when R' Simchah Bunim of Pesishcha was just 5 years old, visitors came to his father. The Rav prepared a meal for them. As they ate, he called over his son and said, "Go, my son, and find a *chiddush* (original Torah thought) on the topic of *hachnasas orchim*."

The boy went into another room. After a while, he returned to his father.

"Have you come up with a *chiddush*?" asked his father.

"Yes," said young Simchah Bunim.

The guests, who had already heard of the child's brilliance, thought that the father had no doubt asked him to say some novel halachic thought. After they had finished their meal, the Rav said, "Let us go together and see what *chiddush* my son has prepared."

They walked into the other room, and the Rav showed them the "*chiddush*" that his son had come up with regarding the "laws" of *hachnasas orchim:* There stood several beds, well supplied with pillows and blankets. The Rav bade them lie down and enjoy a good sleep.

The guests were astounded at the young boy's wisdom and goodness.

Quick Thinking

וְהוּא עֹמֵד עֲלֵיהֶם תַּחַת הָעֵץ וַיֹּאכֵלוּ
He stood over them beneath the tree and they ate.
(*Bereishis* 18:8)

R' Shmuel of Shinov related the following:

"My Rebbe, R' Simchah Bunim of Pesishcha, very much admired

R' Akiva Eiger. He used to tell a story about how R' Akiva Eiger was hosting a guest in his home, when the guest accidentally knocked over a cup of wine, staining the beautiful white tablecloth.

"Immediately, R' Akiva Eiger took his own cup of wine and 'accidentally' knocked it over as well, saying, 'It seems that the table is crooked.'"

Through the Window

כִּי יְדַעְתִּיו לְמַעַן אֲשֶׁר יְצַוֶּה אֶת בָּנָיו וְאֶת בֵּיתוֹ אַחֲרָיו וְשָׁמְרוּ דֶּרֶךְ ד'

For I have cherished him, because he commands his children and his household after him that they keep the way of Hashem

(*Bereishis* 18:19)

A man once came to seek the Gerrer Rebbe's advice. "I am considering buying a new apartment. Do you think it is worth buying?" And he went on to describe the apartment, with all its assets and flaws. The Rebbe stopped him and asked, "Tell me, which direction do the windows face? What will your children see when they look out the windows? Will they see good, instructive sights or, Heaven forbid, other things?"

The Rebbe continued. "In that neighborhood there is a youth center. If the apartment's windows face this center — don't buy it. If they don't, you can go ahead and buy it. Educating our children is the most important thing of all!"

Tzedakah the Right Way

לַעֲשׂוֹת צְדָקָה וּמִשְׁפָּט

Doing charity and justice

(*Bereishis* 18:19)

A poor man from a distinguished family came to the city of Ostrov wearing clothes that were tattered and stained. When R' Elyakim Getzel offered to outfit him with a new set of clothes, the poor man declined. "I have no need for that," he said.

That night, as the poor man slept, R' Elyakim Getzel summoned a tailor to sew a coat in the same measurements as the torn one. When he was done, R' Elyakim Getzel switched the ragged garment for the new one.

In the morning, when the poor man awoke, he searched in vain for his old coat. In its place, he found a brand-new one that fit him perfectly. He went to his host and told him what had happened.

R' Elyakim Getzel listened, then said, "If the coat fits you, it is a clear sign that Heaven arranged this."

The Meeting

זַעֲקַת סְדֹם וַעֲמֹרָה כִּי רָבָּה

The outcry of Sodom and Amorah has become great
(*Bereishis* 18:20)

When R' Levi Yitzchak accepted the position of Rav of Berditchev, he made one condition: The community must not trouble him to participate in every public meeting it chose to hold. Only when they desired to institute a new law or custom would he involve himself.

One day, the leaders of the community decided to create a new law in their town: Poor people would no longer be permitted to go from door to door collecting money. Instead, public funds would go to support the poor on a regular monthly basis.

Because this was a new law, the Chief Rabbi was invited to the meeting. Upon R' Levi Yitzchak's arrival, the community leaders presented him with their proposal.

With an astonished expression, R' Levi Yitzchak said, "But I told you when I became Rav of this town I did not want to be troubled to participate in meetings unless there was a new law to be enacted!"

The city council members were stunned. "But, Rebbe — isn't this a new law?"

R' Levi Yitzchak answered, "You are mistaken. This law is not new at all. In fact, it is an ancient law — dating from the days of Sodom and Amorah, who decreed that its poor could not collect from door to door."

The proposal, of course, was struck at once from the meeting's agenda.

Humility

וְאָנֹכִי עָפָר וָאֵפֶר
"I am but dust and ash."
(*Bereishis* 18:27)

Over 200 years ago, R' Yehudah ben Attar, known to his fellow citizens by the term "Rabi Elkabir" ("The Great Rabbi"), served as *Av Beis Din* of the city of Fez.

One afternoon, after *Minchah*, R' Yehudah ben Attar stepped out of the *beis midrash* and began walking home to eat lunch and to take a short rest. On his way, he passed by the marketplace. The Jewish merchants rose to their feet and greeted him respectfully, while the Arabs, who knew him as a holy man, called out, "Greetings to you, Rabi Elkabir!" And R' Yehudah warmly returned all their greetings.

On one corner stood a coal merchant's shop. It was hard to even call it a "shop"; it was narrow, cramped, and dark, filled to the brim with sacks of coal. The merchant would move some of the sacks to the street each morning and, seated on a small wooden stool, call out to passersby to buy his wares.

Seeing R' Yehudah approaching, the coal merchant called, "Rabi, can you do me a favor?"

"What kind of question is that? A favor for a fellow Jew? Of course I'll do it!" R' Yehudah answered readily.

"I am very hungry, and it's hard for me to drag my sacks back into the shop. If you're willing to wait here with my coal, I'll run home, eat some lunch, and return immediately!"

The other merchants who overheard this request dropped their jaws in amazement. How dare that coal man belittle Rabi's honor in this way? But R' Yehudah was glad to do the mitzvah that had chanced to come his way. "All right, my son. Go on, and enjoy your meal!"

The coal merchant went home, and Rabi sat down at the shop's entrance reviewing the Talmud from memory. Presently, a friend of his came walking by. It was the *dayan* (judge), R' Yaakov.

"Rabi!" R' Yaakov cried out in surprise. "What is Rabi doing here?"

"The shopkeeper gave me the privilege of doing a mitzvah," R'

Vayeira / 87

Yehudah answered happily. "I'm looking after his store while he eats lunch."

R' Yaakov grew very angry. "How dare that stupid coal merchant belittle our Rabi in this way!"

"*Chas v'shalom!*" R' Yehudah said. "He is not stupid, only naive. Because of him, I now understand the words of R' Yehudah *Hanasi* in *Talmud Yerushalmi* (*Kesubos* 12): 'Whatever a person asks of me — I will do it for him!'"

R' Yehudah ben Attar went on, "Had someone asked R' Yehudah *Hanasi* for a loan or charity and R' Yehudah complied, what would have been so great in that? He was a wealthy man, and by Jewish law was obligated to give a loan or charity. If he were asked to intercede on someone's behalf and pay a visit to the king — that, too, would have been his obligation. To try to bring about peace between people, or to attend a *seudas mitzvah* — all these were obligations. But R' Yehudah meant what he said: If a coal merchant asked him to look after his shop, he would do that, too, with joy.

"And if *Rabbeinu Hakadosh* was prepared to make light of his own honor in fulfilling a coal man's request," concluded R' Yehudah ben Attar, "how much more so should I, his servant."

True Hospitality

וַיָּבֹאוּ שְׁנֵי הַמַּלְאָכִים סְדֹמָה

The two angels came to Sodom
(*Bereishis* 19:1)

R' Levi Yitzchak of Berditchev once came to the city of Lvov. He entered a rich man's home and requested permission to stay for the night. Not recognizing him, the rich man refused.

R' Levi Yitzchak went next to a poor *melamed* (schoolteacher), who received him with joy.

Over the course of the next few hours, the news began to spread throughout the city: "The Berditchever Rav has come!" Great crowds began to gather around the *melamed's* house. Among them was the rich man who had turned R' Levi Yitzchak away. He had come to beg the *tzaddik's* pardon.

"I didn't recognize the Rav," he explained. "Now I beg of you to move into my home, where I can give you proper honor!"

But R' Levi Yitzchak declined the invitation. "What was the difference," he asked, "between Avraham and Lot? Both of them welcomed guests into their home. But we only praise Avraham for his hospitality, not Lot. Why?

"Lot saw angels and received them into his home. This is welcoming angels, not guests! But Avraham *Avinu* saw three men, apparently poor travelers, covered with dust, and he ran out to greet them. That is true hospitality!"

No Excuse

וַיָּבֹאוּ שְׁנֵי הַמַּלְאָכִים סְדֹמָה בָּעֶרֶב וְלוֹט יֹשֵׁב בְּשַׁעַר סְדֹם וַיַּרְא לוֹט וַיָּקָם לִקְרָאתָם וַיִּשְׁתַּחוּ אַפַּיִם אָרְצָה

The two angels came to Sodom in the evening and Lot was sitting at the gate of Sodom; and Lot saw and stood up to meet them and he bowed, face to the ground.

(*Bereishis* 19:1)

The Beis HaLevi, R' Yosef Dov Soloveitchik, had the custom, when traveling, of exchanging his rabbinical clothing for simple ones so that he would not be recognized. He would take off his big black hat and don the kind of cap that plain workmen wore in those days.

One frigid winter's night, R' Yosef Dov was traveling by wagon to the city of Baranovitch. The cold was intense. Seeing that it was impossible to travel further that night, the wagon driver pulled up by the roadside in front of a Jewish inn. He knocked on the door, but there was no reply. Because it was dangerous for them to remain outdoors, R' Yosef Dov urged the driver to pound on the door with all his might. At last, after repeated banging, the innkeeper awoke and opened the door for them. In a raging temper, he told them curtly that there was no room for them at his inn. "Some guests are expected at any minute," he added.

They pleaded with the innkeeper, reminding him that they would be risking their lives remaining outdoors in such freezing weather.

They would be content, they assured him, even with a simple attic room in which to find shelter from the cold until morning.

After lengthy coaxing, the innkeeper finally let them come in and sleep on the floor in the hall. R' Yosef Dov lit a candle in order to learn quietly from a *sefer*. Immediately, there came the innkeeper's furious voice: "Put out that candle at once. Do not disturb our rest!"

R' Yosef Dov extinguished the candle and continued to learn by heart, his lips moving silently.

A few hours later, hoofbeats, and the noise of wagon wheels, were heard approaching. The wagons stopped at the inn. Without delay, the innkeeper ran to light the lanterns and throw open the door. He greeted the newcomers pleasantly. They were R' Aharon of Koidenov and some of his *chassidim*.

The innkeeper and other members of his household scurried about fetching glasses of hot tea for their chilled guests. After resting awhile from his travels, the Rebbe began to prepare himself to *daven Ma'ariv*. As he passed through the hall in order to wash his hands, he glanced at a Jew sleeping on the floor. He took another, closer look and saw none other than R' Yosef Dov, the Brisker Rav! Emotionally, he cried out, "R' Yoshe Ber! R' Yoshe Ber! Brisker Rav! Why are you sleeping here?"

When the innkeeper heard the Rebbe's words, he grew pale. Fear and shame overcame him. Whom had he treated with such scorn and disdain? None other than the *gaon,* the Brisker Rav! With shaking knees he approached R' Yosef Dov to beg his forgiveness, for he had not known who he was.

The Brisker Rav replied that he would forgive him only on one condition: that the innkeeper come stay in his home in Brisk for two weeks, and learn the laws of *chesed* and *hachnasas orchim*. R' Yosef Dov added, "I've always been amazed: In *Parashas Vayeira* we find two wonderful stories, one about Avraham *Avinu's* hospitality to his guests, and one of Lot's hospitality to the angels. The surprising thing is that the Torah places greater worth on Avraham's mitzvah of *hachnasas orchim* — though Lot's was performed with greater sacrifice and risk to his life.

"The difference is this: Avraham thought that his guests were Arabs, yet he still served them eagerly and devotedly. But Lot knew right away that angels had come to his home. It is no great act of heroism to offer hospitality to angels, and it is no wonder that he was prepared to sacrifice his life for their sake."

R' Yosef Dov finished, "It is not an excuse to say, 'I didn't know it was the Brisker Rav knocking on my door!'"

The innkeeper accepted the condition. He traveled to Brisk and stayed in the Rav's home, where he was able to witness with his own eyes R' Yosef Dov's compassion for the poor and the downtrodden.

He saw — and became a new man. Those two weeks under R' Yosef Dov's roof transformed that innkeeper into the biggest *machnis orchim* in the entire area.

Hospitality to the Rescue

וַיֹּאמֶר הִנֶּה נָּא אֲדֹנַי סוּרוּ נָא אֶל בֵּית עַבְדְּכֶם וְלִינוּ וְרַחֲצוּ רַגְלֵיכֶם

And he said, "Behold now, my lords; turn about, please, to your servant's house; spend the night and wash your feet"

(*Bereishis* 19:2)

A lumber merchant had the custom of coming to Radin for the High Holy Days, in order to *daven* with the Chofetz Chaim.

After one such Rosh Hashanah, the merchant went to see the Chofetz Chaim to discuss a serious legal dispute with several non-Jewish locals in which he was involved. The ruling in the case was due to be handed down after Yom Kippur. The Chofetz Chaim ordered him to return home immediately so that he might be on hand in case legal matters arose requiring his presence. Though it pained the merchant to miss the Yom Kippur *davening* in Radin, he obeyed his Rebbe and returned home.

That very night, a mighty storm arose. Strong winds, rains, thunder, and lightning rampaged through the area. Suddenly, at the height of the storm, there came a frantic pounding on the merchant's door. It was a group of Poles who had been on their way to the nearby forest when the storm caught them by surprise.

The merchant welcomed them warmly into his home and supplied them with everything they needed. And it turned out that one of his guests was none other than the judge in the merchant's dispute.

The judge was grateful to the Jew who had helped him in his hour of need. On the appointed day, his ruling went in favor of the lumber merchant.

An Outstanding Host

וְלִינוּ וְרַחֲצוּ רַגְלֵיכֶם
"Spend the night and wash your feet"
(*Bereishis* 19:2)

The door of R' Boruch Mordechai Tcherny's house was always open wide for everyone. Poor people could make themselves at home there. So outstanding was R' Boruch Mordechai's *chesed* that he did not mind at all what people did to any of his belongings beneath his roof. In fact, he treated himself exactly the way he treated his guests.

Once, a poor man came to his house and remained for several weeks without recognizing that R' Boruch Mordechai was his host. In his innocence, the guest thought that R' Boruch Mordechai — who always dressed simply, in the manner of those he welcomed into his home — was merely another poor guest. After a lengthy period, the poor man turned to R' Boruch Mordechai and said, "I see that you are an old-timer here. You surely know how things work in this place. Tell me: Do you think anyone will mind if I stay on another few days?"

R' Boruch Mordechai shrugged. "I think you can stay. Look at me; I've been here for quite some time, I sleep here and eat here at the host's expense, and no one says a word."

Running After Chesed

וַתַּגְדֵּל חַסְדְּךָ אֲשֶׁר עָשִׂיתָ עִמָּדִי לְהַחֲיוֹת אֶת נַפְשִׁי
"And Your kindness was great which You did with me to save my life"
(*Bereishis* 19:19)

In his early years as a rabbi, the Beis HaLevi was approached by a blacksmith who had a question regarding Pesach. "Tell me, Rebbe, can I fulfill my obligation of the four cups at the *seder* by drinking four glasses of milk?"

R' Yosef Dov asked a question in turn. "Is your health bad that you are afraid to drink wine?"

"No," answered the blacksmith. "Thank G-d, I am healthy. But this year I don't have the money for four cups of wine each for me and all of my family."

Hearing this, R' Yosef Dov immediately asked his wife to give the blacksmith twenty-five rubles. The man refused to take it, saying, "I came to ask a halachic question, Rebbe — not to take charity!"

R' Yosef Dov answered, "Take it, my dear man. The money is a loan, until Hashem broadens your horizons."

Persuaded, the blacksmith took the money and left.

After he had gone, R' Yosef Dov's wife asked her husband, "For just two or three rubles, that blacksmith could have bought enough wine for his family to drink four cups each. Why, then, did you instruct me to give him twenty-five rubles?"

R' Yosef Dov explained. "You are right. However, from his question to me I understood that he cannot afford to buy the rest of his Pesach needs, either. Since he asked if it is permissible to drink milk instead of wine, it's clear that he has no money for meat and other foods for Pesach. Therefore, I asked you to give him enough money to help him buy everything he needs for the holiday!"

Filling the Quota?

הֲלֹא מִצְעָר הִוא וּתְחִי נַפְשִׁי
"Is it not small? And let my soul live."
(*Bereishis* 19:20)
"And are not its sins few [because it is a new city], and You are able to spare it."
(*Rashi*)

One *Shabbos Shuvah* afternoon, as the sun set and shadows filled the *beis midrash* of Yeshivas Eitz Chaim, R' Isser Zalman Meltzer addressed his students.

"We are all believers, and the sons of believers. Now the Day of Judgment is approaching, the day when every living being passes before the King of kings. But where is the fear? How is it that we are not terrified? Where is our fear of the Day of Judgment?

"The answer is that we have grown used to these Days of Judgment. We have already lived through a number of Rosh Hashanahs. For forty-five years, say, Rosh Hashanah has come and gone, and nothing has happened—"

Slowly, the great room became even darker. Shabbos was already over, but no one made a move to turn on a light. The darkness joined R' Isser Zalman's deep voice in creating the proper awe-inspiring atmosphere for the Day of Judgment.

"But really," R' Isser Zalman continued, tears on his cheeks, "This way of thinking is fundamentally flawed. In Slobodka, we once heard R' Yitzchak Blazer say that when Lot and his daughters fled from Sodom, Lot asked the angels to send him to the city of Tzo'ar. Why did Lot wish to go to that specific city?

"Rashi explains that Tzo'ar was founded one year after Sodom, and so its sins were fewer than Sodom's. Tzo'ar was still not filled to the brim with sin and did not yet deserve to be destroyed. 'Is it not small? And let my soul live.'

"And maybe," the *gaon's* voice trembled as he wept, "maybe on Rosh Hashanah of last year, I fell into the category of 'Tzo'ar.' Maybe last year my quota of sin was not yet filled to the brim, and was not yet worthy of the death sentence.

"But this year, after another full year without repenting, have I reached, Heaven forbid, the category of Sodom? Has my quota for sin been filled this year?"

Look at the Pot!

כִּי אָמַרְתִּי רַק אֵין יִרְאַת אֱלֹקִים בַּמָּקוֹם הַזֶּה

"Because I said, 'There is but no fear of G-d in this place'"
(*Bereishis* 20:11)

Word went out that a well-known Jewish lecturer was seen frequently in the company of *maskilim,* men who had thrown off the yoke of Torah and mitzvos. In short, the speaker did not practice what he preached.

One day, this speaker arrived in the city of Brisk, where R' Chaim Soloveitchik was rabbi. Upon learning of the man's doubtful behavior, R' Chaim forbade him to speak in any shul in the city.

The speaker came to R' Chaim and said, "Please, let the Rav come hear me speak. That will prove that I am 100 percent kosher. From beginning to end, my entire *derashah* (sermon) is filled with wisdom culled from works of *mussar* that have been accepted among our people for generations. Why, then, does the Rav forbid me to speak in any shul in Brisk?"

"Even if your words are true and correct," R' Chaim answered, "I will not change my mind and let you speak in this city. You are no doubt aware, even if meat is slaughtered by an experienced *shochet* and *kashered* in accordance with every halachic requirement, if it is then cooked in a *treif* pot, it becomes completely unkosher.

"Similarly, concepts that emerge from the mouth of a man lacking fear of Heaven must have a negative influence on those who hear them!"

The Proper Way to Receive a Traveler

רַק אֵין יִרְאַת אֱלֹקִים בַּמָּקוֹם הַזֶּה

"There is but no fear of G-d in this place"

(*Bereishis* 20:11)

A guest who comes to a city, [is it] regarding matters of eating and drinking [that people] should ask him...

(Rashi)

The Chofetz Chaim was a close friend of R' Chaim Ozer Grodzinsky, Rav of Vilna. Together, the two labored on behalf of the people and tended to their spiritual and physical needs.

Once, when the Chofetz Chaim was staying in a city near Radin, he received word that R' Chaim Ozer was on his way to see him, in order to help him organize aid for poor Jews in Russia. Overjoyed at the news, the Chofetz Chaim hurried to put on his Shabbos clothes in his guest's honor. When R' Chaim Ozer arrived, the Chofetz Chaim's happiness knew no bounds.

Vayeira / 95

One of his students turned to the Chofetz Chaim and said, "Rebbe, now we will be able to *daven Minchah* with a *minyan*. Together with R' Chaim Ozer, we now number ten men!"

The Chofetz Chaim answered, "One must make sure a guest rests and has enough to eat and drink, but nowhere in the Torah does it say that one must ask a guest if he wishes to *daven*." And, turning to his guest, he asked, "R' Chaim Ozer, would you like something to eat or drink?"

"No, thank you," R' Chaim Ozer replied.

"In that case," said the Chofetz Chaim, "I'd like to ask you to go rest a little. You must be very tired from your journey." And the Chofetz Chaim personally saw to his beloved and illustrious guest's every need.

On One Condition

וַיִּתְפַּלֵּל אַבְרָהָם אֶל הָאֱלֹקִים וַיִּרְפָּא אֱלֹקִים אֶת אֲבִימֶלֶךְ

Avraham prayed to G-d, and G-d healed Avimelech

(*Bereishis* 20:17)

A large number of people were waiting their turns to see R' Yitzchak Meir, the Gerrer Rebbe and author of the *Chiddushei Ha-Rim*. His aide, R' Bunim, stood by to keep order. One man, however, refused to take his turn in an orderly fashion. When R' Bunim denied him entry before the others, the man grew angry and slapped R' Bunim. Everyone was stunned by the action and by the force of the blow.

R' Bunim went and told the Rebbe what had happened but did not reveal the attacker's identity. One by one, the people took their turns, and entered the Rebbe's room. When the man who had slapped R' Bunim stepped inside, the Rebbe knew immediately that he was the one. The Rebbe refused to even hear the reason for the man's coming to see him, and rebuked him strongly for what he had done.

The man felt genuine remorse for his action, and he wept brokenly. He had no children and had come to ask the Rebbe to plead with Hashem that he be blessed with offspring. R' Yitzchak Meir told the man that he would not hear him out until he had begged forgiveness from R' Bunim. Only after R' Bunim forgave him would the

Rebbe agree to hear the man's story.

The man did as he was told. He went to apologize to R' Bunim. The Rebbe's aide went with him into R' Yitzchak Meir's room and announced, "Rebbe, I will forgive this man on one condition."

"And what is that?" asked the Rebbe.

"That the Rebbe will bless this man with living offspring."

Pleased with his assistant's good-heartedness, the Rebbe agreed to the condition and his blessing soon bore fruit.

Fire

וַיִּטַּע אֶשֶׁל בִּבְאֵר שָׁבַע

He planted an "eshel" in Be'er Sheva

(*Bereishis* 21:33)

A villager came to the Maggid of Koznitz to complain about the harshness of his lot. He had always been hospitable to strangers, opening his house to them, he said — but Hashem had decreed that a fire burn down his home and everything in it.

The Maggid questioned the man closely. "Did you feed your guests?"

"Of course!"

"Did you give them to drink?"

"All they wanted."

"And did you set aside a sleeping place for each of them?" the Maggid persisted. "And did you afterward fulfill the mitzvah of accompanying them when they departed?"

"A-as for sleeping arrangements," the villager stammered, "it was not always possible for me to be scrupulous with this mitzvah. There were many guests and my home is small. And I also did not find the time to accompany my guests when they left."

"Hashem, may His Name be blessed, has commanded us to supply our guests with the letters '*eshel*' [aleph, shin, and lamed]," the Maggid explained. "That stands for '*achilah*,' food; '*shesiyah*,' drink; and '*linah*,' a place to sleep. Some say that '*levayah*,' accompaniment, is also included.

"Because you left out the '*lamed*' of '*eshel*,' only two letters were left. They spell '*eish*' — fire!"

One Precious Life

בִּנְךָ אֶת יְחִידְךָ אֲשֶׁר אָהַבְתָּ
"Your son, your only one, whom you love"

(Bereishis 22:2)

An interesting anecdote is told about R' Mordechai of Rachmastrivka and his awesome love of his fellow Jew.

R' Mordechai had a precious *sukkah* which had been passed down to him from his holy ancestors. One day, he took the wooden walls of that *sukkah* and burned them. It was a time of famine and dearth, when firewood was in short supply. But R' Mordechai had heard of a very sick boy, battling for his life, who needed to be kept warm.

Because of their origin, the planks of that *sukkah* were very valuable. In the *Beis Shlomo,* the story is told of a very wealthy man who visited Jerusalem in the year 5668 and wished to purchase those *sukkah* boards. He offered a very large sum of money — an amount on which R' Mordechai might have lived out the rest of his days. Although R' Mordechai was living in great poverty, he refused to consider the proposal.

But when he realized that it was in his power to save one Jewish life, he did not hesitate even one minute before burning the planks to provide warmth for a sick child.

The Competition

וַיַּשְׁכֵּם אַבְרָהָם בַּבֹּקֶר
So Avraham arose early in the morning

(Bereishis 22:3)

As a young man, R' Yaakov Yitzchak of Peshischa lived with his in-laws, who supported him while he learned Torah. Their home was near a blacksmith's shop. Each day, as he passed the shop, he would see the sparks flying from the white-hot metal and compare the sight to the study of Torah. Even something as strong as steel, if heated sufficiently, can be made to bend.

It was the sound of the blacksmith's ringing hammer that awakened R' Yaakov Yitzchak each morning. He would leap out of his bed, *daven,* and sit down to learn Torah. One morning, he thought: "I should be ashamed of myself. That blacksmith wakes up earlier than I do, and for physical purposes only. How much earlier should I awaken to perform Hashem's work!"

The next day, R' Yaakov Yitzchak got out of bed before the blacksmith.

When the blacksmith entered his smithy, he heard the melodious voice of Torah coming to him from his neighbor's house. And the blacksmith said to himself: "Look at that young man who does not have to rise early in order to earn a living, yet gets up so early to do his job. I, who am responsible for supporting my wife and children, must wake up earlier than he!" On the third day, the blacksmith got up earlier and was at work before R' Yaakov Yitzchak awoke.

Hearing the ringing of the blacksmith's hammer, the young Torah scholar felt the same sense of inadequacy as before. He decided to arise before dawn from then on. The blacksmith removed himself from the competition.

In later days, when R' Yaakov Yitzchak stood revealed as a holy *tzaddik,* he often said, "For everything I've accomplished and everything I am today, I owe thanks to that blacksmith!"

Yiras Shamayim to Its Depths

עַתָּה יָדַעְתִּי כִּי יְרֵא אֱלֹקִים אַתָּה
"Now I know that you are G-d-fearing"
(*Bereishis* 22:12)

R' Yehoshua Leib Diskin related that, as a boy, he would observe everything his father, R' Binyamin, did. When a halachic question arose about a certain cooked food, even if R' Binyamin ruled favorably, he would tell his wife to feed it to the children. Little Yehoshua Leib was insulted. He did not understand why he was any different from his father. If R' Binyamin had accepted a stringency upon him-

100 / STORIES MY GRANDFATHER TOLD ME

self, why was he being lenient with his son?

One day, a fire broke out in a nearby village. The flames penetrated the village shul and licked at the *sifrei Torah,* burning a portion of them. When the fire was finally subdued, the villagers prepared a message for R' Binyamin, asking for his instructions in this matter.

The messenger arrived in the city, carrying the scorched parchments that had been saved from the flames. When he reached R' Binyamin's house, Yehoshua Leib came out to greet him, asking the purpose of his visit. The messenger told him about the fire that had broken out in the nearby village and about the burnt *sifrei Torah.* Excitedly, the boy brought the man in to see his father.

The messenger opened the door to R' Binyamin's inner room. R' Binyamin lifted his eyes and caught sight of the scorched scrolls. He collapsed on the floor in a faint.

His household was thrown into an uproar. Family members and students alike attempted to revive him. After great effort, R' Binyamin was restored to consciousness. Very slowly, he regained his strength, and was finally able to deal with the question of the burnt Torah scrolls.

"From that moment on," R' Yehoshua Leib would say long afterward, "I understood that there *was* a difference between my father and myself."

Like Master, Like Servant

וַיִּקְרָא אַבְרָהָם שֵׁם הַמָּקוֹם הַהוּא ד' יִרְאֶה אֲשֶׁר יֵאָמֵר הַיּוֹם בְּהַר ד' יֵרָאֶה

And Avraham called the name of that site "Hashem Yireh," as it is said this day, on the mountain Hashem will be seen.

(*Bereishis* 22:14)

Guests from abroad once came to stay at R' Yehoshua Leib Diskin's house in Jerusalem. They looked around at the Rabbi's simple home and asked in surprise, "Why did his honor, the Rav, choose to live in such a simple place?"

R' Yehoshua Leib gestured at the *Har Habayis,* which could be seen from his window. "It is sufficient for a servant to be like his master." In other words, if the *Shechinah* hovered over the ruins of the destroyed *Beis Hamikdash,* how could he, R' Yehoshua Leib, live in a beautiful house?

The guests inquired further: "But doesn't it reflect poorly on the Torah for the greatest rabbi in Israel to live in such a simple dwelling?"

"It's not true that I am the greatest in Israel," the *gaon* answered modestly. "But if I've accomplished a little, it is because I did not desire fancy houses and did not pursue luxuries."

פרשת חיי שרה

Parashas Chayei Sarah

The Truth in His Heart

וַיִּשְׁקֹל אַבְרָהָם לְעֶפְרֹן אֶת הַכֶּסֶף אֲשֶׁר דִּבֶּר בְּאָזְנֵי בְנֵי חֵת אַרְבַּע מֵאוֹת שֶׁקֶל כֶּסֶף עֹבֵר לַסֹּחֵר

And Avraham weighed out to Efron the money that he had mentioned in the hearing of the children of Ches, four hundred silver shekalim in negotiable currency

(*Bereishis* 23:16)

A Jewish merchant — a stranger in town — once approached R' Shraga Feivel Frank (father-in-law of R' Moshe Mordechai Epstein, *Rosh Yeshivah* of Slobodka, and R' Isser Zalman Meltzer, *Rosh Yeshivah* of Eitz Chaim) with an order for a large quantity of leather skins.

"What kind of discount will you give me for such a large order?" the merchant asked.

R' Shraga Feivel replied, "This is my price. I sell for a price that will leave me with a certain amount of profit. I am not prepared to lower it or to bargain with you. Whoever is not interested in buying at my price can buy from the other merchants in town!"

With that, R' Shraga Feivel gave the visiting merchant the addresses of the town's other leather shops.

The merchant left the shop and went off to buy his leather someplace else. But after going from one shop to another, he discovered that R' Shraga Feivel's price was the best in town. The merchant returned to him, saying that he had decided to buy the skins from him after all — at the stated price.

"I will sell them to you," R' Shraga Feivel said, "but not at the price I quoted earlier. I am going to give you a discount, as you requested."

The merchant was astonished. "But you refused to give me a discount before, even though you saw that unless you lowered the

Chayei Sarah / 105

price I would not buy from you. Now, when I've come to buy at your stated price, you're lowering it without my even asking?"

"Let me explain," said R' Shraga Feivel. "After you left my shop, I thought the matter over. The quantity you were interested in purchasing was much larger than the norm, so that even with a discount I would be left with a nice profit from the sale. I told myself that, in this case, I should not have stood stubbornly by my usual business principles.

"Now that you've come back and wish to buy from me, I must fulfill what I was thinking before. After all, David *Hamelech* said, 'Hashem, who may sojourn in Your tent? Who may dwell on Your Holy Mountain? One who walks in perfect innocence, and does what is right, and speaks the truth from his heart.' And every morning we say, 'May a man always fear Heaven in private and in public, and speak the truth from his heart.'

"David *Hamelech* showed us the way to live, and I must fulfill what I say each morning. Because I had determined, in my heart, that I'd made a mistake in not giving you the discount you asked for — now that you've returned I must sell you the leather skins at the price I'd decided upon after you left my store. Each one of us is required to 'speak the truth from his heart'!"

Something "Fishy"

וַיָּקָם שְׂדֵה עֶפְרוֹן . . . לְאַבְרָהָם לְמִקְנָה לְעֵינֵי בְנֵי חֵת

And Efron's field... stood... as Avraham's as a purchase in the view of the children of Ches

(*Bereishis* 23:17-18)

The Chofetz Chaim's wife, together with a neighbor, once bought a large fish. The two women agreed that, at noon, the neighbor would come to the Chofetz Chaim's house, where they would divide the fish between them.

Noon came and went, with no sign of the neighbor. From time to time the Chofetz Chaim's wife went to the window to see if she was coming. Soon it was time to cook the fish, but the neighbor still had not come. Seeing that it was growing late, the Chofetz Chaim's wife divided the fish on her own. She reserved the larger portion for her neighbor and kept the smaller one for herself. Quickly, she placed her share of the fish into a pot to cook it.

When it was time to eat, the Chofetz Chaim washed his hands, made a *berachah* on a piece of bread, and began to eat it. After consuming a *k'zayis,* he recited the 23rd psalm, "Hashem is my shepherd, I shall not want." His wife, in the meantime, placed the cooked fish on the table.

The Chofetz Chaim did not seem to notice; he continued eating bread. His son, R' Leib, thought that perhaps his father did not know there was fish on the table, and moved the plate closer to him. But the Chofetz Chaim pushed the plate aside and continued eating bread.

R' Leib understood that there was something behind all this. He went into the kitchen and asked his mother to tell him everything she knew about the fish. She explained that the fish had been too big, so she had bought it together with a neighbor. Seeing that the neighbor had not yet come to divide the fish, she had undertaken to divide it herself, reserving the larger portion for the neighbor.

"Now I understand!" R' Leib said to himself. "There is a halachah in the *Shulchan Aruch, Choshen Mishpat,* dealing with the laws of partnership (*siman* 176, *se'if* 18): 'If a time limit for the partnership was not specified... and one partner wishes to divide [the goods] without his friend's knowledge, he must divide [it] in front of three people, etc.' This fish certainly falls into that category so my father cannot eat it. The division was not a proper division, and the fish still belongs partially to the neighbor! Can the author of *Mishnah Berurah* stoop to stealing?"

R' Yechezkel Levenstein related this story in the year 5699, when he served as spiritual administrator for the Mirrer Yeshivah. R' Yechezkel added, "It says of the *Mashiach*: '*V'haricho b'yira'as Hashem'* — 'He will be imbued with a spirit of fear for Hashem.' There is a spiritual sense through which it is possible to 'smell' sin. People who have elevated themselves to a very high spiritual level have this sense: They can 'smell' a spiritual flaw, a suspicion of theft, and the like."

The Pearl

וְכָל טוּב אֲדֹנָיו בְּיָדוֹ

With all the bounty of his master in his hand
(*Bereishis* 24:10)

When it came time for R' Aryeh Leibush, author of *Ari Devei Elai*, to marry, he wed the daughter of a respected man from Premishlan. His father-in-law promised to support him so that R' Aryeh might devote all his energies to Torah. It was not long, however, before the young wife expressed a desire for her husband to become involved in business. As R' Aryeh had no wish to give up his Torah learning, the marriage dissolved.

Afterwards, another young woman was suggested as a wife for him. It was Chanah, daughter of the "Yismach Moshe." So eager was the Yismach Moshe to acquire R' Aryeh for a son-in-law that he promised a larger dowry than he could afford, so that R' Aryeh might be able to live off the income and devote himself entirely to Torah.

The wife of the Yismach Moshe protested. "Why should we take a son-in-law whom others have sent from their home? And why obligate ourselves to such a large dowry, when many very wealthy young men are being suggested for our daughter?"

The Yismach Moshe replied, "I will tell you a parable that describes this situation.

"A farmer was once plowing his field when the plow came across a casket filled with pearls. Never having laid eyes on a pearl in his life, the farmer thought that they were beans that had been planted in the ground. He brought them home, put them in a pot with water, and began to cook them!

"When hours passed and the 'beans' had grown no softer, he went to ask a neighbor's advice. The more educated neighbor glanced into the pot and saw that it was filled with pearls. He offered to exchange the defective 'beans' for some fresh green ones. Both were happy with the trade, each according to his own knowledge."

The Yismach Moshe turned to his wife. "That is what happened here," he said. "That first father-in-law turned a precious pearl out of his house and took instead a 'bean' more suited to his aspirations. Let us hurry to acquire this pearl!"

He had already sold all the dishes to help pay for the dowry, but there was still not enough. The Yismach Moshe asked his wife to sell her jewelry and an embroidered shawl that she had brought from her father's home, in accordance with our Sages' words: "A man should sell everything he owns and marry off his daughter to a *talmid chacham*" (*Pesachim* 49).

The Rebbetzin went at once to do as her husband asked, and sold her jewelry for the privilege of acquiring a "pearl" of a son-in-law.

A Bed for the Night

גַּם מָקוֹם לָלוּן
"As well as place to lodge"
(*Bereishis* 24:25)

Late one cold winter's night, a traveler arrived in the town of Gustynin. Every house in town was dark, save for one: the home of R' Yechiel Meyer.

The traveler quickly made his way to that house and knocked on the door. R' Yechiel Meyer opened it and, with a smile, invited the stranger in. He gave the man food and drink and showed him a bed where he could spend the night.

The traveler lay down to sleep, but R' Yechiel Meyer stayed awake all night, learning Torah.

In the morning, when the traveler awoke, R' Yechiel Meyer took him to shul. There the man learned, to his shock, that his host was none other than the rabbi of the town! He approached R' Yechiel Meyer after *davening* to beg his forgiveness for troubling him — for disturbing his learning and sleeping in his bed.

"I will forgive you," R' Yechiel Meyer said, smiling, "on one condition."

"What condition is that?" the startled traveler asked.

"That whenever you return to our town, you will be my guest."

❧

A young man from Jerusalem once traveled to Bnei Brak to see R' Yaakov Yisrael Kanievsky, the Steipler Gaon, author of *Kehillos*

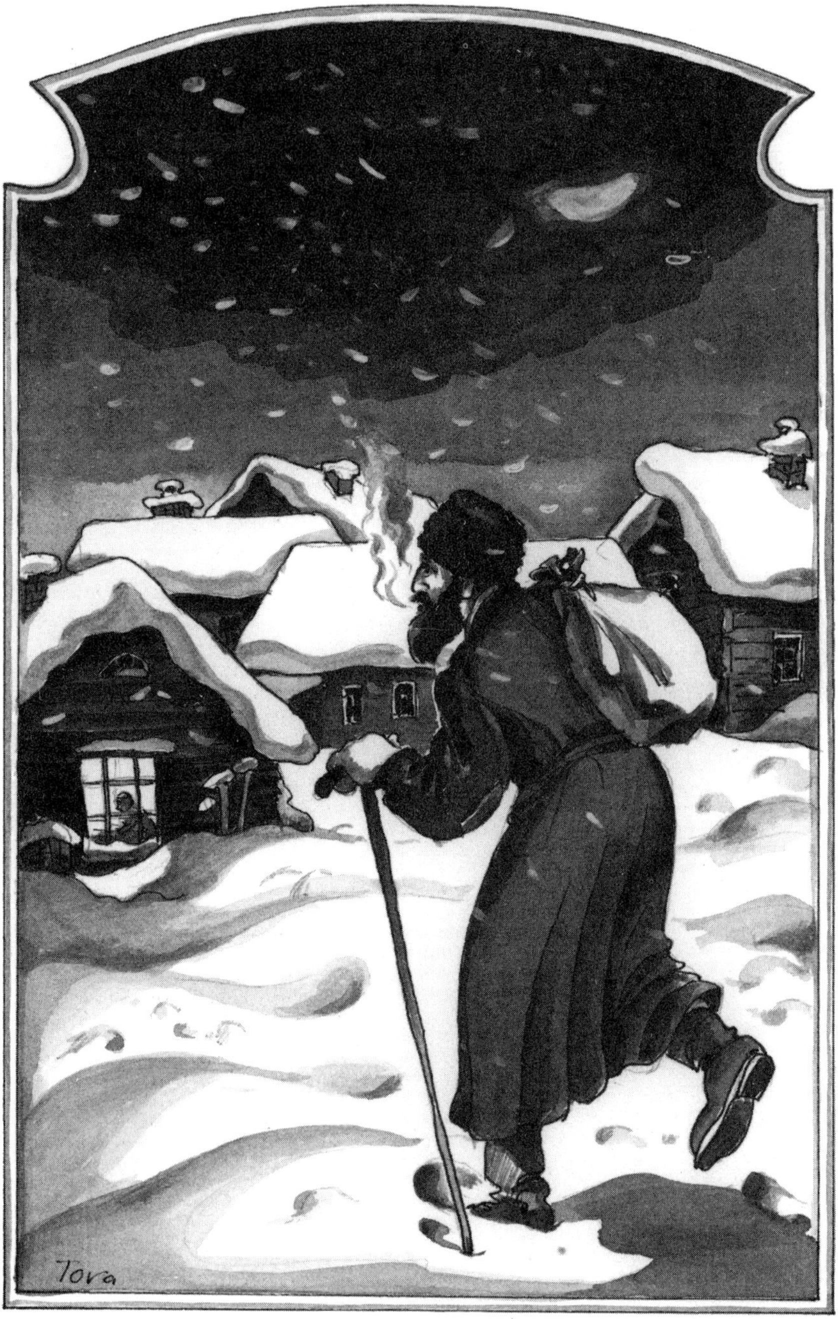
Tora

Yaakov. There was a long line of people waiting to see the Rav. When the young man's turn finally came and went, it was too late for him to return home to Jerusalem. Knowing no one in Bnei Brak, he asked a member of the Steipler's household if he knew of a place where he might spend the night.

"Go to Lederman's shul, not far from here," he was told. "You'll find a man there who will know of a place where you could stay."

The young man did as he was told.

When the Steipler heard about this, he stood up and went in search of the young man himself. After finding him, he invited him to spend the night in his own house. With his own hands, the Steipler arranged the man's bed. And in the morning, after *Shacharis,* the Steipler personally served his guest breakfast.

Afterwards when someone mentioned to the Steipler that the incident was written up in one of the newspapers, he replied dryly, "Soon they'll be writing that I put on *tefillin!*"

Scrupulous in Business

וַיָּבֹא הָאִישׁ הַבַּיְתָה וַיְפַתַּח הַגְּמַלִּים

So the man came into the house and he unfastened the camels
(Bereishis 24:32)

"And he unfastened": He untied their muzzle, for [whenever they traveled] he would obstruct their mouth so that they should not graze along the way in fields belonging to others (Rashi)

R' Yisrael Meyer, the Chofetz Chaim, opened a grocery store. His share of the work was to keep the accounts, while his wife managed the store. This way, the Chofetz Chaim was able to continue learning during the day.

Each night, on his return from the *beis midrash,* he would sit down to tally up the day's accounts. On market days, when there was extra work to do, he would help his wife in the store.

The Chofetz Chaim's management of the store was unique. He and his wife would close up shop in the middle of the day in order not to harm the competition. "They need a livelihood, too," he would explain. Every day, he would go into the store to make sure that the weights and measurements were accurate. If any merchandise had become even slightly damaged, he would not permit it to be sold in the store.

The Chofetz Chaim was constantly on the alert not to transgress in any way with respect to his business. If a man bought merchandise and still owed money on it, the Chofetz Chaim made sure not to pass near that man's house, lest the customer think that he was coming by to remind him of his debt. In this way, he fulfilled the commandment, "Do not be like a usurer."

Once, a non-Jewish customer accidentally left behind a salted fish in his shop. R' Yisrael Meyer was unsuccessful in discovering the man's identity. Here was a problem of stealing from a gentile! What did he do? On the following market day, the Chofetz Chaim distributed salted fish, free of charge, to every non-Jewish customer who came in.

On another occasion, he discovered that a certain non-Jewish woman had inadvertently received a little less salt than she had paid for. After great effort, he managed to discover which village the customer lived in, but was unsuccessful in learning her name.

The Chofetz Chaim did not procrastinate. He hired a driver and wagon and sent him to that village, with a sack of salt and instructions to distribute the salt among all the women in the village.

Is there anyone who would not prefer to shop in this sort of store than anywhere else? Gradually, the stream of customers to the Chofetz Chaim's store became greater and greater. Everyone wanted to buy from him.

As the number of his customers increased, the Chofetz Chaim became concerned: What would happen to the other shopkeepers? He instructed his wife to regularly lock the door that fronted the street.

"That way," he explained, "the only ones who will enter the store will be neighbors who know about the back way."

But these measures did not help for long. Customers quickly learned of the back door, and continued to patronize the store. The Chofetz Chaim was greatly worried that he might be stealing other shopkeepers' livelihood. He decided to close the store. That was the end of an unusual and interesting chapter in his life: the Chofetz Chaim as a shopkeeper.

But the story did not end there. Though he had always tried to run the store faithfully and honestly, he remained worried all through

Chayei Sarah / 113

his life that his integrity might have been less than perfect during the period when the store was open. In his old age, as the Chofetz Chaim prepared to move to Eretz Yisrael, he visited every Jew in his town and asked forgiveness for anything he might have done to wrong them. In order to compensate for any possible problem, he followed the advice of our Sages (may their memory be blessed): He donated the sum of 500 gold coins to the public fund. With this money, the town built a well from which any person might draw water, free of charge.

On the Path of Truth

אֲשֶׁר הִנְחַנִי בְּדֶרֶךְ אֱמֶת
"Who led me on a true path"
(*Bereishis* 24:48)

R' Pinchas of Koritz had a faithful disciple named Raphael of Bershad. R' Raphael's outstanding trait was *emes,* truth. Truth was stamped on his every action and his every word. He never spoke falsely; indeed, R' Raphael went to great extremes to distance himself from falsehood.

There was once a certain Jew who traded in contraband items. He was caught, and thrown into prison. The judges were inclined to give him a long prison sentence, but they agreed to let him go free if R' Raphael of Bershad and R' Moshe of Savran testified to the man's innocence.

R' Moshe of Savran, judging that this was a case in which a life was in danger, ruled that it was permissible to testify falsely on behalf of the prisoner. But R' Raphael of Bershad, who had struggled all his life to embrace the truth, was not able to do that. He could not bring himself to swear falsely.

The accused man's wife and children gave R' Raphael no peace. They came to his home to cry and plead from morning to night, begging him to testify on the prisoner's behalf. On the last day before the testimony was to be submitted, the man's family did not budge from R' Raphael's house. They wept bitterly and supplicated him ceaselessly to change his mind.

Night fell. R' Raphael closeted himself in his room, broken and anguished. He knew that it lay in his power to save the accused man on the following day and return him to his family — but how dare he utter a lie? All his life he had battled on behalf of *emes*. Morning, noon, and night he had taught his own students that falsehood is the father of evil and that truth is the seal of Hashem Himself, the foundation of all of man's service and the most basic of all the basics.

Weighed against this was the knowledge that it was up to him alone to rescue a Jew and his family. How could he harden his heart and not bring about that rescue?

What an impasse! R' Raphael paced his room, tears streaming. Finally, lifting his voice, he cried, "Please, Hashem, take my life from me! Remove me from this world — only do not let me utter a false word!"

He wept and pleaded all night long, until his soul burst from his body and rose in purity to Heaven.

In the morning, a messenger hurried to R' Raphael's house to give him the news: The accused man had come forward to admit his guilt. He did not wish two holy men to swear falsely on his behalf.

When R' Raphael's aide opened his door, he found the *tzaddik* lifeless. Hashem had heeded his cries and granted his plea. R' Raphael had sacrificed his very life on the altar of truth!

An Honest Question

אֲשֶׁר הִנְחַנִי בְּדֶרֶךְ אֱמֶת
"Who led me on a true path"
(*Bereishis* 24:48)

The Kotzker Rebbe went through a period of seclusion that lasted nearly twenty years. He hardly ever left his room. He was seen only on rare occasions, once every few months. *Chassidim* who wished to see him and receive his blessing before departing for their homes were sometimes forced to wait in the *beis midrash* for weeks at a time. He stopped conducting a "*tish*" and received very few people.

With all this, it was said that more holiness emanated from the Kotzker Rebbe's closed door than from many open doors of other rebbes.

One day, a simple Jewish villager arrived to complain about his cow, which had suddenly stopped giving milk. The Rebbe, to everyone's astonishment, received him warmly, answered his questions, and sent him on his way with a blessing.

The Rebbetzin asked in surprise, "There are learned *chassidim* here, devoted servants of Hashem, but you are not interested in seeing them. Yet you let that simple man in without any delay?"

In his characteristically sharp-witted way, the Rebbe answered, "Those *chassidim* come asking me about spirituality, while deep in their hearts they really want my blessing for — money! I want to have nothing to do with that. But that simple villager came to me about his cow, and really meant it. The truth, with no hypocrisy, is something I do want!"

The Right Way to Teach

וַיַּעַן לָבָן וּבְתוּאֵל

Then Lavan and Besuel answered

(*Bereishis* 24:50)

R' David of Lelov listened as the *melamed* taught his son *Chumash*. They had just learned that Eliezer, servant of Avraham, reached Besuel's house and asked for Rivkah's hand in marriage on Yitzchak's behalf. They reached the *pasuk*, "Then Lavan and Besuel answered." The teacher explained the *Rashi* on those words: "'Then Lavan and Besuel answered' — why does it say 'Lavan' first, and then 'Besuel'? Because Lavan was a *rasha*, an evildoer, and jumped ahead to answer before his father."

The Rebbe turned to the *melamed* and said gently, "Let me show you how to teach this."

The teacher was amazed. "But what did I do wrong? These are *Rashi's* own words!"

"True, those are *Rashi's* words. But you must read them properly. This is how we teach them."

And R' David read: "'Lavan and Besuel'? How can that be?" He banged on the table and cried aloud, "He was a *rasha,* and jumped ahead to answer before his father! He was an evil man!"

His listeners trembled to hear him. The Rebbe ended his lesson, "That is how to teach; so that the message will tunnel deep into their hearts!"

A Grand Gesture

וַיְבִאֶהָ יִצְחָק הָאֹהֱלָה שָׂרָה אִמּוֹ וַיִּקַּח אֶת רִבְקָה וַתְּהִי לוֹ לְאִשָּׁה

And Yitzchak brought her into the tent, Sarah his mother; he married Rivkah, she became his wife

(*Bereishis* 24:67)

A group of *chassidim* once traveled to Lublin in a wagon whose driver was a simple, uneducated man. Upon their arrival in Lublin, the *chassidim* hurried to prepare their "*kvittels*" (notes) to present to their rebbe. The driver, seeing the reverent preparations they were making in order to greet their rebbe, asked them to write a *kvittel* for him as well. He handed his *kvittel* to one of the *chassidim* and went off to an inn.

The *chassidim* went to see the rebbe, *kvittels* in hand. When the *chassid* handed the rebbe the wagon driver's note, the rebbe said without unfolding it, "This man shines in all worlds." Knowing the wagon driver to be a simple individual, the *chassidim* were taken aback by their rebbe's words. They decided to follow the man and investigate his actions. Perhaps he would turn out to be one of the 36 hidden *tzaddikim* that are said to exist in every generation!

The *chassidim* went to seek out the wagon driver at the inn. Before they reached the inn, they could hear sounds of laughter and merriment emanating from within. Peeking inside, they saw their driver, face glowing, dancing energetically in front of a bride and groom.

They approached the wagon driver and told him what their rebbe had said about him. "Please, explain to us what he meant!" they begged.

The driver told them his story:

"When I came to this inn, I heard the sounds of quarreling. A poor bride and groom were waiting to stand under the *chupah,* but the bride did not have enough money to fulfill her dowry obligations and the groom refused to marry her. When I saw how distressed everyone was, I asked how much money was in question. It was a large amount, but I decided to offer all my savings so that the match would not break up. The couple patched up their quarrel, and now I am as happy as though I'd just married off my own son."

The *chassidim* saw that their rebbe's holy eyes had glimpsed the change in the wagon driver, who had purchased his World to Come with a single grand gesture.

A Blessing for Long Life

וַיִּגְוַע וַיָּמָת אַבְרָהָם בְּשֵׂיבָה טוֹבָה זָקֵן וְשָׂבֵעַ

And Avraham expired and died at a good old age, an old man and content

(*Bereishis* 25:8)

A righteous woman by the name of Blumke Wilenkin lived in Minsk. When the townspeople made life difficult for the Sha'agas Aryeh during the time he served as *Rosh Yeshivah* there, it was Blumke who supported him with money and food. She also had a special *beis midrash* built for him, which was known until World War II as "Blumke's Kloiz" (Blumke's *beis midrash*). In later years — again with Blumke's support — R' Chaim of Volozhin and his students established a yeshivah in this *beis midrash*. The greatest Torah scholars of the time served as *Roshei Yeshivah* there.

It is said that the Sha'agas Aryeh blessed this generous woman, saying that she would merit building one *beis midrash* in Minsk and another in Eretz Yisrael. Many years after she received this blessing, she wished to fulfill the *tzaddik's* prediction and move to Eretz Yisrael. She asked R' Chaim Volozhin for his opinion. She was, after all, getting on in years.

R' Chaim answered, "Since you have the Rav's blessing in your pocket, why rush to move? Who knows how long you will live afterwards? You have been assured that you will build a *beis midrash* in

Eretz Yisrael. It is better, therefore, to wait and see how things turn out."

Blumke heeded R' Chaim's advice and remained in Minsk. Only years later, when she was at a remarkably advanced age, did she make the trip to Eretz Yisrael. True to the Sha'agas Aryeh's promise, she erected a *beis midrash* there as well. And indeed, immediately upon its completion, the righteous woman passed away.

True Repentance

וַיִּקְבְּרוּ אֹתוֹ יִצְחָק וְיִשְׁמָעֵאל בָּנָיו

His sons Yitzchak and Yishmael buried him
(*Bereishis* 25:9)

From here [we see] that Yishmael repented and let Yitzchak walk ahead of him [out of respect, even though Yishmael was older]. This is the "good old age" which was said about Avraham [in the preceding verse].
(*Rashi*)

A lone, cloaked figure walked along the streets of Chevron. People on their way home recognized him as their rabbi, R' Chaim Chizkiyah Medini, author of *S'dei Chemed*.

"Where is the Rav headed?" they asked him respectfully.

"To Baruch the blacksmith's house," he answered. "I wish to fulfill the mitzvah of *bikur cholim* — visiting the sick."

The people glanced at one another in astonishment. Baruch the blacksmith was known throughout Chevron as a sinner. He hardly ever appeared in shul, and many tales were told of his unworthy behavior. Everyone kept their distance from him — except for the town's few other sinners.

"To Baruch the blacksmith's house?" they repeated in wonder. "Why would the Rav trouble himself to visit a sinner who has practically left the bounds of our people?"

The townspeople's reaction did not surprise R' Chizkiyah. He, too, knew who Baruch the blacksmith was. But this did not deter him from going to visit him.

"You all know," he said gently, "that even a sinning Jew is as full of mitzvos as a pomegranate, and in the merit of those mitzvos he deserves to be visited when he is ill. Moreover, I am not only visiting the sick, but also the *Shechinah* that hovers over the sick man's bed. Should I stay away from a place where the *Shechinah* is?"

Moved by the Rav's words, the others joined him in his mitzvah.

When they arrived at the blacksmith's house, Baruch's eyes popped in amazement.

"To *me*? The Rav of the city has come to see *me*?" he asked. "The Rav surely has no idea of who I am or what I've done. If he did, he would not trouble himself to come to my house!"

R' Chizkiyah spoke to him soothingly, explaining in heartfelt words that before time ran out for the blacksmith there was still time for him to mend his ways. The visit wound to a close and the visitors went home, the incident all but forgotten.

Some days later, Baruch the blacksmith's condition began to improve. He was soon back at work. But he was not the same man as before. R' Chizkiyah's visit had had its effect. Baruch had known no rest since then.

"If R' Chizkiyah sees fit to visit me and bless me, then apparently I *am* capable of improving!" Numerous scoldings and even threats had not had the power to help him in the way that that brief visit had helped him.

Baruch began to return to his forefather's ways. To their amazement and wonder, the townspeople began to see him in shul every day. Within a short period, the blacksmith was a new man, pious and honest — a *ba'al teshuvah* through and through.

פרשת תולדות
Parashas Toldos

R' Yosef Chaim Sonnenfeld Says a Prayer

וַיֶּעְתַּר יִצְחָק לַד' לְנֹכַח אִשְׁתּוֹ כִּי עֲקָרָה הִוא וַיֵּעָתֶר לוֹ ד'

Yitzchak entreated Hashem opposite his wife, because she was barren. Hashem allowed Himself to be entreated by him

(*Bereishis* 25:21)

In a city in Hungary, there lived a Jewish couple who owned a prosperous business enterprise. The couple was very wealthy. The wife ran the business, while her husband sat and learned Torah all day.

Money was plentiful, but the couple lacked one thing, and this distressed them sorely: They had no children. Ten years had passed since their marriage, and still they had not been blessed with offspring.

One day, the woman appeared at the home of the city's Chief Rabbi with four hundred gold coins, an awesome amount of money at that time. "I want to give this money to the greatest *tzaddik* of our generation," she said, "so that he will pray for me to merit bearing children."

The Rabbi replied, "My advice is this: Send the money to R' Yosef Chaim Sonnenfeld, who lives in Jerusalem. In my opinion, he is the man whose prayers can help you!"

The woman gave the money to the Rabbi, who sent it that same day to Jerusalem. In order to ensure that it reached the proper hands, the Rabbi sent it to the Austrian ambassador, with instructions to forward it to R' Yosef Chaim Sonnenfeld.

When the ambassador received the money, he became very curious to learn its purpose. He sent it to Jerusalem with his secretary, resolved to follow the matter privately.

Meanwhile, some days later, the woman's husband learned of the large sum that his wife had sent to Jerusalem. He grew very angry, and went with his wife to confront the city's Rabbi. Furious, he complained that the Rabbi should not have sent the money without his knowledge.

Uncomfortable, the Rabbi made his apologies. He had had no idea that the woman had sent such a large sum without her husband's consent. The man was somewhat mollified, but insisted that the Rabbi send a telegram to Jerusalem asking that the money be returned.

Instead, the Rabbi offered to pay back the irate husband out of his own pocket. He wished at all costs to avoid a situation where a *tzaddik* like R' Yosef Chaim Sonnenfeld might be embarrassed. They were still discussing the matter when the door opened and the postman handed the Rabbi a letter that had just arrived from Jerusalem.

The letter was from R' Yosef Chaim Sonnenfeld himself — and enclosed in the envelope was a check for the equivalent of 400 gold coins. The Rabbi handed this immediately to the husband.

"Please," the couple said to the Rabbi, "read us the letter." Emotionally, the Rabbi picked up the letter and began to read.

"I received your honor's letter, in which you write that the money was brought to you by a woman who came herself. This made me suspect that she might have acted without her husband's consent. Therefore, I am returning the money, and beg your forgiveness for troubling you to see that it finds its way back to the sender.

"Of course, my prayers on behalf of the woman will not be diminished in the slightest. May her salvation come from Hashem in the blink of an eye—"

Warm tears trickled down the couple's faces. They had never in their lives encountered such greatness, such caution with another's money. Humbly, the man asked the Rabbi to send the check back to Jerusalem. "I will be happy indeed if my money reaches the hands of such a *tzaddik*!"

The money was sent again to Jerusalem, with a note attached giving the husband's consent.

The Austrian ambassador, who had tracked the money from Hungary to Jerusalem, then back to Hungary and back again to Jerusalem, also found himself greatly moved by R' Yosef Chaim's nobility. He decided to meet the great man himself.

The ambassador went to visit R' Yosef Chaim Sonnenfeld in Jerusalem, and the two had a long talk together. From that day on, the ambassador held R' Yosef Chaim in the greatest esteem, and showed him every honor.

Mother Power

וַיֶּעְתַּר יִצְחָק לַד׳ לְנֹכַח אִשְׁתּוֹ כִּי עֲקָרָה הִוא וַיֵּעָתֶר לוֹ ד׳

"Yitzchak entreated Hashem opposite his wife, because she was barren. Hashem allowed Himself to be entreated by him"

(*Bereishis* 25:21)

One Yom Kippur eve, R' Levi Yitzchak of Berditchev sent word to his townspeople: Whoever wanted R' Levi Yitzchak to pray for them should write his name, along with his mother's name, on a piece of paper, and submit it to him together with a certain sum of money for *tzedakah*. The townspeople, happy to have this rare opportunity, hurried to write their own and their mothers' names on slips of paper, and to bring them to the Rabbi along with the *tzedakah*.

The day wore on. Most of the city had already brought in their requests, but still R' Levi Yitzchak waited. Just a little while before the onset of Yom Kippur, a woman came running up. She placed a slip of paper and money for *tzedakah* in front of R' Levi Yitzchak.

Glancing at the paper, R' Levi Yitzchak told the woman, "You have written two names here. Therefore, you were supposed to bring a double portion of *tzedakah,* one for each person."

"I have written my own name and that of my son," she replied respectfully, "but what could I do? Though I went around all day trying to borrow money, I did not manage to get more than one portion of *tzedakah*."

R' Levi Yitzchak stood firm. "For this amount, you can write down only one name for me to pray for."

"In that case," the woman answered, "I will leave out my own name. Please, *daven* for my only son. I am prepared to give up my life for his sake."

When R' Levi Yitzchak saw how devoted the mother was to her son, he stood up with a radiant face and started off to shul for *Kol Nidrei*. As he went, he said repeatedly, "I am going now on the strength of that loving mother, who agreed to give herself up in order to save her son's life. '*Ha-ben yakir li Efrayim im yeled sha'ashuim*' — 'My son Efrayim is as precious to me as a child at play.' Just as a father has mercy on his children and a mother on her

Toldos / 125

child, so, too, Hashem, have mercy on Your beloved children!"

Saying these words, the *tzaddik* entered the shul, walked up to the *bimah*, and began to recite *Kol Nidrei*.

Right Place, Right Time

וַיֶּעְתַּר יִצְחָק לַד׳ לְנֹכַח אִשְׁתּוֹ כִּי עֲקָרָה הִוא וַיֵּעָתֶר לוֹ ד׳

"Yitzchak entreated Hashem opposite his wife, because she was barren. Hashem allowed Himself to be entreated by him"

(*Bereishis* 25:21)

The Vizhnitzer Rebbe, author of *Tzemach Tzedek,* once stayed at a health spa in Marinbad. He was sitting on a balcony whose floor was made of wooden planks, reading a note from one of his *chassidim,* when a plank suddenly broke. The Rebbe and his armchair plummeted several stories to the ground below.

The Rebbe was found unconscious, and the doctors feared internal injuries. They despaired of his life.

At that same time, in Baden, the Sanzer Rebbe (author of *Divrei Chaim*) paced to and fro crying emotionally, "And I will put a person in your place!" (*Yeshayahu* 43:4). No one had yet heard about the Vizhnitzer Rebbe's fall, and no one understood the meaning of the Sanzer Rebbe's words.

Against all medical predictions, the Vizhnitzer Rebbe regained consciousness and slowly began to recuperate. A German Jew, staying at the same spa, offered to attend to the Rebbe's needs. He remained there several weeks, wholeheartedly serving the Rebbe. Every time he finished performing some service, he would sit down and recite *Tehillim* in a sweet tune, to the accompaniment of tears. The man remained in Marinbad, serving the Rebbe faithfully, until the Rebbe recovered from his injuries and was ready to return home.

The Rebbe instructed R' Yankel, his aide, to pay the stranger generously for his trouble. But the man came to the Rebbe first, holding a slip of paper and a hundred gold coins, a very large sum of money in those days. The Rebbe asked the man how he could help him. The man replied that he lived in Freisin, where he owned a business worth a million marks. During the summer months, he normally opened an additional store in Marinbad for vacationers, but this year he had abandoned this store in order to serve the Rebbe devotedly and faithfully.

Deeply moved, the Rebbe said that Heaven had apparently sent the businessman to that place to provide the "remedy before the blow," both in terms of his service to the Rebbe and the *Tehillim* that the man had constantly recited. And he quoted the *Gemara* which states that Hashem brings a person to the very place where there will be someone on hand to plead for Hashem's mercy and to say *Tehillim* for him.

All Consuming

וְיַעֲקֹב אִישׁ תָּם יֹשֵׁב אֹהָלִים
But Yaakov was a wholesome man, abiding in tents.
(*Bereishis* 25:27)

So deep and all consuming was R' Meshulem Igra's involvement in Torah, that his mind was busy with Torah thoughts even as he walked in the street. Not surprisingly, he was completely unaware of what was happening around him.

One day, as he walked down a city street, deeply absorbed in a thorny halachic debate between the Rambam and the Raavad, a coach driven by four horses came rattling along. The horses swerved unexpectedly, striking R' Meshulem and throwing him to the ground.

Passersby ran quickly to the Rabbi's aid. Carefully, they extricated R' Meshulem from beneath the coach's wheels. Imagine their amazement when they saw his lips moving, and heard him murmuring, "...and so, according to this, the Raavad's view must take precedence over that of the Rambam..."

R' Shlomo of Radomsk once noticed a *chassid* who had fallen asleep over his *Gemara*. He approached the man, roused him, and said, "Have you already answered the sea captain's question?"

The *chassid* was bewildered.

"I am referring to," explained the Rebbe, "the sea captain's question to Yonah HaNavi. 'Why are you sleeping? Get up, call out to your G-d.'"

※ ※ ※

On the thirteenth day of Elul in the year 5669 (1909), R' Yosef Chaim, head of the Jewish community in Baghdad, departed this world. R' Yosef Chaim was a *gaon* and a *tzaddik*, and is famous to this day as the author of the halachic work, *Ben Ish Chai*.

The funeral procession set out through the city near midnight on a *Motza'ei Shabbos*. Men, women, and children walked with bowed heads, weeping bitterly. The darkness around them was reflected in the darkness within their own hearts.

One of the children present was a nine-year-old boy, Salman Mutzafi. His face wore a woebegone expression, as he was filled with pain at the loss of this great *tzaddik*. At the sight of so many people crying sorrowfully, a resolution formed in Salman's young heart. Firmly, decisively, he whispered to himself, "I promise now, near the grave of R' Yosef Chaim, that I will learn Torah with great diligence and will make all my actions holy. I promise!"

From that day on, Salman's parents saw their son advance steadily in Torah. Salman noticed that his father had the habit of waking at midnight and learning Torah until dawn. He asked for permission to do the same.

But his parents feared for their son's health. "You are young yet," they told him. "You need your sleep at night. If you don't sleep enough, your body will grow weak and you will not be able to learn Torah during the day, either."

Salman had no wish to distress his parents — but he still longed, with all his heart, to wake up in the night to learn Torah. He considered ideas for waking up without his mother's and father's knowledge. Finally, he hit on a strategem.

Every night, before he went to bed, Salman would take a long string, tie one end to the doorknob and the other end to his wrist. At midnight, when his father opened the door, the string tugged at

Salman's hand, waking him instantly. His father left for the *beis midrash,* his mother was still asleep, and Salman hurried to get dressed. Then he, too, would go to the *beis midrash* where, in a hidden spot, he would learn and pray without anyone seeing him.

Night after night, Salman woke up at midnight and learned until daybreak — until one night when his father happened to notice the string tied around the doorknob. Investigating, he discovered that the other end of the string was tied to his sleeping son's wrist. Out of concern for the boy's health, he removed the string from the doorknob.

Now Salman was faced with a difficulty once again. "How will I wake up without my parents' knowledge?" After much thought, he devised a new plan.

Salman had a friend, also very diligent in his learning, who woke up at midnight to pore over the Torah. When night came, Salman once again tied a string around his wrist. The other end he dropped outside his window to the street below.

His friend, passing the house in the dark of the night, would tug at the string and wake Salman. It took just minutes for Salman to wash his hands, get dressed, and come out into the street. Then, he and his friend made their way to the *beis midrash* to learn together in secret until morning.

With the passage of years, Salman grew to become a *gaon* in both the revealed and the hidden Torah.

~ ~ ~

R' Yitzchak Silberstein, rabbi of the Ramat Elchanan neighborhood in Bnei Brak, told the story of a Jew in our own generation who set aside time for learning Torah in the *beis midrash* on a regular basis. He was very strict about never missing a day.

Something once occurred that prevented this man from attending his regular *shiur.* He remained at home and learned on his own. He reached a difficult passage which he was unable to understand even with *Rashi's* help, and he experienced great anguish. At length, he fell asleep — and had a dream.

In the dream, a man with a noble countenance appeared before him, saying, "Come, I will explain the difficult passage in *Rashi.*" And he went on to expound the section in a new way.

The dreamer asked him, "Please tell me, what is your name?"

The other answered, "My name is Rashba."

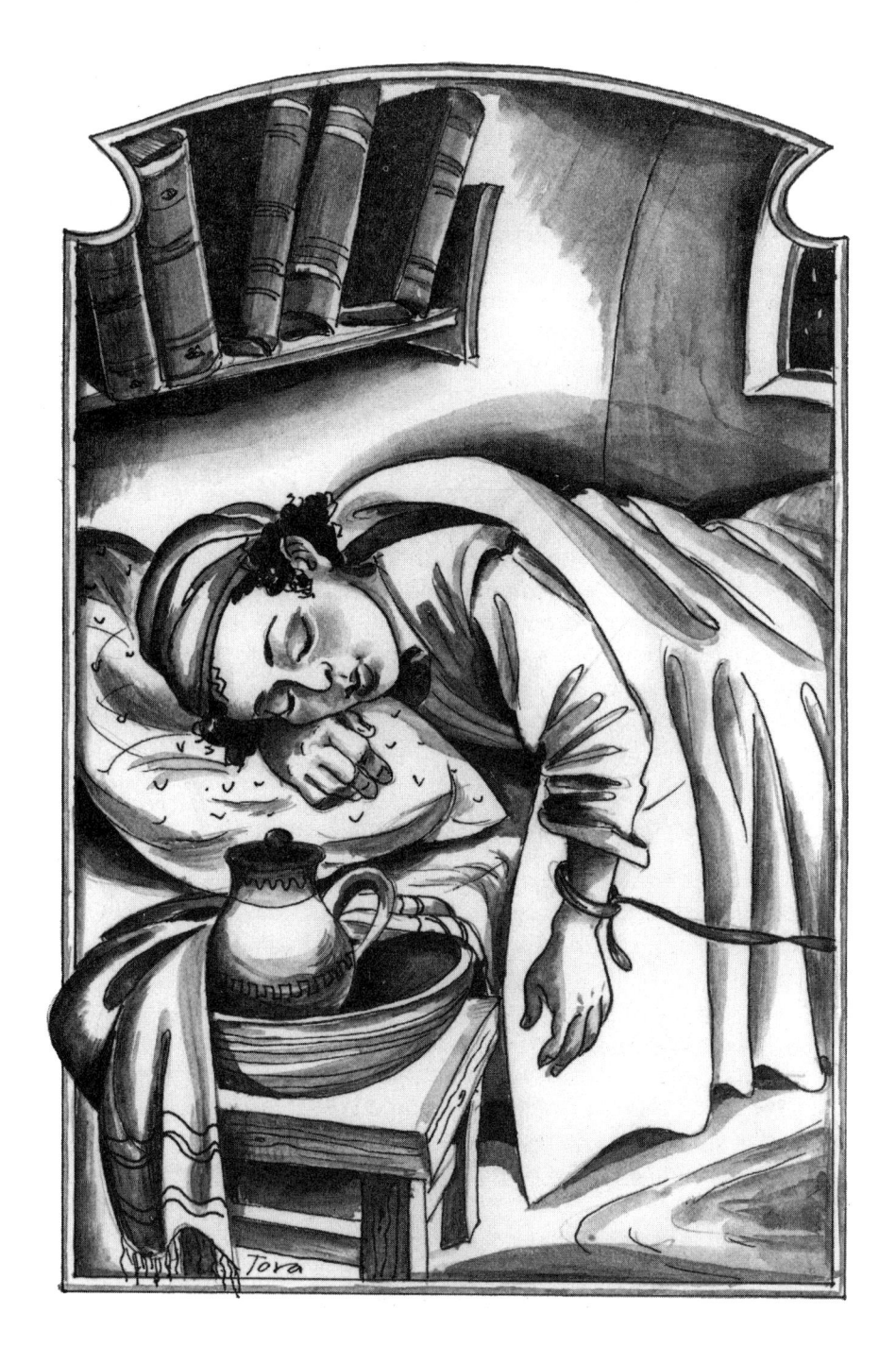

130 / STORIES MY GRANDFATHER TOLD ME

The next day, the man related the dream to his *maggid shiur* who found the explanation for the difficult *Rashi*, word for word, in a *sefer* written by the Rashba!

The *maggid shiur* was dumbfounded. The man who had had the dream was incapable, on his own, of understanding a single line of the Rashba — and he did not even own a copy of the Rashba's *sefer*! It seemed the man had indeed been privileged to have the holy Rashba, himself, speak to him in a dream.

This story, which took place in our own time, shows us the power of diligence and a genuine desire to learn and grasp Torah. If we learn regularly, our limited understanding will be helped along by Heaven itself!

The Wellsprings of Torah

וַיָּשָׁב יִצְחָק וַיַּחְפֹּר אֶת בְּאֵרֹת הַמַּיִם אֲשֶׁר חָפְרוּ בִּימֵי אַבְרָהָם

And Yitzchak returned and he dug the wells of water which they had dug in the days of Avraham

(*Bereishis* 26:18)

R' Yechezkel Abramsky told a parable about the Ponovizher Rav:

The Torah tells us that Yitzchak *Avinu* returned and dug the wells of water that his grandfather, Avraham, had dug, and that the Philistines had sealed up after Avraham's death. Yitzchak gave the wells the same names that Avraham had given them.

The evil Nazis not only destroyed the "wells" of Torah in Europe by uprooting its noble yeshivahs, but also sealed them up with sand. They destroyed those who taught Torah, in the hope that Torah might never revive.

The Ponovizher Rav not only came along and re-dug the old wells, renewing the study of Torah, but he also called them by their old and illustrious names: Ponovizh, Grodno, Vilkomir...

In this way, said R' Yechezkel Abramsky, we are able to see with our own eyes the actualization of *Chazal's* prediction that the yeshivahs of the Diaspora will come to be established in Eretz Yisrael.

After he was saved from the Holocaust, the Ponovizher Rav decided to establish a large yeshivah in Eretz Yisrael. Suddenly, without warning, he fell ill. The doctors, fearing a fatal illness, forbade him to talk and ordered complete bed rest.

The Rav sat up in bed and said softly, "You all know that the Lithuanian farmer, as a rule, is terribly lazy. It is impossible to get him to stir. But when harvest season arrives, he immediately turns into the most incredibly energetic fellow. And if, at the height of the harvest, the skies darken and rain threatens, the farmer hurries like the wind. The work burns in his bones as he struggles to beat the rain.

"Why won't you understand me? I have decided to found a holy yeshivah during the height of the harvest season and the skies have turned dark. The Nazis, may their names be blotted out, are destroying Torah centers and murdering those who learn in them. How can I rest peacefully?"

Honor Thy Father and Mother

וְעַתָּה בְנִי שְׁמַע בְּקֹלִי

"So now, my son, heed my voice"

(*Bereishis* 27:8)

R' Yisrael of Vizhnitz was scrupulous in honoring his parents. When his father, author of *Imrei Baruch,* passed away at an early age, R' Yisrael continued to honor him even after his death. Each year, on his father's *yahrtzeit,* the twentieth day of Kislev, he would travel to Vizhnitz in order to pray at his father's grave.

R' Yisrael continued this custom even when the roads were treacherous. Although everyone close to him pleaded with him to give up the journey, he continued year after year to make the trip, often courting death on the way.

"I am doing this in order to fulfill my obligation to honor my father," he explained. "Because he died young, his greatness was not sufficiently recognized. Because I make the trip each year, his name will not be forgotten."

On his final journey to his father's gravesite, before his own passing, R' Yisrael said, "My strength is failing and this trip is very hard. But I have a *chazakah* (a long-standing custom) in the mitzvah of honoring my father."

❦

Some years after the Chazon Ish moved to Eretz Yisrael and settled in the Givat Rokach neighborhood of Bnei Brak, his elderly mother arrived, too. She settled near her son.

His mother was always careful to *daven* together with a *minyan* so the Chazon Ish quickly organized one in his home. Every morning, his mother would come to his house, go quietly into a side room, and wait for *Shacharis* to begin.

The Chazon Ish was overjoyed at this opportunity to honor his mother. Every morning, he personally brought her a *shtender* on which she placed her *siddur*.

"It's too heavy for you," the Chazon Ish's wife would protest, fearful for his health. "Someone else can carry that for you."

But the Chazon Ish would inevitably answer, "Honoring a mother comes first!"

A "Last Request"

הַקֹּל קוֹל יַעֲקֹב וְהַיָּדַיִם יְדֵי עֵשָׂו

"The voice is Yaakov's voice, but the hands are Esav's hands."
(*Bereishis* 27:22)

The Rabbi of Tabrik, in Lithuania, was known for his exceptional scholarship and diligence in Torah. During the First World War, when the line of battle was not far from Tabrik, Russian troops noticed a light burning in one of the town's houses late one night. Furious (the town was supposed to enforce a complete blackout), the Russians hurried to the house, certain that it contained a spy for the German side who was using his candle to signal to the enemy.

Bursting into the house, they found R' Aharon, the town's Rabbi, absorbed in learning. The sight did not change their minds about the presence of a spy. They informed R' Aharon in no uncertain terms that they intended to execute him immediately, on the charge of treason.

Knowing full well the cruel reputation of the Russian soldiers, the Rabbi answered, "If it is decreed that I am to be killed, I accept the decree. But I have one favor to ask of you. Please, fulfill my last request. I am completely absorbed at the moment in trying to understand a difficult passage of the Rambam. Please, give me a little time to understand this difficult passage!"

The soldiers' shock was boundless. Who had ever heard of such a thing? Their surprise worked in the Rabbi's favor. The soldiers told him to go ahead and clarify the matter; they would wait.

While they waited for the Rabbi to finish learning, the tide of battle suddenly shifted. The Germans made a surprise attack on Tabrik, and the Russian troops fled for their lives. And so, in the merit of his extraordinary diligence in learning Torah, the Rabbi of Tabrik was saved from the hands of those who would have destroyed him. "And you, who cling to Hashem — you are all alive today!"

Seize the Mitzvah

הַקֹּל קוֹל יַעֲקֹב וְהַיָּדַיִם יְדֵי עֵשָׂו

"The voice is Yaakov's voice, but the hands are Esav's hands."

(*Bereishis* 27:22)

A certain *tzaddik* delivered a *Gemara shiur* to his students every day. One of these students was an outstanding youth who had lost his father. Once, in the middle of learning, the Rebbe began to delve into a difficult passage. The boy knew that once his teacher began this process, he would concentrate exclusively on the subject matter for some time. Therefore, the boy decided to slip out and go home in the meantime. He felt weak and needed to eat to replenish his strength.

When he had finished eating, he got up quickly in order to return to his Rebbe's house. At that moment, however, his mother asked him to go up to the attic and bring down something she needed from

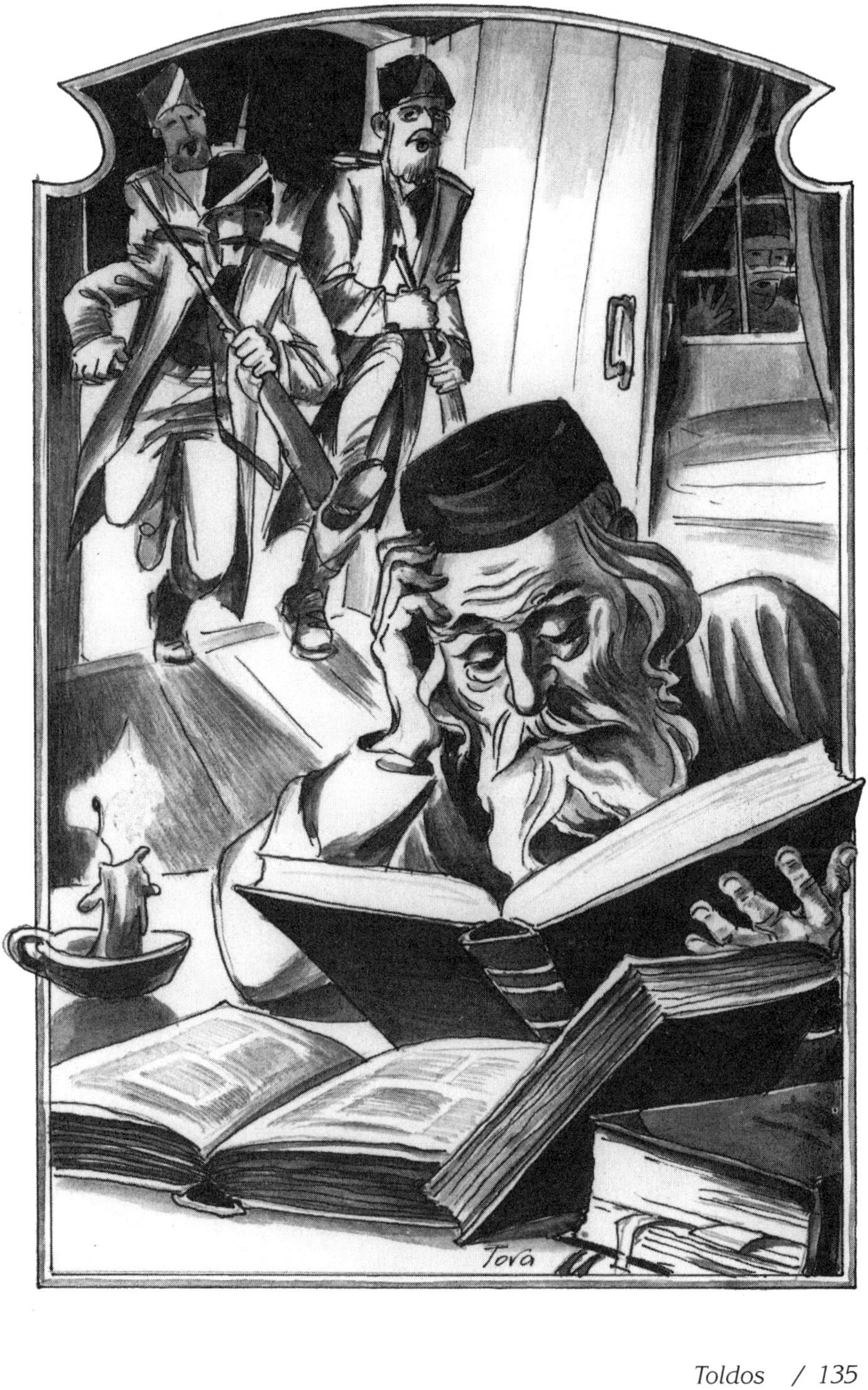
Tova

there. He refused, saying that his Rebbe might already have resumed the *shiur*. On his way back to the Rebbe's house, however, a thought suddenly occurred to him. Isn't the essence of learning to observe and perform what one has learned? Here was a chance to perform the mitzvah of *kibbud av v'em*, of honoring one's parents — how could he not seize it?

He ran back home and hastened to fulfill his mother's request. Only then did he return to his Rebbe's house.

When the youth opened the door, the Rebbe was aroused from his thoughts. Standing up to his full height, he asked, "Which mitzvah did you do just now?" For he had seen the image of the Amora Abaye accompany the boy into the house, and at the same time he had found the answer to the difficult question which he had been trying to unravel!

The boy told him what had just happened at his mother's house. The *tzaddik* turned to his students and said, "The *Gemara* tells us that Abaye had neither a father nor a mother. That is why he was called 'Abaye,' which stands for the initials, '*Asher becha yerucham yasom*' ('That the orphan will find compassion in You'). When a person fulfills the mitzvah of honoring his parents, Abaye walks with him, so that he might have a portion of this mitzvah [which, as an orphan, was denied to him during his lifetime]!"

The Burning Candle

וַיֹּאמֶר רְאֵה רֵיחַ בְּנִי כְּרֵיחַ שָׂדֶה אֲשֶׁר בֵּרְכוֹ ד׳

He said, "See, the fragrance of my son is like the fragrance of a field which Hashem has blessed."

(Bereishis 27:27)

The fragrance of the Garden of Eden came in with [Yaakov].

(Rashi)

The Tzemach Tzedek of Vizhnitz raised his two young grandsons in his home. They would grow up to be the Ahavas Yisrael of Vizhnitz and the Nimukei Chaim of Antania. All day long, from early morning until the wee hours of the night, they learned Torah together. In order to safeguard her grandsons' health, the Tzemach Tzedek's wife asked her husband to set a specific bedtime for the boys. Even then, the boys continued to learn. Hearing their grandfather's footsteps as he came to check on them, they would hastily snuff out their candles and pretend to be asleep. Afterwards, they would resume their learning.

Once, they did not hear their grandfather's approach. He stood on the other side of the door and took great pleasure in the sweet sounds of their Torah. At last, he opened the door. The boys were startled, and afraid that he would be angry with them. But the Tzemach Tzedek smiled understandingly.

"It says, 'When one tastes the sweet taste of Torah, we don't snuff out the light at night.'"

Mired in Mud

וַיֹּאמֶר רְאֵה רֵיחַ בְּנִי כְּרֵיחַ שָׂדֶה אֲשֶׁר בֵּרֲכוֹ ד׳

He said, "See, the fragrance of my son is like the fragrance of a field which Hashem has blessed."
(*Bereishis* 27:27)
The fragrance of the Garden of Eden came in with [Yaakov].
(*Rashi*)

One winter's day, as a heavy windswept rain fell on the sleeping town, the two young sons of R' Baruch of Vizhnitz, Yisrael and Chaim, sat learning together. When the clock showed it was very late at night, Chaim wanted to sleep a little.

His brother protested, "My dear brother! Imagine a wagon driver traveling on such a stormy night. Heavy rain is falling on his head and the wagon is moving with difficulty, its wheels stuck in mud. Would the wagon driver say, 'I'm tired,' and take a nap by the roadside? If he did, the wagon would only sink deeper into the mud, and it would be very difficult to extricate it in the morning.

"Shall we, sitting here in such a pleasant well-heated room, stop learning and go to sleep? Please, sit down and let us learn more of Hashem's Torah, that brings peace of mind."

And the two brothers continued learning until morning.

The Personal Touch

קוּם לֵךְ פַּדֶּנָה אֲרָם . . . וְקַח לְךָ מִשָּׁם אִשָּׁה
"Arise, go to Paddan-aram... and take a wife from there"
(*Bereishis* 28:2)

R' Moshe Chaim, the brother of Rabbi Yitzchak Meir, the Gerer Rebbe, was very wealthy. He managed mighty business enterprises and traveled in a lavish carriage drawn by four horses, in the manner of the nobility.

When R' Moshe Chaim traveled to Warsaw, he made a detour to visit his elderly parents — his father, R' Yisrael, and his mother, Rebbetzin Chayah — who lived in Ger. As his carriage approached Ger, R' Moshe Chaim noticed a woman walking ahead at the side of the road, bent under a large load of straw. When the carriage drew alongside the woman, R' Moshe Chaim saw, to his shock, that it was his own mother!

Aghast, he leaped from the carriage, asking, "What is this?"

The Rebbetzin answered, "This is for an orphaned bride. (Straw was used to stuff mattresses in those days.) Are my legs exempt from the obligation to do mitzvos?"

"Mother!" R' Moshe Chaim said at once. "I will give you enough money for ten mattresses — just throw off that straw!"

Calmly, his mother replied, "Certainly, give money — the bride needs money, too, in addition to the mattress."

Learning Honesty From Rashi

וַיִּשְׁלַח יִצְחָק אֶת יַעֲקֹב וַיֵּלֶךְ פַּדֶּנָה אֲרָם אֶל לָבָן בֶּן בְּתוּאֵל הָאֲרַמִּי אֲחִי רִבְקָה אֵם יַעֲקֹב וְעֵשָׂו

And Yitzchak sent off Yaakov; and he went toward Paddan-aram, to Lavan the son of Besuel the Aramean, brother of Rivkah, mother of Yaakov and Esav.

(*Bereishis* 28:5)

I do not know what this [mention of the fact that Rivkah was the mother of Yaakov and Esav] teaches us.

(*Rashi*)

Honesty was the touchstone of R' Shlomo Zalman Auerbach's life, and guided his every action. He walked in truth from the time he was young. Through this, he grew to greatness in Torah and piety.

When R' Shlomo Zalman's name was offered as a candidate for the post of *Rosh Yeshivah* of Yeshivas Kol Torah, he was summoned to meet the yeshivah's administration, so that they might talk with him and see whether he was worthy of that illustrious position.

During the Torah discussion, the *gaon*, R' Yonah Merzbach, asked R' Shlomo Zalman a question in Talmud. R' Shlomo Zalman replied at once, "I don't know the answer."

On his return home that evening, R' Shlomo Zalman told his wife all about the interview. It was his conviction that the yeshivah would decline to appoint him *Rosh Yeshivah* because he had not known the answer to the question that R' Yonah had asked.

They were still talking, when R' Yonah himself came to their door. He came with a "request" that R' Shlomo Zalman serve as *Rosh Yeshivah*. The administration had decided unanimously that he was the man for the job.

R' Yonah added, "When you answered 'I don't know' to my question, I saw the light of truth shining in your eyes. Although you knew that you were being tested, you did not betray a single sign of evasiveness, but answered simply and honestly, 'I don't know.' At that moment, I knew that you were the man that Hashem sent to lead our yeshivah. Our students will learn from you to strive for truth, as well as to grow in their understanding of the Torah and the correct paths in life."

R' Shlomo Zalman confided that he had actually had several answers to R' Yonah's question, but because he was not fully certain that any one of them was absolutely true, he had preferred to say, "I don't know."

He became *Rosh Yeshivah* of Yeshivas Kol Torah, where, over a period of fifty years, he disseminated Torah to thousands.

Rashi, referring to the verse above, says of the words "mother of Yaakov and Esav": "I do not know what this teaches us." Why, the commentators wonder, did Rashi bother saying this? If you have nothing to say, then write nothing!

The Sifsei Chachamim explains, "The holy Rashi knew that he might interpret the text in various ways, the way other commentators have done. But Rashi did not have a clear insight into the true meaning of the text, and therefore chose to write, 'I don't know!'"

פרשת ויצא
Parashas Vayeitzei

Earthquake!

מַה נּוֹרָא הַמָּקוֹם הַזֶּה
"How awesome is this place!"
(*Bereishis* 28:17)

On the 24th day of Teves, 5597 (1837), the ground shook under Tzefas and the city was reduced to rubble. Some 2,000 Jews were killed in the earthquake, and thousands of other people were pinned under the ruins.

Scholars of the day declared, "From the day the *Beis Hamikdash* was destroyed, there has not been such a great destruction." The Rabbi of Tzefas, R' Shmuel Halir, was found alive, buried in stone up to his chin. His arms and legs were broken and he remained crippled till the end of his life.

R' Avraham Dov Meyerowitz was miraculously spared, unharmed. The earthquake had taken place between *Minchah* and *Ma'ariv*. As the earth began to shake, the Rabbi called the worshipers to gather around him in his *beis midrash,* assuring them that a miracle from Heaven would occur. Only half the roof fell in; the second half, the part over the congregants' heads, remained in place and the men's lives were spared.

To this day, the *beis midrash* that was rebuilt on that spot bears a plaque describing the miracle, under the banner, "How awesome is this place." It goes on to say: "The *beis midrash* of R' Avraham Dov, the Obritzer Rebbe, who witnessed the great earthquake in Tzefas in the year 5597 (1837), and in whose great merit half the *beis midrash* was saved from destruction and the Rebbe and his disciples remained alive."

The Obritzer Rebbe worked heroically to rebuild the holy city of Tzefas, to encourage bereft families, and to help bring the city back

Vayeitzei / 143

to life. On the first anniversary of the earthquake, the Rebbe made a *seudas mitzvah*, at which he gave a speech.

"We see that R' Yosi ben Kisma's students asked, 'When will ben David [*Mashiach*] come?' He told them, 'When this gate [*sha'ar*] falls down and is rebuilt, and falls again and is rebuilt, and falls again, and they will not have time to rebuild it before ben David comes.'

"The letters of '*sha'ar*' (*shin, ayin, resh*) can be reassembled to read '*ra'ash*' (earthquake) and its *gematria* (numerical equivalent) is Tzefas. Tzefas has been hit twice before by earthquakes, in which many people were killed. But this earthquake is the final 'fall' before it is rebuilt; ben David will surely come!"

A Crumbling Shul

מַה נּוֹרָא הַמָּקוֹם הַזֶּה אֵין זֶה כִּי אִם בֵּית אֱלֹקִים

"*How awesome is this place! This is none other than the abode of G-d*"

(*Bereishis* 28:17)

A shul in a certain Galician town was in very poor repair. Indeed, pieces of it fell regularly onto those standing inside. Once, R' Meir of Premishlan entered the shul to *daven*. As he opened the door, R' Meir stood and surveyed the wreckage inside. Then he called out, "*Mah nora hamakom hazeh. Ein zeh ki im beis Elokim*." ("How awesome — or, in this case, awful — is this place! This is none other than the abode of G-d.")

The *chassidim* who accompanied him were at a loss to understand these words. Surely, they thought, there must be some hidden meaning to them. Noticing their bewilderment, the Rebbe explained, "*Mah nora hamakom hazeh*" — How awful is this place; it is truly dangerous to walk in here. "*Ein zeh ki im beis Elokim*" — and the reason for that is because this building has no owner to care for it. All the other houses in town are in good repair, while this shul appears ready to crumble to its foundations."

The Essence of Joy

אִם יִהְיֶה אֱלֹקִים עִמָּדִי . . . וְנָתַן לִי לֶחֶם לֶאֱכֹל וּבֶגֶד לִלְבֹּשׁ

"If G-d will be with me... and He will give me bread to eat and clothes to wear"

(*Bereishis* 28:20)

There were always several students at the yeshivah in Meknes, Morocco, who remained during *Yom Tov* and summer vacation. These were generally boys from distant towns who lacked the means to travel back home.

One of these was a 14-year-old orphan who lived far from the yeshivah and could not travel home for the holidays. One *erev Pesach*, when R' Raphael Baruch Toledano walked into the yeshivah, he saw this boy sitting alone in a corner, preoccupied and sad. R' Baruch approached him and asked what was wrong.

Hanging his head in shame, the boy did not answer.

R' Baruch continued to gently coax the boy to share his sorrow. At last, the orphan said brokenly, "In a few hours, *Yom Tov* will begin. All my friends have new shoes in its honor, except for me —" Tears fell, preventing any further talk.

Looking down, R' Baruch saw the torn shoes on the boy's feet, with his big toes sticking out through the holes. He thumped the boy's shoulder encouragingly, spoke warmly to him, and promised to try, with Hashem's help, to supply what he needed.

It was already late in the afternoon on *erev Pesach*. The Jewish streets were bustling with last-minute holiday preparations. Most of the shops were already closed, except for the grocery stores — but R' Baruch needed a shoe store. He must find a new pair of shoes for the unfortunate orphan before Pesach began!

He sent someone to scour the town for an open shoe store, but all were closed. Thinking furiously of a plan to acquire shoes at such a late hour, he suddenly remembered that the owner of a shoe store lived not far from his home. R' Baruch rose immediately and went in person to visit the storekeeper.

R' Baruch quickly explained the situation. He ended forcefully, "We will not lean back around the *seder* table tonight until that child gets shoes!"

The man went with R' Baruch to his store and gave him what he

Vayeitzei / 145

needed. R' Baruch was filled with great joy. With shining eyes, he brought the shoes to his student.

This was the true *simchah* of *Yom Tov* — one in which he was able to bring joy to a poor orphan child. The Rambam says that we do not fulfill our obligation to feel happy on *Yom Tov* unless we also bring happiness to orphans and widows. This is the essence of joy!

Words to Warm the Heart

וַיֹּאמֶר לָהֶם יַעֲקֹב אַחַי מֵאַיִן אַתֶּם

Yaakov said to them, "My brothers, where are you from?"
(*Bereishis* 29:4)

R' Yaakov Kamenetsky once asked a question about Yaakov *Avinu's* criticism of the shepherds. A total stranger, he approached them and reminded them that the day was still long and it was not yet time to bring in the flocks. "Water the flock and go on grazing," he advised. Why, asks R' Yaakov, did the shepherds accept this criticism so mildly? One would think that such words, from a stranger, would make them bristle.

The answer lies in Yaakov's opening words: "My brothers." Though his message was one of rebuke, he began his speech with words of warmth and friendship!

A public issue once arose in the city of Kovno, with the community arguing on one side and a certain wealthy and respected member opposing the general opinion. In the end, the matter was resolved according to the majority view. Insulted, the wealthy individual retreated from contact with the community. He also nursed a grievance against R' Yitzchak Elchanan Spektor, Rabbi of Kovno, and cut off all contact with him as well.

Years passed, and the man's sense of injury only grew stronger. The man lived his life in isolation, refusing to attend public meetings or to interest himself in any community affairs.

By chance one day, this individual participated in a *seudas mitzvah*, at which the Rabbi of Kovno was also present. Contrary to custom, the rich man did not go over to greet the Rabbi or even stand up to honor him. Instead, R' Yitzchak Elchanan approached him, thrust out a hand in the most natural manner possible, and greeted the man. Taken aback by the Rabbi's humility, the man hurried to greet him in turn. The past was reconciled.

In the coming days, it became clear that the reconciliation between the man and the Rabbi would have far-reaching effects.

It was shortly afterwards that a devastating message reached the Rabbi: A false accusation had been made against the town's Jews, and the ruler had decreed that every Jew must leave Kovno. R' Yitzchak Elchanan tried through various means to influence a change in this decision, but his efforts came to nothing. Messengers were sent to speak to central figures in the government, but they, too, returned empty handed and unsuccessful. There seemed to be no escape from the harsh decree.

Suddenly, a ray of hope appeared. Someone told the Rabbi that the ruler was on good terms with the wealthy man who had severed relations with the Jewish community so many years before. R' Yitzchak Elchanan hastened to send messengers to this now-elderly man, to plead for his help. Now that whatever happened between them was forgiven, the man responded favorably to this request. He spoke to the ruler and the decree was rescinded.

When the excitement had died down, R' Yitzchak Elchanan remarked to his secretary, R' Yaakov Lifshitz, author of *Zichron Yaakov*, "When I made peace with that gentleman, people complained that I had overlooked my own honor to do so. But who was right — I, who took the first step to reconciliation, or those who were so careful of my honor? How has my honor been damaged by what I did? And if we had not made peace, what would have been the fate of all the families doomed to exile and homelessness?"

Beyond the Call of Duty

וַיִּגַּשׁ יַעֲקֹב וַיָּגֶל אֶת הָאֶבֶן מֵעַל פִּי הַבְּאֵר וַיַּשְׁקְ אֶת צֹאן לָבָן אֲחִי אִמּוֹ

Yaakov came forward and rolled the stone from the mouth of the well and watered the sheep of Lavan, his mother's brother.

(*Bereishis* 29:10)

R' Yisrael Salanter was traveling by train from Kovno to Vilna. As was his custom, he traveled alone, without companions, and was

Vayeitzei / 147

dressed as a simple man. A young yeshivah man sat beside him.

It was the smoking section, and R' Yisrael sat in his seat smoking a cigarette. The yeshivah man beside him turned on R' Yisrael and declared that he could not tolerate cigarette smoke. R' Yisrael made no attempt to justify himself by pointing out that the compartment was one set aside for smokers. He merely asked the man's pardon, and extinguished the cigarette.

A few minutes later, the same man muttered angrily, "It is simply impossible to sit near that old man! He's opened the window and let in cold air to freeze our bones!"

R' Yisrael said gently, "Pardon me. It was not I who opened the window, but if it disturbs you, I will close it." And he stood up and closed the window.

When the train reached Vilna, a large crowd was on hand to greet R' Yisrael Salanter. Seeing them, the young yeshivah man was surprised. "What are you all here for?" he asked someone.

Now it was the other man's turn to be surprised. "Don't you know? R' Yisrael Salanter is arriving!"

Discovering his seatmate's identity, the young man turned pale. All that night, he was unable to sleep. Whom had he berated angrily? Whom had he abused and degraded?

The following morning, the man went to the home of R' Yisrael Salanter's son-in-law, where the great man was staying. Before he could say a word, R' Yisrael said, "Please, sit down! How are you? Have you rested a little after the journey?"

The yeshivah man was astonished at this warm reception. Bursting into tears, he begged the *tzaddik* to forgive him.

R' Yisrael assured him that he held no grudge at all in his heart, and encouraged him to cheer up. Then he engaged the young man in a discussion of *middos* and *mussar.*

When the yeshivah man stood up to go, R' Yisrael asked him, "Tell me, please — why did you come to Vilna?"

The yeshivah man explained that he had come to receive *semichah,* in order to become a *shochet.*

"In that case," R' Yisrael said happily, "I can be of use to you! My son-in-law is one of the town's leading rabbis. I will see to it that he gives you what you need."

Doors opened in front of the young man. R' Eliyahu Eliezer Grodenski, R' Yisrael's son-in-law, received him at once and began discussing the laws of *shechitah* with him. Unfortunately, it turned out that the man was as devoid of knowledge as he was of good *middos*.

"You are doubtless still tired from the journey," R' Yisrael said encouragingly. "Go rest a little, and come back in a few days!"

With difficulty, the man found the door and disappeared.

Some days passed, but the young man did not return. R' Yisrael, who had made sure to get the man's address, went personally to see him at his inn, and to ask why he had not made a second appearance.

"I am grateful to the Rebbe," the young man said. "He has opened my eyes. I now know my place, and will return home at once."

But R' Yisrael did not let him off that easily. He insisted that the young man study the laws of *shechitah,* and even found him an expert *shochet* to teach him all the relevant laws. R' Yisrael supplied all the young man's needs during this period.

Before long, R' Yisrael's efforts began to bear fruit. The young man learned the halachos diligently, and became a proficient *shochet*. He received *semichah* from several rabbis. But even then, R' Yisrael did not stop. He worked until he had found a community in which the young man could settle down respectfully to his profession.

When asked why he labored so hard on the man's behalf, R' Yisroel replied, "When he came to beg my forgiveness, I told him that I forgave him absolutely and that I held no grudge against him and I said those things with a full heart. But being only human, I was afraid that some measure of dislike would linger in my heart. Therefore, I tried to strengthen my *middah* of compassion, and to find all sorts of ways to help and benefit that man, so that every trace of a grudge might be erased!"

Vayeitzei / 149

The Difference

וַתִּקְרָא שְׁמוֹ רְאוּבֵן
And she called his name Reuven
(*Bereishis* 29:32)
She said, "See what is [the difference] between my son and the son of my father-in-law [Esav]"
(Rashi)

R' Levi Yitzchak of Berditchev, who always sought to find the good in any Jew, would parade his people's merits before *Hakadosh Baruch Hu*, declaring, "Israel is foremost among the nations."

Once, at midnight, R' Levi Yitzchak told his *shamash*, "Take a bottle of whiskey and a glass and come with me."

The two went to the bathhouse, where the town's poor and destitute slept at night — miserable and hungry. R' Levi Yitzchak instructed his *shamash* to pour a glass of whiskey. Then he woke up one of the poor men and asked, "Would you like some whiskey?"

The man opened his eyes, saw the glass of whiskey, and said, "Sure, Rebbe. But without washing my hands and saying '*Modeh ani*'?"

R' Levi Yitzchak went on to another man, and then another. With each of them, the reaction was the same. Not one of the destitute and starving men would touch the whiskey.

R' Levi Yitzchak then roused the "Shabbos goy," who was asleep among the others, and said to him, "Ivan, would you like a glass of whiskey?"

"Hand it over!" cried the gentile, and swallowed the drink in one gulp.

Raising his eyes skyward, R' Levi Yitzchak said, "Master of the Universe, look down from Heaven and see who is like Your nation, Israel, a pure and holy people! No Jewish man will touch food or drink until he has washed his hands and rendered Your praise. Your Children are pleasing to You and You are pleasing to Your children."

A Proper Diet

כִּי רָאָה ד' בְּעָנְיִי
"Because Hashem has discerned my humiliation"
(Bereishis 29:32)

A wealthy man once came to see the Maggid of Mezritch. The Maggid asked him, "What do you eat each day?"

"A piece of bread and salt, like a poor man," the other answered.

The Maggid grew angry, and ordered the rich man to begin that very day eating meat and drinking sweet drinks like other wealthy people. After his visitor had gone, his students asked the reason for the Maggid's anger and his instructions.

The Maggid said, "If that rich man eats meat and drinks sweet drinks every day, he will understand that the poor man must at least have bread and salt. But if he himself eats nothing but bread and salt, he may end up thinking that the poor man can eat stones!"

The Washerwoman's Tale

הָבָה לִי בָנִים וְאִם אַיִן מֵתָה אָנֹכִי
"Give me children — if not, I am dead."
(Bereishis 30:1)

R' Shlomo of Zvil's blessings were always fulfilled to the fullest. In Jerusalem, the story is told of the woman who washed clothes in R' Shlomo's home. She was a pious and good woman. One day, after she had finished her work, she stood in the door of the Rabbi's study and asked him to bless her with children.

R' Shlomo regarded her for a few moments, then shook his head. "I cannot help you."

Then he added, "I bless you with this: that in your merit others will be remembered and find salvation."

For years afterwards, the washerwoman lived with the memory of that promise. In the year 5724 (1964), she died and was buried

Vayeitzei / 151

on Har Hamenuchos. On her gravestone were etched the words: "Here lies the woman Miriam, daughter of Maman, *a"h,* who passed away on the 24th day of Teves, 5724 (1964)."

In the year 5753 (1993), twenty-nine years after the washerwoman's death, a former neighbor of hers saw Miriam in a dream. In the dream, Miriam said, "I was a washerwoman in Rebbe Shlomo'le of Zvil's house. I had no children, and asked him for his blessing. The Rebbe told me that he could not help me, but blessed me that in my merit others would be remembered and saved. I ask that they come up to my grave and pray for the elevation of my soul. I promise that barren women will be remembered."

From that day, many women have ascended to visit Miriam the washerwoman's grave on Har Hamenuchos and, in the merit of the many prayers they poured out at that grave, many have indeed been remembered and have gone on to bear the children they so dearly craved.

<hr>

The room where the "Chiddushei HaRim" learned with his students was not large enough to hold them all, but the Rebbe refused to take the time away from Torah study in order to enlarge the room. Under normal circumstances, the job would take several consecutive days.

The small room became so cramped and uncomfortable that at last the Rebbe said, "If someone would undertake to construct the expansion in just one day, I would be very happy!"

One of the *chassidim,* hearing this, went to see a certain prosperous builder in Warsaw who had no children. "An opportunity has arisen for your salvation! Go expand the room where the Chiddushei HaRim learns, and in this merit you will have a son. There is just one condition: You must complete the work in one day."

The contractor was not a *chassid,* but he listened attentively to the offer. At once, he began to prepare all the necessary materials for the job. Gathering together a large work force, he managed in a single day to widen the room beautifully.

When the *chassid* saw his Rebbe's pleasure and peace of mind, he said, "We promised this man a son."

The Rebbe was silent for a few minutes. Then he said, "Hashem will help him."

A year later, the Chiddushei HaRim was invited to act as *sandak* at the *bris* of the builder's son.

A Personal Honor

נָתַן אֱלֹקִים שְׂכָרִי
"G-d has granted me my reward"
(*Bereishis* 30:18)

R' Levi Yitzchak of Berditchev's father-in-law was a wealthy man who regularly had many guests eating at his table. It was R' Levi Yitzchak's custom, while he was living with his in-laws, to serve these guests, to bring them straw to sleep on and to spread the straw out himself.

His father-in-law once asked him, "Why do you trouble yourself in this way? Don't you think I can afford to pay a gentile a penny or two to carry in the straw?"

"It's not right to honor a gentile with this mitzvah," R' Levi Yitzchak responded, "and, on top of that, to pay him for it!"

Suspecting the Innocent

מַה פִּשְׁעִי מַה חַטָּאתִי כִּי דָלַקְתָּ אַחֲרָי: כִּי מִשַּׁשְׁתָּ אֶת כָּל כֵּלַי מַה מָּצָאתָ מִכֹּל כְּלֵי בֵיתֶךָ

"What is my sin, that you have pursued me? When you rummaged through all my things, what did you find of all your household objects?"
(*Bereishis* 31:36-37)

R' Shmuel Strashon (the "Rashash"), a leading Torah light in Vilna known for his work, *Hagahos HaRashash al Shas*, was a great *gaon* conversant with all portions of the Torah. At the same time, he was also very active in public affairs. One of his projects was an interest-free loan fund (*gemach*) for those in need. He managed this fund very carefully, lest it be used up over time.

One day, a Jew came to borrow the sum of 100 rubles from this *gemach*. The sum was due to be repaid in four months. When the time came, the borrower went to see R' Shmuel at home. Not finding him there, he went to the *beis midrash* where R' Shmuel often sat and learned.

When the man walked into the *beis midrash,* the Rashash was totally absorbed in the Gemara lying open before him, unaware of the people coming and going around him. The borrower approached him and placed a 100-ruble note on the *Gemara,* saying that it was for repayment of his debt.

Still absorbed in his learning, R' Shmuel nodded his head.

The man took the nod as an acknowledgment that all was well. In actuality, however, R' Shmuel's attention was so fully focused on his learning that he had noticed neither the man nor the money. Later, when he had finished, he closed his *Gemara* with the 100-ruble note inside, replaced the volume on its shelf, and went home.

It was the Rashash's habit to go over his list of borrowers every day, in order to see if there was any loan due. On this day, upon his return from the *beis midrash,* he discovered that it was time for the 100-ruble loan to be repaid and that the money had not yet come in.

In the goodness of his heart, he decided to wait a few more weeks. Only at the end of that time did he send word to the man, requesting that he repay the loan.

In short order, the man arrived, protesting, "But I repaid the loan on the day the debt fell due! I gave the money to the Rav in person, as he sat learning in the *beis midrash.*"

R' Shmuel, who remembered nothing of this, assumed that the other man was lying. Afraid of letting public funds be stolen, he summoned the man to a *din Torah.*

The news quickly spread. All who heard were astounded at the man's temerity. "How can it be that he is not ashamed to lie? And apart from that, he is repaying a favor with injury!" The more people whispered about him, the greater grew the man's shame and distress, and those of his family as well. Matters reached the point where the man's son, thoroughly shamed by his father's alleged action, was forced to leave Vilna and relocate to another city to escape the embarrassment.

Then the day came when R' Shmuel had occasion to open the same *Gemara* that he had been studying when the man came to repay his debt. Turning the pages, he suddenly came across the 100-ruble note the man had given him! Great waves of guilt overcame the Rashash over the pain and aggravation he had caused the other man. He sent for him at once, and asked, "Tell me how I can compensate you for the harm that was caused because of my suspicion. Would you like me to publicly ask your pardon, so that all will know the truth?"

"What will it help me if you ask my pardon? People will think you only did it in order to spare me shame. In the eyes of the world, I will remain a liar forever. And what will asking my pardon do for my son, who left the city in shame?"

Hearing these words, the *gaon* sat sunk in thought for several moments. Suddenly, he turned to the man and said, "Send for your son, the one who left the city, and I will take him as a son-in-law, husband to my own daughter! In that way, I hope to prove to the entire city that you are honest and innocent."

And, indeed, a short time later an engagement party took place and *tena'im* were signed between the two *mechutanim:* the Rashash and the borrower.

An old woman once appeared at the home of R' Avraham Shag's grandson, with a request that he help her locate his grandfather's grave on the Mount of Olives.

"I have come especially from abroad in order to *daven* at your holy grandfather's grave!" she said. Then she told her story.

"About a hundred years ago, my mother, worked as a maid in R' Avraham Shag's house. One day, a large sum of money was brought to him for safekeeping. As was his custom, he placed the money in an envelope and wrote the owner's name on it. He was involved in his learning at the time, and instead of placing the envelope in its accustomed drawer, he left it lying between the pages of the *sefer* he was learning.

"Some time later, the owner came to ask for his money back. R' Avraham went to his drawer and found, to his dismay, that the envelope was not there! He suspected that the maid, my mother, might have taken it, as she had access to every part of the house.

"Not wishing to shame a Jewish woman, R' Avraham paid the money out of his own pocket and said nothing to the maid. He only told his wife to keep an eye on her.

"Some months later, on *erev Pesach,* R' Avraham was shaking out his *sefarim,* in order to make sure they were clear of *chametz,* when the envelope of money suddenly fell out of one of them!

"R' Avraham was beside himself with anguish. In tears he went to the maid and asked her to forgive him for suspecting her. He begged her to take whatever she wished from his home. But she answered, I forgive you with a full heart, and I do not want any of your possessions. Just one thing I ask: I have been married for fifteen years now, and have not yet had the merit of giving birth to a child. Please bless me, Rabbi, to have living children."

"R' Avraham blessed her with a child that very year, and with long life."

The old woman stopped talking, then continued in a choked voice, "I am that maid's daughter. All her life, my mother longed to come to Eretz Yisrael to visit the holy *tzaddik's* grave. Now Hashem has granted me the privilege of fulfilling my mother's wish."

Midnight Watch

הָיִיתִי בַיּוֹם אֲכָלַנִי חֹרֶב וְקֶרַח בַּלָּיְלָה וַתִּדַּד שְׁנָתִי מֵעֵינָי

"This is how I was: By day heat consumed me, and snow by night; my sleep drifted from my eyes."
(*Bereishis* 31:40)

One winter's night, R' Yechiel Meyer of Gostynin sat learning until very late. Suddenly, someone knocked at his door. The Rebbe opened it to find a Jewish wagon driver standing there, covered from head to toe in snow, his hands and feet turning blue from the cold. R' Yechiel Meyer took him in at once, served him a glass of hot tea to warm him, and offered him food as well.

"I can't take the time to eat," the wagon driver explained. "My horse and wagon are outside. I'm afraid they'll be stolen."

"Eat, then," smiled the Rebbe. "I will watch them for you."

The Rebbe went outside to watch over the man's horse and wagon, his head covered only with a yarmulka. He had refrained from putting on his rabbinical hat, fearing that the wagon driver would not let him help once he knew who he was. After eating his meal, the wagon driver fell asleep and slept through the night.

"I stood outside to guard his horse and wagon all night long," recounted R' Yechiel Meyer afterwards. "I said I would watch his horse and wagon, and watch them I did."

One cold winter's day, R' Zev Wolf of Ozhiran traveled to attend a *bris milah*. He went inside the house where the celebration was to be held, but remained there only a short time. Then he went out to his wagon.

"Go indoors and warm up," he told the driver, who was waiting in the freezing air.

"I can't leave my horses alone," the driver replied.

R' Zev Wolf persuaded the man to enter the house, promising to keep an eye on his horses for him. The driver went inside and began to drink. He soon forgot who was guarding his horses.

An hour passed, then two. The people inside began to wonder about the Rebbe's absence. No doubt he was alone somewhere, *davening* or immersed in meditation, they thought.

The day drew on and it began to grow dark. Then someone stepped outside and saw R' Zev Wolf vigorously pacing beside the wagon, flailing and thumping his arms to keep them from freezing.

One Fearful Night

זֶה לִי עֶשְׂרִים שָׁנָה בְּבֵיתֶךָ עֲבַדְתִּיךָ אַרְבַּע עֶשְׂרֵה שָׁנָה בִּשְׁתֵּי בְנֹתֶיךָ וְשֵׁשׁ שָׁנִים בְּצֹאנֶךָ וַתַּחֲלֵף אֶת מַשְׂכֻּרְתִּי עֲשֶׂרֶת מֹנִים

"This is for my twenty years in your household: I worked for you fourteen years for your two daughters, and six years for your flocks; and you changed my wage ten countings."
(*Bereishis* 31:41)

לוּלֵי אֱלֹקֵי אָבִי אֱלֹקֵי אַבְרָהָם וּפַחַד יִצְחָק הָיָה לִי כִּי עַתָּה רֵיקָם שִׁלַּחְתָּנִי

"Had not G-d of my father, the G-d of Avraham and the Dread of Yitzchak, been with me, you would surely have now sent me away empty handed"
(*Bereishis* 31:42)

The king of Morocco once lost a valuable jewel-studded sword. His men searched the palace grounds, but to no avail. Immediately, though without any proof, the Jews were blamed. An order was issued to search the Jewish ghetto.

It was the middle of the night. Everyone was asleep. Suddenly, with great shouting and noise, the king's soldiers burst into Jewish homes, dragged people from their beds, and forced everyone — men, women, and children — to walk to the outskirts of the town.

Stunned and trembling, the Jews stood in the fields outside the city crying "*Shema Yisrael*" and reciting *Viduy*. Every heart wondered fearfully what edict was about to be decreed against them. All night long they begged Hashem to rescue them, reciting *selichos* amid torrents of tears.

Among the rest of the townsfolk stood R' Chaviv Toledano, the community's representative and adviser to the king. When the soldiers had burst into his house, he had been learning, and he still held in his hand the Halachah *sefer* he had been studying when forced to leave his house.

During the night, the king's soldiers conducted a house-to-house search in the Jewish quarter, but the sword was not found. Thanks to Hashem's mercy, messengers from the king came to inform the Jews that they were free to return to their homes. Even more miraculous, the soldiers did not damage or steal any Jewish property at all.

R' Chaviv Toledano wrote down the events of that night on a blank page in the *sefer* he carried, so that Hashem's salvation would not be forgotten. He opened with the words, "Through Hashem's mercy, I will relate His compassion and abundant lovingkindness to His people, who revere His Name, as a reminder to myself and to my children."

This *sefer* was discovered about 200 years ago, along with the story written in R' Chaviv Toledano's hand.

Vayeitzei / 159

פרשת וישלח
Parashas Vayishlach

A Special Mitzvah

קְטֹנְתִּי מִכֹּל הַחֲסָדִים וּמִכָּל הָאֱמֶת אֲשֶׁר עָשִׂיתָ אֶת עַבְדֶּךָ

"I have been diminished by all the kindnesses and by all the truth that You have done Your servant"

(*Bereishis* 32:11)

R' Yechezkel was serving as *gabbai* in charge of *tzedakah* when a case came before him of a poor couple who lacked the money to marry. The groom was an orphan and the bride's family was unable to contribute much, as the family was impoverished, the father ill, and the expenses great.

"I went to a number of people," R' Yechezkel later related, "and I collected what I could but I was still missing a considerable sum. Then I remembered another man whose hand was always outstretched to help with any mitzvah. I was certain that he would give generously for the important mitzvah of *hachnasas kallah*.

"Immediately after *Shacharis* I went to see him, as I knew I'd find him at home at that hour. As I stood near the door, it seemed to me that I heard the sound of muffled sobs. I hesitated: Ring the bell, or wait until a better time? But I was a messenger for a mitzvah, time was pressing, and I could not disappoint the bride and groom and their families. I pressed the bell lightly.

"I heard hurried footsteps approaching the door. It opened, and there stood my acquaintance, the owner of the house. His face was very pale and his eyes looked red and tired, as though he had not slept all night. He welcomed me in a weak voice.

"'What's the matter? Is someone sick?' I asked. 'Apparently, I haven't come at a good time but the matter I wished to speak to you about is both important and urgent.'

"The man motioned for me to sit by the table and tell him what I needed. I told him all about the poor *chasan* and *kallah*, about the many necessities they lacked, and about the large sum I still needed to collect on their behalf, a sum I hoped to receive from him.

"He apologized. 'I'm sorry, I cannot become involved in anything right now. Please forgive me, and return another time. My head is not clear this morning. Our only son has been stricken with a life-threatening illness. His condition continues to worsen and he is breathing only with difficulty. We are waiting for the doctor to come at any moment. But even if he comes, what can he do? My son is barely clinging to life!'

"I hardly knew what to say to the poor father, whose only son lay dying. Perhaps it was best that I just go quietly away. But what would be the fate of that poor young couple if I did? Suddenly, an idea flashed into my mind. I remembered something I had once heard in the name of our great men of Torah.

"I seized the man's sleeve and said excitedly, 'Please, listen to me for just a moment. You know what we say every morning: "These are things of which a man consumes the fruit in this world, and the interest remains for him in the World to Come... and visiting the sick and *hachnasas kallah* and accompanying the dead..." Our Sages, of blessed memory, placed *hachnasas kallah* in the middle, between visiting the sick and accompanying the dead. This is no coincidence. In their divine wisdom, our Sages come to teach us that the mitzvah of *hachnasas kallah* has the power to stand guard between life and death! There is a special power in this mitzvah to help the ill recover, so that they will not have to reach the condition of "accompanying the dead," Heaven forbid.'

"The despairing father listened attentively, considered for a few seconds, then made his decision. He went into another room and soon returned, bearing the sum that was needed to supply what the young couple lacked. Tears sprang to my eyes. I blessed him with all my heart, 'Hashem will send a speedy recovery to the sick boy among the other sick members of Israel!' And I left.

"Wonder of wonders! Only a few hours had passed, when that same man appeared at my house, overcome with joy. He grabbed my hand emotionally and said, 'Heaven sent you to me today, to save my son's life! Immediately after you left my house, the doctor arrived. He was extremely surprised at the sudden improvement in my son's condition. In fact, he could not find the words to express his astonishment! The situation continues to improve, and the boy is completely out of danger. He is growing stronger by the minute. My boy was spared from certain death — and was granted life!'

The Wheels of Providence

קָטֹנְתִּי מִכֹּל הַחֲסָדִים וּמִכָּל הָאֱמֶת אֲשֶׁר עָשִׂיתָ אֶת עַבְדֶּךָ

"I have been diminished by all the kindnesses and by all the truth that You have done Your servant"

(*Bereishis* 32:11)

In the year 5700 (1940), after the Nazis overran Poland and terrible difficulties began to plague the Jews, the Brisker Rav, R' Yitzchak Ze'ev Soloveitchik, decided that it was necessary to leave Poland and move to Vilna. Preparations were made in haste: Suitcases were packed, bundles tied up, and the family was ready to set out. They lacked only a wagon to transport them.

Members of the Rav's family searched for a fairly new wagon with rubber wheels that would help them make the journey in relative comfort but there was none to be found. All the rubber-wheeled wagons had already left. There was not one remaining in the whole city.

Disappointed, the family climbed onto an old-fashioned wagon that had wooden wheels. Travel in such a vehicle was difficult and tiring. Every bump in the road jolted the passengers unmercifully.

At the city gates, the wagon was stopped. A long line of wagons stood there ahead of them, all waiting to leave. The Brisker Rav's driver tried to find a place to move forward, but was unsuccessful.

"What happened?" the family asked. "Why have all the wagons been stopped?"

Word passed down along the line: "The Germans are confiscating wagons! Every wagon with rubber wheels is being taken away!"

Slowly, the line inched forward, until the family was able to see for themselves what was happening up ahead. The passengers of the more modern wagons were being turned out of their wagons and abandoned at the side of the road. Their pleas and entreaties fell on deaf ears. At last came the Rav's turn.

The officer threw a glance at the squeaking wooden wheels and waved his hand in a dismissive gesture. "Go!" he told the driver. "We have no need for such a wagon."

The passengers heaved a sigh of relief. The driver flicked his whip at his horses and continued down the road, at the end of which they hoped to find respite.

"You see?" the Brisker Rav told his family. "Everything is from Hashem!"

No Tomorrow for the Wicked

הַצִּילֵנִי נָא מִיַּד אָחִי מִיַּד עֵשָׂו כִּי יָרֵא אָנֹכִי אֹתוֹ פֶּן יָבוֹא וְהִכַּנִי

"Rescue me, please, from the hand of my brother, from the hand of Esau, for I fear him lest he come and strike me"

(*Bereishis* 32:12)

The year 5703 (1943) was a very difficult one for the Jews of Tunis. The Nazis had invaded northern Africa, where they hoped to implement the same "Final Solution" that they had set in motion in conquered Europe.

On Shabbos, the eighth day of Adar *Alef*, a group of Gestapo officers came to the shul where R' Moshe Calphon HaKohen — a member of the *beis din* of Gerba — was *davening*. They wished to speak to him.

R' Moshe was in the middle of reciting the *Kedushah* of *Musaf*. He was not one to break off a session with his Creator for any human being. He completed his *tefillah* with concentration and devotion, and only then went out to speak to the Germans.

"We are certain," the arrogant officers told him, "that you, the Jews, have prepared ways to signal the English and show them where to drop their bombs!" Without waiting for an answer, they ordered, "You must collect fifty kilograms of gold from the Jews of Tunis and Gerba. You have three and a half hours in which to do so. If not, we will destroy the Jewish communities in both places!"

The Nazis had a detailed list of the wealthy members of each community and exactly what their assets were. Should the demanded sum not be forthcoming, these rich men would be the first ones to be taken out and shot.

R' Moshe knew that the Nazis were very capable of carrying out their terrible threat. He called an urgent meeting of community leaders, to plan a strategy and seek a solution. Everyone understood that there was no choice but to satisfy the enemy's greed.

Some thirty-five kilograms of gold were gathered in the first hour, with the rest promised to the Germans by the next day.

But, for the evil Nazis, tomorrow never came. In Heaven's mercy, the next day Allied forces descended upon Tunis and overcame the German troops. Salvation had come to the Jews once again!

Scrupulousness in Small Things

וַיִּוָּתֵר יַעֲקֹב לְבַדּוֹ

And Yaakov was left alone
(Bereishis 32:25)
He had forgotten some small jars and went back for them
(Rashi)

R' Eliyahu Dushnitzer, *menahel ruchani* of the Lomza Yeshivah in Petach Tikvah, once climbed aboard a bus together with two companions. He paid his fare without realizing that the driver had neglected to give him a ticket.

When he remembered, he was not sure how to act. He discussed the matter with his companions, saying, "If I ask the driver for a ticket now, he may suspect me of not paying him at all — and that will cause a *chillul Hashem*. However, if I leave the matter alone and do nothing, the money I paid the driver will go into his pocket instead of going to the bus company that employs him, and I will have caused him, unwittingly, to steal. Moreover, if a bus official comes aboard [to make a spot check, as is their custom] and finds me with no ticket, he will suspect me of riding the bus without paying my fare and, again, I will have been the cause of a *chillul Hashem!*"

In the end, he found a solution.

"I absolve the driver completely of the money I've already paid him. Let him keep the money. Now I'll go pay him again, and get a ticket!"

And that was what he did.

❧

A Dubious Exchange

וַיִּוָּתֵר יַעֲקֹב לְבַדּוֹ
And Yaakov was left alone
(Bereishis 32:25)
He had forgotten some small jars and went back for them
(Rashi)

The *shochet* of Salant, a pious and learned man, once came to R' Yisrael Salanter and said, "I want to leave my profession. I'm afraid of the responsibility toward all my fellow townspeople of making sure they don't eat meat that is not kosher."

"And what will you do for a living instead?" asked R' Yisrael Salanter.

"I'll open a store and earn my living in trade."

"I'm surprised at you!" exclaimed R' Yisrael. "*Shechitah* has only one prohibition, and you want to leave it. Yet trade and business are open to many prohibitions from the Torah. 'Do not steal,' 'Do not lie,' 'Do not delay your worker's salary,' the laws of weights and measurements, and many, many more!"

R' Yisrael continued, "Just as the rabbi of a town is obligated to check his *shochets'* knives to make sure they have no flaw that would make the chickens *treif*, so, too, must he go from store to store to check whether the shopkeeper's scales are exact."

It is important to remember that the halachos pertaining to honest business transactions are mitzvos from the Torah — no less serious than all the other halachos.

What Is Heaven Saying About Us?

וַיֹּאמֶר לֹא יַעֲקֹב יֵאָמֵר עוֹד שִׁמְךָ כִּי אִם יִשְׂרָאֵל כִּי שָׂרִיתָ עִם אֱלֹקִים וְעִם אֲנָשִׁים וַתּוּכָל

He said, "No longer will it be said that your name is Yaakov, but Yisrael, for you have striven with the Divine and with men and you have overcome."

(Bereishis 32:29)

"And with men, Esav and Lavan."

(Rashi)

R' Yitzchak Ze'ev Soloveitchik, the Brisker Rav, was imbued with a powerful faith in Hashem's ability to send salvation in any situation. Even in the most difficult of circumstances, he would emphasize that it was not the situation that decided matters, but rather, "What are they saying about us in Heaven?"

In the anthology, *Sha'arei Torah*, the following story is written.

When the Brisker Rav was in Vilna in the year 5700 (1940), the Russians began confiscating apartments for use by its army officers. First they would issue an eviction notice for certain apartments, then they would send interested officers to the apartments to choose the ones they liked for themselves. When an army officer found a place he liked, its owner was forced to vacate it within 48 hours. In exchange, he received an apartment in a distant location, outside the city.

One day, when the Brisker Rav's sons returned home, he told them that the Russians were in their apartment and an eviction notice had been issued. The family was very downhearted, especially when they discovered that the apartment they had been given in exchange was very far from the city, with no means of transportation, and was hardly habitable as it had no windows.

Seeing their sad faces, the Rav said, "This week we will be reading *Parashas Vayishlach*. It says there, 'No longer will it be said that your name is Yaakov, but Yisrael, for you have striven with the Divine and with men and you have overcome.' And Rashi explains the words 'and with men' refers to Esav and Lavan.

"These matters require further study. It is true that Yaakov had already overcome Lavan. But he had not even met with Esav yet.

How, then, can we say 'and you have overcome'?

"The explanation is that the man who struggled with Yaakov was Esav's angel, and we learn that the dust they raised in their battle reached the Throne of Glory. In other words, their struggle was to see who would prevail in Heaven. We find, therefore, that when Yaakov overcame Esav's angel in Heaven, he was already victorious over Esav here on earth, even though they had not yet met.

"In the same way," the Brisker Rav concluded, "the main thing we must concern ourselves with is what they will say about us in Heaven. If good fortune is decreed for us there, then there is nothing we need fear from people!"

And so it turned out. Even though his apartment in Vilna was large and handsome, it did not find favor in the eyes of any of the Russian officers who came to see it. It was only after the Rav left his apartment willingly and moved to Eretz Yisrael, did someone finally come along who liked the apartment, and rented it.

※

A Jewish tradeswoman went to a nobleman's home one morning, as usual, to sell her wares. As a rule, the nobleman's wife would come out to the courtyard to inspect the wares. This time, however, it was the maid who came.

"What's the matter?" the tradeswoman asked the maid. "Where is your mistress?"

"Haven't you heard? The master and mistress's only son is very sick!"

"I know, I know. I heard about his illness," the Jewish woman said, settling down for an enjoyable chat. "And do you know what else I heard? Our rabbi says that if the nobleman would only release the Jewish merchant he's got in his jail, his son would recover from his dreadful illness!"

Thrilled, the maid rushed off to pass the news on to her master and mistress.

Meanwhile, the Jewish woman beat her breast in remorse and frustration. "What have I done? I always get in trouble with my big mouth! I didn't hear anything of the kind from the rabbi!"

She was still standing there in distress when the nobleman himself came out to the courtyard.

"Is what you told the maid true?" he demanded.

"Y-yes!" she answered, panicked. What dire punishment might befall her if she admitted she had lied?

Soberly, he said, "The Jewish merchant transgressed some of our laws in running his business, and has been imprisoned for some time now, awaiting a serious punishment. But for the sake of my son, I am prepared to do everything in my power to have him released."

As soon as she could make her escape, the tradeswoman staggered toward the *beis midrash* of the city's rabbi, R' Yehoshua Leib Diskin. With a heavy heart, she poured out her tale. She begged his forgiveness for dragging him into her troubles, then burst into bitter tears.

"Salvation is in Hashem's hands," the rabbi comforted her.

Near evening, when the nobleman's messenger arrived at the Maharil's home to ascertain whether the tradeswoman had spoken honestly, the rabbi said, "Free the prisoner, and the boy will recover from his illness!"

The next day was one of joyous thanksgiving in the home of the Jewish merchant, newly released from jail. "Blessed is He Who frees the imprisoned!" And in the home of the nobleman, they were celebrating as well: celebrating the miraculously speedy recovery of a cherished only son.

Every Minute of the Day

כִּי רָאִיתִי אֱלֹקִים פָּנִים אֶל פָּנִים

"For I have seen the Divine face to face"
(*Bereishis* 32:31)

When the Maggid of Mezritch passed away, his *chassidim* convened to discuss the choice of a new rebbe to take his place. In the end, they decided to appoint R' Elimelech of Lizhensk. A group of *chassidim* went to R' Elimelech to escort him back.

Not wishing to travel at night, they stopped at an inn. The *chassidim* signaled to the innkeeper to prepare a separate room for R' Elimelech.

When R' Elimelech entered his room, he lay down at once and fell into a deep sleep that lasted for several hours. The *chassidim* were embarrassed: Was it possible that their new rebbe, appointed in place of the great Maggid of Mezritch, would sleep so long instead of learning Torah? They began to regret their choice.

R' Elimelech's brother, R' Zusha, was among their party. The *chassidim* went to him and asked him to wake his brother. At the door to R' Elimelech's room, R' Zusha placed his hand on the mezuzah. R' Elimelech woke up immediately and got out of bed.

The *chassidim* were astounded. "How," they asked R' Zusha, "did your touching the mezuzah affect your brother?"

R' Zusha replied, "The words *'Shivisi Hashem l'negdi samid'* ('I place Hashem before me always') hover constantly before my brother's eyes. During sleep, when the eyes are closed, this is not possible — so we must rely on Hashem's Name that is written in the mezuzah. When I rested my hand on the mezuzah and covered the Name, my brother awoke at once, so that he could once again see the letters of Hashem's Name before his open eyes."

When the *chassidim* heard this, they cried out with deep emotion, "*Baruch Hashem,* Who has not left us like a flock without a shepherd!"

Common Sense

עַל כֵּן לֹא יֹאכְלוּ בְנֵי יִשְׂרָאֵל אֶת גִּיד הַנָּשֶׁה אֲשֶׁר עַל כַּף הַיָּרֵךְ עַד הַיּוֹם הַזֶּה

Therefore the Children of Israel are not to eat the displaced sinew on the ball of the thighbone to this day

(*Bereishis* 32:33)

One *erev Shabbos*, R' Shmuel Salant sat in his house in Jerusalem, learning Torah with several of his top students from Yeshivas Chofetz Chaim. Suddenly, a young girl came in, holding a slaughtered chicken.

R' Shmuel stopped learning and asked the girl what she wanted.

"My mother asked if the Rav would look at this chicken and tell me if it's kosher."

R' Shmuel checked the chicken, then straightened up and told the girl, "Tell your mother to send me the second chicken she had slaughtered!"

The girl left. After a short time, she returned a second chicken in her hand. And this chicken indeed had a questionable halachic status.

Seeing this, R' Shmuel's students were amazed. "It's *ruach hakodesh* (Divine insight)!" they exclaimed.

"It is no such thing," retorted R' Shmuel. "When I saw the first chicken, it was clear that there was no problem at all with it. So I said to myself, 'It is not possible that the mother sent me a chicken that has no question at all. In that case, there were surely two chickens, and she accidentally sent me the good one in place of the questionable one.'"

※

A man who *davened* in R' Shmuel Salant's shul told a friend, "One of the chickens in my chicken yard is always much dirtier than all the others."

R' Shmuel, overhearing this, approached the man and said, "In my opinion, a chicken that is very dirty is not kosher!"

Hearing this, those present were taken aback. One of them ventured to ask, "Will the Rebbe explain to us how he came to the conclusion that the chicken is not kosher?"

"While it is true that this is not mentioned in any halachic works," R' Shmuel answered, "it stands to reason that, if the chicken is not able to turn its head around to clean off the dirt that has clung to it, as chickens usually do, it apparently has a broken joint."

When the chicken was examined, it indeed turned out that its joint was broken!

At a Single Glance

וַיִּשָּׂא יַעֲקֹב עֵינָיו וַיַּרְא וְהִנֵּה עֵשָׂו בָּא וְעִמּוֹ אַרְבַּע מֵאוֹת אִישׁ

Yaakov raised his eyes and saw and behold, Esav was coming, and with him, were four hundred men

(*Bereishis* 33:1)

R' Yehoshua Leib Diskin had remarkable abilities, only a small portion of which were revealed to the general public.

It is said that he was blessed with clear vision until a ripe old age. Once, the *shamash* of the shul stated his intention of taking down the plaque from the shul's western wall that held the names of deceased patrons. The names were handwritten, in small letters, and difficult to read from a distance. By taking the plaque down, the names could be read and *mishnayos* could be learned in their memories.

R' Yehoshua Leib, standing in his place by the eastern wall, told the *shamash* that there was no need to take down the plaque. Without moving a step closer, he began reading off the names in precise detail, while everyone stood by and marveled.

On another occasion, someone brought R' Yehoshua Leib a multipaged letter that he had received. He wished to be advised about a certain problem explained in the letter. R' Yehoshua Leib turned the pages very rapidly, then answered the man's question. The man did not believe that it was possible in such a short space of time to genuinely understand the problem.

"How is it possible to read the letter so quickly?" he wondered silently.

R' Yehoshua Leib, noting the man's doubts, said, "The letter has this number of words." And he named a figure.

Out of curiosity, the man actually went and counted the words in the letter. Sure enough, the number of words was exactly as R' Yehoshua Leib had said — no more, no less!

R' Yehoshua Leib's doctors recommended a daily walk in the fresh air. Near dusk, he would stroll out of the Old City walls, accompanied by a few of his students or respected members of Jerusalem's community.

One afternoon as they were walking, a herd of goats passed in front of them. "There are this many goats in the flock," R' Yehoshua Leib remarked, naming a number.

His students exchanged astonished glances. How, in a single fleeting glance, could their Rebbe know the number of goats in the flock?

One of the students went up to the shepherd and asked, "How many goats are there in your flock?"

When he heard the answer, his amazement grew. The figure that the shepherd gave was the exact number that R' Yehoshua Leib had stated!

On another occasion, R' Yehoshua Leib passed near the Old City wall, and stated the number of stones in that section of wall.

"Where does this ability come from, to count a large quantity at a single glance?" asked his companion.

Vayishlach / 175

"Is this something new?" R' Yehoshua Leib countered. "It says clearly in the Torah: 'Yaakov raised his eyes and saw — and behold, Esav was coming, and with him, were four hundred men.' In other words, in a single quick glance, Yaakov *Avinu* knew that there were four hundred men — exactly!"

A Joyous Death

וַיִּגְוַע יִצְחָק וַיָּמָת וַיֵּאָסֶף אֶל עַמָּיו זָקֵן וּשְׂבַע יָמִים

And Yitzchak expired and died, and he was brought in to his people, old and fulfilled of days

(*Bereishis* 35:29)

R' Moshe Leib of Sassov married off a poor bride and groom, paying the expenses from his own pocket. He was overjoyed as the *kallah* stepped under the *chupah* to the accompaniment of music. Turning to those standing near him, he said, "If only, when my time comes, they will walk me to my resting place to this music!"

Many years passed, and the comment was entirely forgotten.

On the day of R' Moshe Leib's death, 4 Shevat 5567 (1807), a group of musicians was traveling to the city of Brody to play at a wedding. Suddenly, the horses pulling their wagon began to run of their own accord. They raced up and down the hills, not stopping for anything. It was only when they neared the cemetery did the horses come to a halt. The musicians saw a very large crowd of Jews and understood that they were in the midst of an important man's funeral.

"Who is the man who died?" they asked. And they were told that it was the holy R' Moshe Leib.

Suddenly, the musicians remembered what they had heard R' Moshe Leib say at that poor couple's wedding so many years before. They also remembered the tune that had been played then because they themselves had been the ones playing it. A *beis din* was quickly set up to judge whether it was fitting to play the tune now, as R' Moshe Leib had specifically expressed such a wish. It was decided that the musicians should play, and so they did.

There is no way to describe the incredible *tzedakah* that R' Shlomo of Karlin gave, even at a time when his house was bare of food and he lived in great poverty.

Once, when he literally had nothing in the house to live on, someone gave him a gold coin. Minutes later, however, the coin changed hands as R' Shlomo passed it on to a poor man who had come seeking *tzedakah*.

The door was still swinging on its hinges when R' Shlomo's attendant came in. Knowing that the Rebbe had just received a gold coin, he remarked that there was no other money in the house with which to purchase food for Shabbos.

"The coin is no longer here," the Rebbe said simply.

The attendant ran after the poor man. Catching up to him, he said, "The Rebbe made a mistake. He intended to give you a small coin, but accidentally gave you a large one instead."

The poor man, being an honorable person, agreed to exchange the gold coin for one of lesser value. The attendant returned to the Rebbe.

When R' Shlomo saw the gold coin in his helper's hand, he was overcome by a weakness so great that he fell to the floor, unconscious. It was only with great difficulty that his household managed to revive him.

After he had regained consciousness, the Rebbe said, "You took away my whole life when you asked that poor man to give back the coin." And his spirit would not be at peace until messengers had been sent to find the poor man and return the gold coin to him.

פרשת וישב

Parashas Vayeishev

The Teacher-Student Bond

כִּי בֶן זְקֻנִים הוּא לוֹ
Since he was the child of his old age
(Bereishis 37:3)
Onkelos rendered it: "He was a wise son to him," [because] all that [Yaakov] had learned from Shem and Ever he gave over to him.
(Rashi)

When young Avraham Mordechai Alter, who later became the Gerrer Rebbe, reached the age at which he was capable of learning *Gemara*, his father, the *Sfas Emes*, insisted that his son learn in an expansive and fundamental way and brought in illustrious teachers, men who excelled in the depth and breadth of their knowledge. Not every teacher, however, was able to satisfy the boy, who continually thirsted to learn more and more.

When he was 6 years old, one teacher taught him all through the winter, to Avraham Mordechai's great satisfaction. The boy pleaded with him to remain during the "summer semester" as well. The teacher lived in a distant town and had left his family for half a year in order to earn his living, as many people did in those times. He hesitated, therefore, to give his promise until he had learned his family's wishes in the matter.

In the end, the teacher was able to return after Pesach. Young Avraham Mordechai was overjoyed. In his happiness, he seized the teacher's hands and began to dance with him. This took place in the attic, where the two did their learning together. They danced so energetically that the chandelier fell off the ceiling in the dining room directly below. The Rebbetzin hurried up the stairs to see her young son circling the room with his teacher, radiant with joy.

"Tainted" Food

וַיִּגְעַר בּוֹ אָבִיו וַיֹּאמֶר לוֹ מָה הַחֲלוֹם הַזֶּה אֲשֶׁר חָלָמְתָּ הֲבוֹא נָבוֹא
אֲנִי וְאִמְּךָ וְאַחֶיךָ לְהִשְׁתַּחֲוֹת לְךָ אָרְצָה

And his father scolded him, and said to him, "What is this dream that you have dreamt? Are we to come, I and your mother, and your brothers, to bow down to you on the ground?"

(*Bereishis* 37:10)

In his old age, R' Nosson Tzvi Finkel, the Alter of Slobodka, became ill and required round-the-clock care. His devoted students did not leave him day or night, supplying all their Rebbe's needs with a full heart. Each day, they prepared special food that the doctors had prescribed for his recovery.

The preparation of this special food called for great care and attention to detail. One student, in particular, was skilled at preparing it, and he even imbued the dish with good flavor, to please the Alter's palate and perhaps influence his health for the better.

Seeing how hard his student worked to please him, R' Nosson Tzvi always praised his cooking and expressed his heartfelt gratitude.

One day, that same student had to leave Chevron for Jerusalem. He put another student in his place to serve the Alter that day. When the time came to prepare R' Nosson Tzvi's special food, the student did not know exactly how to do it, and the dish came out much less successful than usual. R' Nosson Tzvi, of course, said nothing. But the other students, in their eagerness to serve their Rebbe, were distressed.

The student returned from his trip and heard what had happened. Immediately, he rushed into the kitchen to prepare one of his tasty meals. He decided to add a special delicacy: a little fresh butter that he had just brought back with him from Jerusalem. In this way, he hoped to make up to the Alter for what he had lacked while he, the student, had been away.

The dish was brought to the Alter — who took one spoonful and felt suddenly, overwhelmingly, nauseated. He exclaimed that he felt as though poison had been introduced into the food, and would not eat another bite.

In the evening, his beloved student came trembling to serve him his supper. R' Nosson Tzvi tasted it, then began to praise the food highly, as usual. He finished his portion to the last bite. The student felt at ease again.

It was only then that the Alter explained what had happened earlier in the day. When the student returned from Jerusalem and hurried to prepare the special food, he had been enjoying the forbidden pleasure of receiving honor at the expense of another's shame. In his heart, he had been thinking, "I am the one who knows how to serve the Rebbe best!" This pleasure was the poison that the Alter had tasted in his food.

But now, in the evening, the student had cooked the meal with no unworthy thoughts, so the food was once again delicious.

Doing a Favor

וַיִּמְצָאֵהוּ אִישׁ וְהִנֵּה תֹעֶה בַּשָּׂדֶה
A man discovered him, and behold! he was blundering in the field
(*Bereishis* 37:15)

A *chassid* once came to see R' Chaim of Sanz, to complain that his daughter had reached marriageable age and he had no money with which to marry her off. The Rebbe gave him a letter of recommendation to a wealthy Torah scholar whom he counted among his *chassidim*. In the letter, R' Chaim asked the rich *chassid* to do the poor man a favor and try to collect money for *hachnasas kallah*.

When the poor *chassid* came to the wealthy one with the letter, the rich man answered, "*Talmud Torah k'neged kulam* (Torah study is weighed against all other mitzvos)!" and refused to take the time to busy himself with matters besides learning.

Some months later, this same prosperous *chassid* came to Sanz to see the Rebbe. The Rebbe, however, refused to extend his hand in greeting. And when the time came for parting, he said, "The Torah tells us (*Bereishis* 32:25), 'and a man struggled with him,' and Rashi explains, 'He was the ministering angel of Esav.' And in *Parashas Veyeishev*, when Yosef gets lost in the field, the Torah says, 'A man discovered him,' and Rashi explains that the 'man' in this case was the angel Gavriel. Why is the word 'man' used for Esav's angel in the first place, and the angel Gavriel in the second?

"The answer is as follows: In the case where Yosef lost his way and a man pointed it out to him, that was the angel Gavriel. But when Yaakov *Avinu* meets up with a man and asks him to do him a favor and bless him, and the 'man' answers that he has no time because 'I must recite song by day' (as Rashi explains there), that kind of man must be *Esav's* angel, because a Jew must do a favor for another Jew under any circumstances!"

The Telltale Hand

לְמַעַן הַצִּיל אתו מִיָּדָם
In order to rescue him from their hand
(*Bereishis* 37:22)

In a small town in Eastern Galicia, the corpse of a gentile farmer was found. Anti-Semitism was rampant in those days, and suspicion fell immediately upon the Jews. The gentiles accused a Jewish innkeeper of murdering the farmer. His arguments and denials fell upon deaf ears. The innkeeper was thrown into prison until his case could be decided.

The Jew's son traveled to the great R' Benzion and poured out his bitter tale. He explained that there were three farmers in their town who were always out for the murdered man's blood; apparently, one of them had finally done it. His father was completely innocent of any part in the grisly affair.

R' Benzion said, "Hurry home at once. You must arrive before the farmer's funeral. Tell the judge who is going to decide this case to take my suggestion and ask all four men — your father and the three farmers — to shake the dead man's hand. The one whose hand will become stuck to the dead man's is the guilty party."

The innkeeper's son did as he was told. The judge, hearing the Rebbe's bizarre suggestion, laughed. But since the Rebbe's reputation was well known in Galicia, the judge decided to respect his wishes.

The Jew shook the dead farmer's hand first, and was able to extricate his own with ease. Next came one farmer, and then another with the same result. When the third farmer's turn came, he began to scream at the top of his lungs that he was afraid to shake the dead man's hand, for fear of revenge! And in front of the judge and all the assembled company, he confessed to the murder.

The Jewish innkeeper was released at once, and a great *kiddush Hashem* took place as everyone saw the truth revealed through the Rebbe's sagacity and wisdom.

Shame — or the Flames?

הִיא מוּצֵאת וְהִיא שָׁלְחָה אֶל חָמִיהָ לֵאמֹר לְאִישׁ אֲשֶׁר אֵלֶּה לּוֹ אָנֹכִי הָרָה

She was taken out, and she sent [word] to her father-in-law, saying, 'By the man to whom these belong I am pregnant."

(Bereishis 38:25)

"I will not make his face pale, i.e., embarrass him..." From here [the Rabbis] said: It is preferable for a person that he throw himself into a fiery furnace, but let him not make his friend's face pale in public. (Rashi)

The only source of heat in the Baranovitch *beis midrash* was a large oven that stood by the back wall. The poor people who passed from town to town depended on the shuls, which were heated throughout the night, to provide them with a warm place to sleep.

It was the job of the *shamash* to make sure that the fire was well stoked, so that the men who came to learn before dawn would find a heated shul. In the Baranovitch *beis midrash,* it was the poor people themselves who kept the fire stoked with wood from the pile of logs the *shamash* kept beside the oven. If there happened to be no poor people sleeping there one night, by morning the shul would be freezing and the *shamash* would be at the receiving end of much criticism from the men who came in early to learn and *daven.*

R' Yisrael Yaakov Lubchansky was Rav of the city. In order to protect the *shamash,* who was neglectful of his duties at times, the Rabbi would leave his home very early every morning, while it was still dark outside, and go to the shul. There he would gather logs, pile them in the oven, light a fire, and fan the flames until the fire caught.

Vayeishev / 185

After a while, the people became accustomed to having the shul well heated when they entered in the mornings. They complimented the *shamash* on the fine job he was doing. The *shamash,* for his part, thought that the oven was being lit by the poor people, who had no desire to sleep in a cold shul.

One frigid winter morning, when it was still dark outside, R' Yisrael Yaakov entered as usual to collect wood for the oven. On that day, the *shamash* also happened to come in early. He saw someone moving around, gathering materials for stoking the fire.

"Good morning!" the *shamash* called, approaching closer.

R' Yisrael Yaakov knew that, if the *shamash* would discover that it was the Rav who was doing his job, he would be greatly embarrassed. He did not respond to the greeting, hoping the *shamash* would continue about his duties, collecting the *siddurim* and returning books to their proper places.

But the *shamash's* feelings were wounded. "Good morning!" he screamed angrily, convinced that he was dealing with an ill-mannered pauper. R' Yisrael Yaakov continued with what he was doing, his face turned toward the oven so that the *shamash* would not recognize him. He merely nodded his head to acknowledge the *shamash's* greeting, then continued tending the fire.

In a fury, the *shamash* came over to the "beggar" until he stood directly behind him, and kicked him. He nearly kicked the Rav into the oven!

"What kind of behavior is this? Don't you know how to answer when someone speaks to you?"

By this time, R' Yisrael Yaakov's face was literally inside the oven. He coughed and choked from the smoke and fumes. The *shamash* gave him one last shove for good measure, and went away.

Now the flames caught hold of the Rabbi's beard.

When he saw that the *shamash* had left, R' Yisrael Yaakov turned around quickly and ran out of the shul, covering his face so that no one would recognize him.

When the Rav arrived in the *beis midrash* later that morning with part of his beard missing, the people thought he was the victim of some sort of accident at home. It was only years later, when R' Yisrael Yaakov was appointed *menahel ruchani* of the Baranovitch Yeshivah, that a family member revealed what had really happened.

Every *motza'ei Shabbos,* in his home, R' Yehoshua Leib Diskin would deliver a *shiur* on the weekly Torah portion. Those attending the *shiur* would be offered a glass of tea, and the Rav would drink along with them.

Once, the person pouring the tea accidentally switched the salt and the sugar. Because of his health, R' Yehoshua Leib required an extra-large portion of sugar. Due to the man's mistake, he received instead several teaspoons of salt in his tea.

He took a sip from his glass, but did not show that anything was wrong. None of the men seated around his table noticed anything amiss.

The Rebbetzin noticed that the helper who had been preparing the tea was holding the sack of salt instead of the one with sugar, and she understood what had happened. She ran into the room and cried out, "There is salt in your glass!"

The students who later tasted what was left in R' Yehoshua Leib's glass marveled at his self-control. He had drunk the heavily salted drink without batting an eyelash.

When his wife asked him why he had allowed himself to drink such salted water, which could have a detrimental effect on his health, the Maharil explained, "Our Sages, may their memory be blessed, said: It is better for a man to throw himself into a fiery furnace than to embarrass his friend in public!"

Confession

וַיֹּאמֶר צָדְקָה מִמֶּנִּי

And he said, "She is right; it is from me."
(*Bereishis* 38:26)

Davening was taking place at the home of R' Nosson Tzvi Finkel, the Alter of Slobodka, when a loud noise was heard. Afterwards, the Alter asked about the source of the disturbance. One of his students came forward and said, hanging his head, "I am to blame. It was I who disrupted the *davening.*"

The Alter's face lit up. "See and learn from his actions!" he praised the student. "This is a marvelous example of good behavior!

You should know, that by acknowledging the truth, in a way this young man did something greater than Yehudah did.

"Yehudah was not guilty in his actions. As our Sages, may their memory be blessed, teach, an angel came down from Heaven and forced him into his deed. And still, his confession was seen as an exalted thing.

"This young man, on the other hand, was guilty. He created a deliberate disturbance during *davening*. If he managed to overcome his shame, and the impulse toward pride, and admit what he'd done — his confession is an exalted thing indeed!"

Prisoners at Prayer

וַיִּקַּח אֲדֹנֵי יוֹסֵף אֹתוֹ וַיִּתְּנֵהוּ אֶל בֵּית הַסֹּהַר מְקוֹם אֲשֶׁר אֲסִירֵי הַמֶּלֶךְ אֲסוּרִים

Then Yosef's master took him and placed him in prison, the place where the king's prisoners were confined

(*Bereishis* 39:20)

During the British mandate in Palestine, the Jewish Yishuv (settlement) lived with constant terrorism from the Arabs and curfews from the British. Early one morning, R' Salman Mutzafi left home, accompanied by a student, and set off for shul, without realizing that yet another British curfew was in effect.

A British patrol car came toward them. The officers stopped R' Salman and his companion and, after a brief interrogation, carried them off to Shneller Base.

At the base, R' Salman found more than 300 other Jews, all in one holding area, idly sitting.

"Can this be?" the Rabbi shouted." How can you sit here and not do a thing? This is a golden opportunity to do something!"

Immediately, he organized everyone in one corner, where he himself served as a *sheliach tzibbur* for three hours. They recited various *tefillos,* including *selichos, tikkun chatzos,* and prayers for peace. The British officers were astounded at the strange spectacle. As soon as R' Salman finished *davening,* they came to release him, along with a large number of his fellow prisoners saying, "We don't want to see you here again!"

Upon his return home, R' Salman told his anxious Rebbetzin, "Have you heard? It was not for nothing that they took me to Shneller base today. Everything is from Heaven!"

Not Forgotten

כִּי אִם זְכַרְתַּנִי אִתְּךָ כַּאֲשֶׁר יִיטַב לָךְ וְעָשִׂיתָ נָּא עִמָּדִי חָסֶד

"At which time, if you would think of me with yourself when you will have benefited, and you will please do me a kindness" (*Bereishis* 40:14)

Yet the chamberlain of the cupbearers did not remember Yosef, and he forgot him. (*Bereishis* 40:23)

Unlike the *sar hamashkim* (chamberlain of the cupbearers), the great leaders of Israel remembered to perform kindnesses even after the passage of a great deal of time. Their absorption in Torah learning and the many other burdens they bore did not make them forget their obligations, even months later.

The *sefer, Chut Hameshulash,* relates the story of R' Akiva Eiger, who remembered to send a letter after nine months, as he had been requested by a poor man.

Whenever a destitute person approached R' Akiva Eiger and said he was dependent on the public for his support, R' Akiva would speak to the necessary people on his behalf. If he lived in another city, R' Akiva Eiger would immediately pen a letter asking for compassion and generosity for the poor man's support.

Once, a poor individual came to R' Akiva with a slightly unusual request. He wanted a letter to be sent to a relative who lived in a different city — but he asked that the letter not be sent at once, but rather nine months later, when the relative would be marrying off his daughter. The man thought that his relative would be in a softened frame of mind then, making it a propitious time to ask for his help.

Neither the many responsibilities that R' Akiva Eiger bore, nor his tremendous involvement in Torah as a leader of his generation, made him forget his promise. On his daughter's wedding day, the relative received the letter!

Vayeishev / 189

The Repentant Cantonist

כִּי גֻנֹּב גֻּנַּבְתִּי מֵאֶרֶץ הָעִבְרִים
"For indeed I was kidnapped from the land of the Hebrews"
(*Bereishis* 40:15)

During the period when he was traveling from town to town selling his *sefarim*, the Chofetz Chaim once came upon a troubling sight. At an inn in Vilna, he watched as a Jew sat down heavily at the table and ordered a portion of roast goose and a glass of whiskey. The Jewish man ate greedily, without making a *berachah* first, and also treated the waitress in an improper manner.

The Chofetz Chaim was shaken at the spectacle, and began to approach the man to rebuke him for his frivolous and unseemly behavior. The innkeeper, divining his intention, quietly came closer to the Chofetz Chaim to try and stop him. He was afraid of an unpleasant scene, as the Jewish guest was a former Russian soldier who was liable to start cursing the *tzaddik* for his criticism, and might even raise a fist to him.

"Please, Rabbi, leave him alone. He won't listen. He's a real boor, caught up in material pleasures. He never had a chance to learn any other way. When he was only 7 years old, he was kidnapped along with other Cantonist children, and taken off to Siberia. Until the age of 18 he lived among the local farmers, after which he was drafted into Czar Nikolai's army for 25 years. In such places, how could he have learned any better?"

The innkeeper paused for breath, then added, "Is it any wonder, after 40 years spent in surroundings where he saw not a single Jewish face, that he did not learn a single letter of the Torah? Better not to start with him, Rabbi. Your honor is too valuable in my eyes!"

A smile, tranquil and friendly, crossed the Chofetz Chaim's face. He said, "Is that the story? Don't worry, I will talk to the man."

The Chofetz Chaim approached the man at the table, extended a hand, and greeted him with a warm "*Shalom aleichem!*" Then, in the most friendly way imaginable, he began to speak.

"The truth is, I've heard all about you. You were snatched as a young child, and taken together with other children to distant Siberia, where you grew up among gentiles and did not have the privilege of learning a single letter of the Torah. You have indeed

Vayeishev / 191

passed through *gehinnom* in this world: terrible difficulties and horrible suffering. Wicked men tried more than once to make you convert, to force you to eat pork and other nonkosher meats, but despite all that, you remained a Jew!"

The Chofetz Chaim saw that the man was listening. He went on, "I would be happy if I had your merits and your portion in the World to Come. Is it a small thing, to demonstrate such sacrifice, to suffer such indignities for over 30 consecutive years — all for the sake of *Yiddishkeit* and Heaven's honor? Why, it's a greater ordeal than that of Chananyah, Mishael, and Azaryah!"

Tears gathered in the former soldier's eyes. He was deeply moved by the Chofetz Chaim's warm and heartfelt words. They revived the Jew's weary soul. When he learned who the speaker was, he burst into strong sobs and began to shower kisses on the Chofetz Chaim.

The Chofetz Chaim continued, "If a man like you, who has been privileged to be counted among the holy people who have sacrificed themselves for Heaven's sake, made up his mind to live the rest of his life as a kosher Jew, there would be no happier man on earth!"

The ex-soldier clung to the Chofetz Chaim until he transformed himself into a true *ba'al teshuvah* and a completely righteous Jew.

The Kesav Sofer's Birthday

יוֹם הֻלֶּדֶת אֶת פַּרְעֹה
The day of Pharaoh's birth
(*Bereishis* 40:20)

It is said that the Kesav Sofer once found himself in Budapest, the capital city of Hungary, on *Rosh Chodesh Adar,* his birthday. He closeted himself in his room all day, with instructions to his *shamash* not to let anyone in. Many people came to pay their respects to the great *tzaddik,* but none were permitted to enter.

One of those who came was a rabbi who had learned at the Yeshivah of Pressburg and had been very close to the Kesav Sofer, the *Rosh Yeshivah.* He decided to ignore the *shamash's* refusal, and he entered the closed room to see the Kesav Sofer. To his shock and consternation, he found the Rosh Yeshivah in tears.

"Rebbe!" he cried. "What happened? Why is the Rebbe crying?"

The Kesav Sofer answered," You should know, my dear student, that this is the day on which I was born. I am *nun-dalet* (54) years old today and I am judging myself. [The letters *nun dalet,* in reverse, spell *dan,* to judge.] How have I spent those years? How have I used my precious time? My conclusion is that I have not used them to good purpose. I have no Torah, no wisdom, no righteousness. So why should I not cry over the waste of my time — time which will never come back? I should be crying endlessly."

What humility! And if the Kesav Sofer judged himself so harshly, what should we be saying to ourselves?

Trust in Hashem

וְלֹא זָכַר שַׂר הַמַּשְׁקִים אֶת יוֹסֵף וַיִּשְׁכָּחֵהוּ

Yet the chamberlain of the cupbearers did not remember Yosef, and he forgot him.

(*Bereishis* 40:23)

The Jews of Russia were having a very hard year. Famine and poverty reigned everywhere.

"I must leave the city," a man told R' Chaim of Volozhin. "I have 800 rubles with me, but I am afraid to travel with so much money. I thought that it might be better to entrust it to you, to be used for meeting the yeshivah's expenses. In a year, G-d willing, when I return to Volozhin, you can repay me."

"Thank you," said R' Chaim." Have a good trip and return safely, and may it be Hashem's will that we live to see better days."

A year passed, and then two. R' Chaim had no word from the traveler who had left him the money. In the meantime, he used it for the yeshivah, as the man had suggested.

Then one day, without any warning, the man turned up again in Volozhin. Seeing him, one of the yeshivah's administrators turned pale. The yeshivah's coffers were empty. Where would they find 800 rubles to return to its proper owner?

The administrator ran to find R' Chaim. "Rebbe!" he cried anxiously, "What will I tell that man? Even if I go all over the city, I will not manage to collect as much as 400 rubles!"

"Don't worry," the *Rosh Yeshivah* soothed him." Tell him that tomorrow, at 4 o'clock in the afternoon at the latest, I will return all the money to him — down to the last penny!"

R' Yitzchak, the *Rosh Yeshivah's* son, was sitting in a corner of the room. Hearing R' Chaim's words, he lifted his head in astonishment. How would his father lay his hands on such a huge sum in just one day? R' Yitzchak said nothing, but sat in silence to see what would transpire.

In the evening, R' Chaim sat as usual and learned with great concentration. Calm and happy, there was no sign of worry or tension on his face. He knew from experience that worry never helps solve a problem. If Hashem willed it, all would fall peacefully into place. As David *Hamelech* had said, "Throw your burden onto Hashem, and he will support you!"

The next morning, R' Chaim got out of bed as he did every day. He *davened* with great devotion, ate his breakfast calmly, and began to prepare his *shiur* for the students. It was as though the debt had completely escaped his mind.

At noon, R' Chaim went to the *beis midrash* and began to deliver his *shiur*. Suddenly, there came a knock on the door. In the doorway stood the nobleman who ruled Volozhin.

"The Rabbi will forgive my intrusion," the nobleman apologized politely. "Perhaps you can help me with a problem? You see, I received a thousand rubles in notes from my tenants today. As you may know, I do not like to hold onto paper notes, but only silver or gold coins. Therefore, I would like to get rid of the notes now. Would you be prepared to do me a favor and take them off my hands?"

The students were amazed. "The hearts of kings and officers are in Hashem's Hand!" they quoted in whispers. On the very day that R' Chaim needed to discharge a large debt, the governor had foolishly decided to get rid of his paper notes at any price!

R' Chaim reacted calmly as usual, as though the incident was a matter of course. He thanked the governor for his gift, and at 3 o'clock that afternoon sent an administrator with 800 rubles to the man to whom they were owed — along with a gracious letter thanking the lender for the use of the money for two years.

פרשת מקץ
Parashas Mikeitz

Standing Before the King

וַיִּשְׁלַח פַּרְעֹה וַיִּקְרָא אֶת יוֹסֵף וַיְרִיצֻהוּ מִן הַבּוֹר וַיְגַלַּח וַיְחַלֵּף שִׂמְלֹתָיו וַיָּבֹא אֶל פַּרְעֹה

So Pharaoh sent and summoned Yosef, and they rushed him from the pit. He shaved his hair and changed his clothes, and he came to Pharaoh.

(*Bereishis* 41:14)

R' Yehonasan Eibeshutz once appeared in the emperor's palace in Vienna, for the purpose of trying to better his fellow Jews' standing with the royal house. As befit one who stood before a king, he wore his best clothes.

One of the ministers, a rabid anti-Semite, was looking for a reason to start up with R' Yehonasan. "Why don't you fulfill what it says in your Torah and in your Sages' writings?" he asked with a sneer.

"What do you mean?"

"King Solomon said: 'Do not adorn yourself before a king.' And the Sages have said, '*Yafah aniyusah l'Yisrael*' ('Poverty is beautiful for Israel'). And here you are, dressed in your best clothes. You're disobeying their instructions!"

R' Yehonasan with his sharp wit came up with a ready answer. "Your two points contradict one another. You refer to what our Sages, may their memory be blessed, have said: 'Poverty is beautiful for Israel.' In other words, poverty is an adornment for the people of Israel. So today, had I appeared before the king in the clothes of a pauper, that would have been an adornment and I would have contradicted the verse, 'Do not adorn yourself before a king'! Therefore, I dressed in nice clothes, which from the Jewish perspective are devoid of beauty and thus did not transgress the words of our Sages!"

Quick Thinking

בִּלְעָדָי אֱלֹקִים יַעֲנֶה אֶת שְׁלוֹם פַּרְעֹה

"That is beyond me; G-d will respond to Pharaoh's welfare."

(Bereishis 41:16)

"The wisdom [to interpret dreams] is not mine. Rather, 'G-d will respond,' [that is,] he will put a response in my mouth"

(Rashi)

When R' Yisrael Salanter appeared in public, he was forced to reveal his wisdom in order to be able to influence others. His brilliance was once unveiled in a remarkable fashion.

Before delivering a *derashah*, R' Yisrael would provide its title, along with a detailed list of sources in the Talmud and commentaries upon which he had based his original thoughts. This gave his listeners an opportunity to look into the sources and prepare for what they were about to hear.

One time, he hung his list on the shul door as usual. The list contained about one hundred sources. When the time came to deliver his talk, he asked the *shamash* to bring the notice in to him, so that he could keep it in front of him and concentrate exclusively on the topics listed there.

Imagine his shock when the notice was brought in and he saw that some frivolous people had exchanged his list for one of their own, changing all the sources! R' Yisrael grew white as a sheet. He remained frozen in place, neither speaking nor moving.

He stood this way, lost in thought, for ten minutes. Then he began to deliver an intricate talk, based on the new sources listed on the changed notice. Everyone present were stupefied at his incredible breadth of knowledge.

The next day, two youngsters came and confessed to having made the switch. They begged R' Yisrael's forgiveness. In their desire to test him, they had come up with a list of disparate sources, having no connection with one another, and had listed them on the notice.

When telling this anecdote, R' Yisrael's great student, R' Naftali Amsterdam, would add, "Do not think that the Rebbe needed ten minutes in order to come up with a new lecture. His talents were beyond our grasp. He was able to come up with complicated original thoughts with the speed of lightning.

"In those ten minutes, R' Yisrael was waging a war within himself. First he thought of telling the audience that he had 'forgotten' his speech, and of stepping down from the dais as though filled with shame in order not to reveal his towering ability.

"But then a second thought came: Perhaps, by degrading himself, he would lose influence with those listening, and all his efforts at spreading *mussar* would have been in vain. It was this struggle that took place in his heart for ten minutes, until at last he was certain to the depths of his being that he was innocent of personal glory-seeking. Only then did he permit himself to astound his audience with the dazzling new lecture that he created on the spot."

From time to time, R' Yosef Zundel of Salant had occasion to travel on business. On one such occasion, R' Tzvi Brody, rabbi of Salant, gave him a letter to deliver to R' Gershon Amsterdam, who was then living in Vilna. As soon as he set foot in Vilna, R' Yosef Zundel hurried to fulfill his job as messenger, going directly to R' Gershon Amsterdam's house to deliver the letter.

It was R' Yosef Zundel's custom to dress in the garb of a simple householder, which led R' Gershon Amsterdam to believe that the man who had brought him the letter was a wagon driver. He instructed his servant to give R' Yosef Zundel a glass of whiskey for his trouble.

R' Yosef Zundel did not refuse the drink. After all, our Sages have advised guests: "Do whatever your host asks of you." As he prepared to leave the house, R' Gershon Amsterdam stopped him and asked, "You are from Salant. Do you happen to know the gaon, R' Yosef Zundel?"

Stammering, R' Yosef Zundel answered, "Y-yes."

R' Gershon began to question the "wagon driver" closely about the *tzaddik's* ways and customs. R' Yosef Zundel found it increasingly difficult to answer. He stammered and muttered and tried to avoid speaking at all. At last, the possibility occurred to R' Gershon: Could this simple wagon driver be none other than R' Yosef Zundel himself?

"What is your name?" R' Gershon asked.

"Zundel," replied the "wagon driver."

Then R' Gershon knew the truth. He leaped to his feet at once, and began to show R' Yosef Zundel the honor worthy of such a great and righteous man.

※

When a new gentile governor was appointed over the Ostrovtza region, R' Meir Yechiel refused to receive him when he came to visit. The governor peeked into R' Meir's room, curious to see what was more important to the Rabbi than welcoming such an important visitor as himself. He found R' Meir immersed in a *Gemara*, completely disconnected from the world around him.

The governor did not become angry. Rather, he remarked with a smile to R' Meir's family, "There are few men today who are able to disassociate themselves from the experiences of this world and to engage only in spiritual matters. I am happy that such a great rabbi lives under my jurisdiction."

And he got up and left the house in a friendly fashion, without speaking with R' Meir at all.

※

When R' Shlomo of Zvil left his hometown to make his way to Eretz Yisrael, numerous residents came to see him off. A great lament rose up from the crowd, a clear testimony to the esteem and reverence in which R' Shlomo was held. But when R' Shlomo arrived in Eretz Yisrael, he decided to conceal his identity from the world. Standing on the ship's deck at the port of Haifa, he remarked to his grandson, R' Mordechai, who had accompanied him on his journey, "We are throwing the mantle of leadership into the sea."

For three years, R' Shlomo lived in extreme poverty, spending his days and nights learning Torah, along with the other students in Yeshivah Chayei Olam. No one knew who he was; they knew only that a former resident of Zvil sat quietly in a corner of the *beis midrash* and learned, day and night. During this time, R' Yosef Chaim Sonnenfeld received money to be given to the Zviler Rebbe in Jerusalem, but he had no idea who the Rebbe was.

Then, one day, a resident of Zvil, on a visit to Eretz Yisrael, stopped at Yeshivah Chayei Olam.

"Who is that, sitting in the corner?" the tourist wanted to know.
"Oh, that's some man from Zvil," he was told.

The tourist looked at the figure more closely, and suddenly realized that the face was familiar to him. It was the face of R' Shlomo!

"It's the Rebbe of Zvil!" he cried aloud.

The students sitting there lifted their heads to stare at the excited tourist. They were astonished to learn that the man who had been learning quietly in their midst for three years was none other than the famous Rebbe of Zvil.

The news spread like wildfire. From that day onward, the Rebbe was forced to take up the mantle of leadership once again. His years of concealment were over.

One Man's Courage

הֲנִמְצָא כָזֶה אִישׁ אֲשֶׁר רוּחַ אֱלֹקִים בּוֹ

"Could we find like this a man in whom is the spirit of G-d?"
(*Bereishis* 41:38)

During World War I, when R' Shimon Yehudah HaKohen Shkop served as Rav, his city was placed in grave danger. The German army was advancing, and the danger of bloodshed appeared imminent.

The town fathers urged R' Shimon to flee to a secure place, but he refused. "As long as there are Jews in this town, it is my obligation as its Rabbi not to leave them in times of trouble."

When he learned that many Jewish families were caught up in the general panic and were thinking about fleeing, R' Shimon decreed that no one was to leave home. Then he instructed community members to prepare gifts for the Russian army, which had been governing the city until then, and now stood poised to leave the area. This plan was duly carried out. No one left the area.

R' Shimon then went, together with some of the community's most respected men, to see the army commander. Hashem helped him find favor with the commander, who received his gift with pleasure and issued an order that no person in town was to be harmed, on penalty of dire punishment.

When the Russian troops did leave the town, the Cossacks came in their place. They began torching every building and property that might be of use to the incoming Germans. At the same time, they stole and pillaged as their hearts desired. The Jews, in grave danger, were afraid to step out into the streets.

R' Shimon instructed his people to give bribes to the Cossacks, as they had to the Russian officers, but no one had the temerity to approach those wild men. At last, R' Shimon took his life in his hands and went out to the rampaging troops. He stood before their leader and placed money into his hand. He and his men left R' Shimon alone — but on his way home a different group of Cossacks fell on R' Shimon, beat him, and stole his watch. He managed to escape with his life.

After the Cossacks came the conquering Germans. They remained in the city until the end of the war.

On the very last day of their occupation, as the last of the German troops were leaving the city, a tragedy occurred: One of the soldiers was accidentally killed by a stray bullet. The Jews were immediately accused of the murder, and the Germans decided on last-minute revenge for their fallen comrade.

At the outskirts of town stood a small cottage, home to a Jewish family. The Germans set the cottage on fire with the family inside. Then they surrounded the city on all sides and started a huge conflagration, which they prevented the citizens from extinguishing. Anyone who attempted to douse the flames could expect to be at the receiving end of a hail of bullets.

Once again, R' Shimon took his life in his hands. Dodging the bullets, he ran to the camp commander and pleaded with him to protect the innocent townspeople. He was answered with curses and mockery, but he did not give up. Again and again he repeated his request, until the commander's heart softened and he issued a permit for the Jews to put out the flames that were roaring through their town.

Permit in hand, R' Shimon ran back into town and went directly to the communal wells. Bullets flew everywhere as he approached the soldiers who stood guard over the wells lest anyone draw water to douse the flames. R' Shimon presented the commander's permit and himself began to draw the first bucket of water from the well.

When the other Jews saw their Rabbi drawing water in front of the soldiers, they understood that permission had been granted to

Mikeitz / 203

fight the fire. They all ran out to join him. Buckets were quickly filled and water sprayed in all directions.

R' Shimon was urged to rest a little, but he did not listen. He ran swiftly from place to place, supervising the firefighting operation, until it seemed as though he was everywhere at once. The town was saved from destruction.

A Miracle Amid Famine

וְהָרָעָב הָיָה עַל כָּל פְּנֵי הָאָרֶץ
And the famine spread over all the face of the land
(*Bereishis* 41:56)

R' Yisrael of Shklov, one of the Vilna Gaon's foremost students, and one of the pioneers of the Jewish settlement in Eretz Yisrael, was privileged to merit a public miracle during one of the most difficult hours that the country as a whole, and Jerusalem in particular, had ever experienced.

A heavy famine reigned throughout the land, and the Jews' sources of food had dried up completely.

As Pesach drew near, R' Yisrael called a meeting of community leaders to form a strategy to help Jerusalem's Jews survive the continuing famine. Pesach added fresh problems, as it was virtually impossible to obtain wheat for flour for baking *shemurah* matzos. Money had been promised from abroad but had not yet materialized. No solution was in sight, and the meeting ended without any definite decisions.

When R' Yisrael left the building where the meeting had been held, a message was brought to him: A group of Arabs, standing down the street, wanted to speak to the Jews' rabbi.

R' Yisrael approached the group and asked what they wanted. They were able to get a large amount of wheat, they replied, and were prepared to sell it all to him.

"I don't have the money to buy it now," R' Yisrael answered regretfully.

To his surprise, the Arabs answered that they did not need the money right away. In fact, they did not even demand a down payment.

They trusted the Rabbi's integrity. All they asked was that he sign his name on a piece of paper, confirming the transfer of the wheat, so that at some future date they might come to collect their money. R' Yisrael happily signed the note.

After Pesach, he waited for the Arab merchants to return for their money — but he waited in vain. They never came back.

Cakes and Compassion

וְהָרָעָב הָיָה עַל כָּל פְּנֵי הָאָרֶץ וַיִּפְתַּח יוֹסֵף אֶת כָּל אֲשֶׁר בָּהֶם וַיִּשְׁבֹּר לְמִצְרַיִם

And the famine spread over all the face of the land, Yosef opened all that was within them and sold to Egypt

(*Bereishis* 41:56)

A blind man used to sit outside the home of R' Yeshayah of Prague, selling cakes from a little stand while he shivered with cold and with fear of the police.

Indeed, a policeman did catch him at it one day, and confiscated his cakes. The poor man wept bitterly. R' Yeshayah passed by the stand at that moment, and he generously compensated the man for the damages he had sustained. From that day on, R' Yeshayah waited for the blind man each day. As soon as he came with his wares, R' Yeshayah immediately bought all his cakes.

R' Yeshayah's friends advised, "Isn't it better to pay the man once a month, and save both of you the bother of going through this every day?"

"No," answered R' Yeshayah. He went on to explain. "Right now, that man believes himself to be a successful businessman, a man who is respectably earning his own living. His sight has already been taken from him; why take away his joy in living as well?"

Bread for Torah

וְהָרָעָב הָיָה עַל כָּל פְּנֵי הָאָרֶץ
And the famine spread over all the face of the land
(*Bereishis* 41:56)

World War I was raging, and so was a terrible famine. In R' Yechiel Mordechai Gordon's home, there was tremendous hunger. There was literally not even a piece of bread in the house.

The Rabbi considered the problem. What to do? While still immersed in his thoughts, there came a knock at the door. A youth stood there, suitcase in hand. He had just arrived in Lomza from the Chofetz Chaim's yeshivah in Radin.

"Now?" the *Rosh Yeshivah* asked in astonishment. "With the war raging and the roads so difficult, weren't you afraid of the dangers of traveling?"

The young man answered, "The Chofetz Chaim blessed me, saying that whoever accepts the yoke of Torah is freed from the yoke of government. So I wasn't afraid."

The *Rosh Yeshivah* invited him to sit down. Within minutes they were deep into the discussion of a complicated *sugya*. R' Gordon quickly saw that the youth merited acceptance to his yeshivah. He sighed, and said, "We have raised questions and answered all of them, but there remains one question still unresolved: Lunchtime is approaching, and there is no bread for the students. How, then, can we accept another one?"

He had scarcely finished speaking when there came another knock at the door. In the doorway stood a sturdy man carrying a sack over his shoulder. The fragrance of fresh bread spread through the room.

"Rabbi," the man said, "my wife baked bread for the yeshivah students this morning."

R' Gordon turned jubilantly to his new student, and exclaimed, "What was it that the Chofetz Chaim told you? He who accepts the yoke of Torah...?"

For the Children

וְהָרָעָב הָיָה עַל כָּל פְּנֵי הָאָרֶץ
And the famine spread over all the face of the land
(*Bereishis* 41:56)

The *Gaon* of Tchebin treated children with extraordinary courtesy. The moment a child entered his house, the Rav would stand up and make sure the child had a chair to sit on. With the same affection with which he welcomed his most outstanding students, he greeted young boys who came, *Chumash* in hand, to be tested.

One Shabbos afternoon, the Rav was awakened from a nap by the sound of pounding on his door. Opening it, he was surprised to find a boy standing on his doorstep, with a request that the Rav test him on the weekly Torah portion that he had learned in *cheder*. In his usual manner, the Rav welcomed the boy with a smile, tested him, and then treated him to sweets.

As the boy stood ready to leave, the Rav turned to him and said gently, "Listen, my dear boy. The next time you need to enter a person's house in the middle of the day, don't bang on the door too much, in case he's taking an afternoon nap."

The boy, taking the hint, began to excuse himself. "Forgive me, Rebbe, but it never occurred to me that the Rav of Tchebin also naps in the middle of the day!"

The Rav enjoyed the boy's answer. In his humility, the weak and elderly *gaon* even found a certain merit in the childish remark.

❦

When R' Shlomo Zalman Auerbach was elderly, he was once sitting in his room, opening the many letters that streamed into his home daily from every part of the globe. Rabbis, *dayanim* (judges), and Torah greats from many different countries turned to him with their difficult questions.

Among the letters, R' Shlomo Zalman noticed a small one, penned by a 9-year-old boy. In it, the boy asked for an explanation of a certain *Tosafos* that he did not understand. R' Shlomo Zalman picked up his pen and wrote the boy a simple explanation of the

Mikeitz / 207

Tosafos, without any elaboration or additions. He wrote clearly and concisely, in easy language suitable to a 9-year-old.

Even at the pinnacle of the Torah world, this great *tzaddik* did not begrudge his precious time, or the toll on his dwindling energy, to answer a child's question. This was Torah, and it was his job to teach it; what difference did it make whether he taught it to a grown man or a young boy?

※

In the neighborhood where R' Elchonon Wasserman, *Rosh Yeshivah* of Yeshivah Ohel Torah in Baranovitch, lived, there was a young 4-year-old boy who liked to collect empty matchboxes and play with them. This small matter came to the *Rosh Yeshivah's* attention, and whenever a matchbox became empty in his house, he would save it for the boy.

R' Elchonon Wasserman, who zealously guarded every precious minute, who busied himself exclusively with Torah and *yiras Shamayim,* who was distressed over the wasted thirty seconds or so each morning that it took him to tie his shoelaces — this same man found within himself the love and patience to provide a child with playthings. He was able to lower himself to the level of a youngster and look for ways to make him happy. And this, in his opinion, was no waste of time at all!

The Guarantor

אָנֹכִי אֶעֶרְבֶנּוּ מִיָּדִי תְּבַקְשֶׁנּוּ

"I will guarantee him; of my own hand you can demand him."

(*Bereishis* 43:9)

A Jewish man came to see R' Yeshayah with a request: "Please lend me a thousand gold coins for six months. This sum will help me avoid bankruptcy."

Since the man was a stranger to R' Yeshayah, he replied as follows. "I am ready to make the loan, on the condition that someone you know in this city cosign it." (The cosigner would be responsible for guaranteeing that the borrower would repay the loan; should the borrower fail to do so, it was up to the cosigner to do it for him.)

The man burst into tears. "I am a stranger in town. I know no one in this area who would agree to cosign such a loan for me! Only Hashem himself knows my situation and my integrity. Only He can guarantee the loan."

"Well, there is no guarantor more reliable than He!" said R' Yeshayah. And he gave the man the sum he wanted.

Six months passed, and the man returned to R' Yeshayah. "Hashem has helped me," he said joyfully, "and success has lit my way! I have come to repay my debt." He set a thousand gold coins on R' Yeshayah's desk.

But R' Yeshayah pushed away the money. "Your Guarantor has already paid back the loan!"

"H-how can that be?" stammered the man in amazement.

"On the very day that I made you the loan, Hashem arranged matters so that a side business of mine produced a profit of exactly one thousand gold coins. I put that sum down to your account."

A Sacrifice for Peace

כִּי נִכְמְרוּ רַחֲמָיו אֶל אָחִיו

Because his compassion for his brother had been stirred
(*Bereishis* 43:30)

R' Shimshon Aharon Polanski of Teplik once arrived at shul on the first day of Sukkos carrying three of the four *minim*: The *esrog* was missing. Before *Hallel*, the Rebbe asked one of the other members of the congregation if he might borrow his *esrog*. The man handed it over at once. The Rebbe joyously recited the blessing and returned it to its owner.

The shul was abuzz with whispered speculation. The Rebbe had been seen, before Sukkos, carefully inspecting and choosing an *esrog*. Where, then, was that *esrog* now?

Some time later, the story emerged.

Early Succos morning, screams and cries were heard from the house next door to the Rebbe's. The Rebbe asked his wife to go over and find out what had happened. It turned out that the neighbor's stepdaughter had been playing with her stepfather's *esrog,* and had accidentally rendered it *pasul* — unfit for use. The little girl's mother knew that her husband had spent a large sum for that *esrog,* and she was afraid of his reaction. In her panic, she hit her daughter, and their wails rose and mingled in the air.

When the Rav heard this, he hurried over to the neighbor's house with his own *esrog.* He checked the broken *esrog,* then handed his own over to the neighbor's wife, saying, "Tell your husband that I saw the *esrog* he bought, and ruled it unfit to have a blessing made over it. Therefore, I am giving him my *esrog* as a complete gift. There is no need to return it."

R' Zelig Braverman was one of the leading Torah lights in Jerusalem. Apart from his greatness as a Torah scholar, he also involved himself in collecting and distributing money and food for poor people. Every *erev Shabbos,* the city's destitute would stream to R' Zelig's home to receive a portion of the food he had collected for them.

One Friday, a poor man arrived at R' Zelig's house just minutes before candlelighting time. He wanted challahs for Shabbos.

"What can I do?" R' Zelig asked sadly. "You've come too late; everything is gone!"

In his distress, the poor man slapped R' Zelig across the cheek. All those who were watching stood shocked and outraged, but R' Zelig paid no heed to the insult. Apparently, the man was very hungry. R' Zelig went immediately into the house next door and asked his neighbors if there was any way they could help. Then he went on to the house after that. In this way, in the last minutes before the onset of Shabbos, he managed to collect a respectable amount of food, which he sent on to the poor man's house.

R' Zelig returned home, where he went into his room and closed the door. One of his family members, listening from the other side of the door, heard R' Zelig berate himself: "*Oy,* Zelig, Zelig! Without getting slapped, didn't you realize the need to care for a poor, unfortunate man? You needed a slap on the face to understand that?"

פרשת ויגש
Parashas Vayigash

At a Single Glance

וְאָשִׂימָה עֵינִי עָלָיו
"And I will set my eye on him."
(*Bereishis* 44:21)

Once, when R' Aharon Leib of Premishlan was traveling to visit R' Menachem Mendel of Riminov, he asked his wagon driver to switch places with him. At R' Aharon Leib's insistence, they also traded hats — the wagon driver gave R' Aharon Leib his battered hat, and put on the Rebbe's *spodek*.

Approaching the town, they found a large group of R' Menachem Mendel's students coming to greet the wagon. Their Rebbe had sent them to meet his prestigious guest.

The students hurried over to the man wearing the *spodek* and greeted him reverently. But R' Naftali Ropshitz went immediately to the "wagon driver," and said, "*Shalom aleichem,* Rebbe!"

"How did you know?" R' Aharon Leib asked.

"I saw the humility with which the 'wagon driver' was leading the horse, and I knew that it was you."

Outrageous Demands?

וְחָטָאתִי לְאָבִי כָּל הַיָּמִים
"I will have sinned to my father for all time."
(*Bereishis* 44:32)

The book *Sipurei Chassidim* (Chassidic Tales) tells a story about R' Yosef of Turchin, the son of the Chozeh of Lublin. One day, just

214 / STORIES MY GRANDFATHER TOLD ME

before the blowing of the shofar on Rosh Hashanah, R' Yossel entered the *beis midrash* and announced, "Let me tell you a story.

"In a certain city, there lived a wealthy *talmid chacham* who earned his living by selling wine. One day, the rabbi of the city decided to honor this man with a visit. Seeing the rabbi approach his house, the wine merchant was overjoyed, and hastened to welcome him with every sign of respect. Then he ordered his servant to go down to the cellar and bring up a bottle of fine wine.

"Some time passed, but the servant did not reappear. The host was surprised and upset. Begging the rabbi's forgiveness, he descended to the cellar himself to see what had delayed the servant. At the entrance to the cellar, he came upon a shocking sight. Some of the wine barrels were uncovered. Others had been tipped over onto their sides, and wine was pouring from them in a steady stream. The cellar itself was a shambles, aside from the loss of his wine! There was no sign of the servant anywhere.

"Brokenhearted, the merchant returned upstairs and began to search for the servant who had caused all the trouble. In the end, he found the man peacefully asleep on top of the stove. When his boss shook him awake, the servant opened one eye and brazenly said, 'I demand a raise in salary!'

"On Rosh Hashanah," concluded R' Yossel, "we are like that servant. All year long we sin and we damage Hashem's world, and on Rosh Hashanah we come before Him demanding that He inscribe us for a good life."

All for the Children

כִּי אֵיךְ אֶעֱלֶה אֶל אָבִי וְהַנַּעַר אֵינֶנּוּ אִתִּי

"For how can I go up to my father if the youth is not with me?"
(*Bereishis* 44:34)

The settlement of Mevasseret Zion, near the entrance to Jerusalem, had two schools: one religious, the other secular. One year, during the season when parents traditionally register their children for school, the settlement was invaded by a group of secular activists whose goal was to eliminate the religious school.

Local parents called on R' Yehudah Tzadkah, *Rosh Yeshivah* of Yeshivah Porat Yosef, to help them in this crucial battle for their children's spiritual lives.

One *Motza'ei Shabbos,* a group numbering several hundred residents gathered in a large hall to listen to important speakers from Jerusalem, including R' Yehudah Tzadkah. It was R' Yehudah who opened the assembly.

"I am Yehudah Tzadkah, of Yeshivah Porat Yosef in the Holy City. I have brought you three important men, men from all sides of the spectrum. One is the wise Yaakov Douek, a businessman by profession and a man of the world. The second is Yosef Edem, a righteous and elevated man, a *chassid* and an ascetic whose every blessing comes true. And the third, R' Naim Eliyahu, a teacher and school principal."

One by one, R' Yehudah introduced the speakers, who had a single message for their listeners: not to heed the call of those who agitated in favor of secular education.

But it was R' Yehudah himself who proved the most inspiring of all. He ascended the dais after the others, and spoke with such fiery conviction that his listeners' hearts were ignited as well. When he finished, emotional cries rang out in the crowded auditorium: "We are ready to follow you through fire and water! We will do whatever you tell us!"

For their precious children's education, no course was too difficult or dangerous.

The Bobover Yeshivah was in debt over its head, and anxiety over his financial difficulties was weighing heavily on the spirit of the Rebbe, R' Ben Zion. The yeshivah's administrators decided that the only course open to them was for the Bobover Rebbe himself to travel to Vizhnitz for Shabbos, in order to collect money with which to satisfy the yeshivah's creditors. On *Motza'ei Shabbos,* a great crowd gathered at the inn where R' Ben Zion was staying, all of whom wished to enter and present the Rebbe with their *kvittels*. To their surprise, R' Ben Zion sent word that he was too tired to see anyone that night. The people were obliged to return disappointed to their homes.

But instead of going to sleep, the Rebbe summoned a certain young man, the son of a Vizhnitz butcher, and had a long conversation with him.

"In a sense, I was your parents' *shadchan* (matchmaker)," R' Ben Zion told the youth. "When someone came to your father's father to suggest a match between your father and your mother, your grandfather became insulted. He said, 'Is it possible that I will ever agree to become connected, through this *shidduch,* with a butcher?' I went to your grandfather then and explained to him that the bride's father is a respected and good man, from a fine family, and that his first son-in-law is a genuine *talmid chacham.* I talked to him until I persuaded him, and the match went forward.

"You should know, however, that I never received a single penny for that *shidduch,*" the Rebbe continued. "I've finally decided not to wait any longer. The time has come for the debt to be paid and I have come to collect it. The payment I require is that you walk a straight path and live in fear of Heaven."

The Rebbe continued to converse with the young man until he had ignited in the other's heart a flame of desire for holiness and piety. When his visitor had departed, R' Ben Zion sent for other youths and spoke to them as well, for many hours. His words of rebuke overflowed from a heart filled with love and compassion.

The next day, the Rebbe again told the innkeeper that he had no strength. The innkeeper, a devoted follower who knew all about the Rebbe's financial worries, could not contain himself. "Of course the Rebbe is tired!" he exclaimed. "Yesterday, the Rebbe sent away all the householders who came with their *kvittels* and money for the yeshivah, with the excuse that he was tired. And then he spent the entire night talking with youngsters!"

The Rebbe knew that the innkeeper's impulsive words came from real concern and loyalty. Patiently, he explained. "Tell me this. Suppose someone owns a large factory from which he earns most of his livelihood, but he also has some small business dealings on the side. Suddenly, all sorts of business problems crop up and he lacks the time to take care of everything. What should he do? Surely we would advise him to set aside his minor concerns, and devote all his energy to running his factory, because that is his primary business and to lose that would be to lose everything.

"Those young boys are my primary 'business.' Even when I had no strength, I felt compelled to find some energy to help them uproot their evil inclination, and to bring them back to the correct path in life before it is too late. Lacking the strength to do both, I decided to put aside the smaller matter of the money."

For Shame

וַיִּקְרָא הוֹצִיאוּ כָל אִישׁ מֵעָלָי וְלֹא עָמַד אִישׁ אִתּוֹ בְּהִתְוַדַּע יוֹסֵף אֶל אֶחָיו

So he called out, "Remove everyone from before me!" Thus no one stood with him when Yosef made himself known to his brothers.

(Bereishis 45:1)

He could not bear that there should be Egyptians standing before him and hearing that his brothers were shamed

(Rashi)

R' Yisrael Salanter used to say that any person who has the power and ability to influence the public has a responsibility to do so. He must not hide himself inside his own state of spiritual contentment, but rather must go out to the people, to teach and guide them.

An incident once occurred in Vilna that touched R' Yisrael deeply. The town's wealthy people used to hold their children's weddings in a certain square. These weddings were lavish and costly. A certain shoemaker in Vilna became very prosperous, and when the time came to marry off his daughter, he too held the wedding in that same town square.

This incensed the town's upper echelons. The rich folk gathered in the square, and when the proud father returned from his daughter's *chupah*, happy and elated, one of them stepped forward holding a torn shoe, and asked the former shoemaker how much it would cost to repair it.

The blood drained from the father's face. He stood in a daze, beside himself with shame and anguish.

When he heard the story, R' Yisrael Salanter was shaken to the core. He stated: "I am positive that the Torah leaders of the previous generation, up in *Gan Eden,* are being judged for this terrible incident, because they did not properly teach the people to distance themselves from such atrocious behavior."

How to Placate an Angry Man

וְעַתָּה אַל תֵּעָצְבוּ וְאַל יִחַר בְּעֵינֵיכֶם
"And now, be not distressed, do not reproach yourselves"
(Bereishis 45:5)

While listening to one of R' Yisrael Salanter's sermons in the Vilna shul, the *gabbai* was certain that the Rebbe's rebuke had been aimed directly at him, and he was insulted. Even before R' Yisrael completed his talk, the *gabbai* raised his voice, publicly railing against R' Yisrael and heaping abuse on what he had said. Then he stood up and left the shul, slamming the door behind him.

The audience expected R' Yisrael to continue his talk as though nothing had happened. Instead, they were surprised to see him quickly descend from the *bimah* and race outside after the *gabbai*.

He caught up with the angry man far down the street. Pulling a handkerchief from his pocket, R' Yisrael began to wipe the droplets of sweat from the *gabbai's* brow. "I can understand your being angry with me," R' Yisrael said softly. "But you are perspiring. How can you go outside in this wind, and risk your health this way?"

The man was visibly moved. After R' Yisrael assured him repeatedly that his words had not been intended for him — in fact, R' Yisrael was not even acquainted with the *gabbai* — the man abandoned his anger and became one of R' Yisrael's most ardent admirers and friends.

Good Apples!

כִּי לְמִחְיָה שְׁלָחַנִי אֱלֹקִים לִפְנֵיכֶם
"For it was as a supporter of life that G-d sent me ahead of you."
(Bereishis 45:5)

A poor woman once came to see R' Chaim, the Sanzer Rebbe. "Rebbe," she cried, "I have no money for Shabbos!"

"It seems to me that you have a stall selling apples in the marketplace," said the Rebbe. "Am I right?"

With downcast eyes, the woman whispered, "For some reason, they say my apples are no good. Lately, no one's been buying anything from me."

R' Chaim stood up at once, picked up his walking stick, and left the house. The woman followed him with a burning curiosity. Where was the Rebbe going? R' Chaim turned right, then left, with the woman at his heels. Suddenly, she saw that he was headed for the marketplace! Quickening his pace, the Rebbe reached the woman's stall, which was heaped with apples. He stood behind it and began calling loudly, "Good apples! Who wants to buy good apples?"

When the passersby saw who was standing behind the stall, they quickly clustered around the stall. They were prepared to pay their Rebbe any sum for the apples! Within minutes, not a single apple was left.

The Rebbe handed the woman the money he had collected.

"See?" he said, smiling. "They were fine apples. It's just that the people of Sanz didn't know it until now."

How to Make a Living

וַיִּשְׁלָחֵנִי אֱלֹקִים לִפְנֵיכֶם לָשׂוּם לָכֶם שְׁאֵרִית בָּאָרֶץ
וּלְהַחֲיוֹת לָכֶם לִפְלֵיטָה גְדֹלָה

"And G-d has sent me ahead of you to insure your survival in the land and to sustain you for a great deliverance."

(*Bereishis* 45:7)

The following story was told by a neighbor of R' Yosef Chaim Sonnenfeld, Rabbi of Jerusalem:

I had the privilege of living near Rav Sonnenfeld for many years. One day, at noon, the Rebbetzin knocked on our door and asked in sorrow and shame if we could lend her a loaf of bread for lunch.

This astounded me. Rebbetzin Sonnenfeld had never borrowed a thing from us before, and especially not food. I went over to the cupboard and picked out a well-done loaf, baked by my wife. I handed it to the Rebbetzin.

The expression on her face revealed that she was in some inner turmoil. My curiosity was too great for me. When she left, I followed her.

Entering the Sonnenfelds' house behind the Rebbetzin, I saw R' Yosef Chaim sitting quietly at the table, waiting for his wife to serve him his lunch. The Rebbetzin came over with the bread she had received at our house. After her husband had recited the "*Hamotzi*," she told him brokenly, "This bread is not ours, either. I had to borrow it from our neighbor." And she burst into bitter tears.

"I don't have a penny," she sobbed. "How shall I feed the children?"

His wife's distress, and his children's hunger, touched R' Yosef Chaim's heart. When he finished *bentching,* he murmured, as though to himself, "I thought that she had *bitachon* (faith), as I do. Apparently that is not the case. I will have to go out and earn a living!" So saying, he got up and left the house.

My curiosity was still upon me. Knowing R' Yosef Chaim's greatness, I decided to follow him and see how he sought to earn his living.

I saw him climb the broad stairs leading up from the neighborhood. I followed. R' Yosef Chaim turned right, preparing to leave through the gate near the Misgav Ladach Hospital, and I was right at his heels. R' Yosef Chaim passed through the gate and walked up the street. I followed every step with my eyes, careful not to miss a thing. Suddenly, I saw him stoop down. I broke into a run. Pulling up beside him, I saw R' Yosef Chaim pick up and hold two gold napoleons in his hands, a huge sum of money at that time.

Seeing me, R' Yosef Chaim smiled. "I can go home now. Now I have something to live on, *baruch Hashem.*"

A Timely Escape

וְעַתָּה לֹא אַתֶּם שְׁלַחְתֶּם אֹתִי הֵנָּה כִּי הָאֱלֹקִים
"And now, it was not you who sent me here, but G-d"
(*Bereishis* 45:8)

With the outbreak of World War II, R' Dov Berish Weidenfeld, the famed Gaon of Tchebin, succeeded in escaping the Nazi dragnet, and he fled to the city of Lvov, capital of Galicia. R' Dov Berish remained in Lvov some nine months until the evil decrees began there, too, growing more severe with each passing month.

The Bolsheviks were heavy-handed oppressors, especially toward those who embraced religious beliefs. The city's large shuls were closed, public Torah study was banned — and finally, there came the order for expulsion.

One Friday night, police and army troops descended on the city and pulled more than 80,000 Jewish refugees from their homes. By Shabbos morning the streets were thronged with heavy trucks in which the Jews were forced to sit. The refugees were taken to waiting trains for transport to Siberia.

The Gaon of Tchebin was among them. Many people pleaded with the authorities to set him free, and indeed, a short time later two commissars arrived and removed R' Dov Berish from the truck. But R' Dov Berish cried out, "I do not wish to be separated from the rest! I will not be parted from my fellow Jews in their hour of trouble!"

After a brief debate, the commissars returned the Gaon to the truck, where he once again took his place among the rest of the Jewish refugees. Together they were sent to the labor camps of Siberia.

It was a horrific and painful sight to see the Gaon, a living *sefer Torah,* desecrated in the hands of those who scorned his nobility. But the sequel later became clear to all. If not for R' Dov Berish's obstinate insistence not to be parted from his Jewish brothers, it is most likely that he would have shared the sad fate of those Jews who remained behind in Lvov and fell victim to Hitler's evil sword. His expulsion to Siberia saved the Gaon of Tchebin's life and allowed him to illuminate the world with his Torah for more than 25 additional years.

❧

For many years after the passing of R' Moshe of Peshvorsk, the *sifrei Torah* and *tefillin* that he wrote continued to be held in special reverence, and fetched a princely sum when sold. It is said that the Divrei Yechezkel of Shinov, when serving as rabbi of Stropkov, once traveled to see his father, the Divrei Chaim of Sanz. On the way, he was robbed of everything including his *tallis* and *tefillin*. When it came time for *davening* in the morning he was still on the road, and went from village to village seeking a pair of *tefillin*. None of the *tefillin* he found, however, found favor in his eyes.

The hour was nearing noon when he arrived at a certain village where he finally found a Jew who owned a pair of *tefillin* that seemed suitable. The Shinover Rebbe put them on, then *davened* with greater than usual intensity and fervor.

After he had finished, he asked the owner of the *tefillin* where they had come from. The man explained that they had been written by R' Moshe of Peshvorsk.

"Now I understand!" the Shinover Rebbe exclaimed. "That's the reason for the special enthusiasm that gripped me when I *davened* — an experience I have never merited until now."

Shortly after this encounter, the robbers were apprehended and all the Shinover Rebbe's belongings were returned to him. Ever afterwards, the Shinover Rebbe would claim that the robbery had taken place solely in order to enable him to *daven* once with the holy *tefillin* of R' Moshe of Peshvorsk.

R' Baruch Ber Honors His Father

מַהֲרוּ וַעֲלוּ אֶל אָבִי וַאֲמַרְתֶּם אֵלָיו כֹּה אָמַר בִּנְךָ יוֹסֵף שָׂמַנִי אֱלֹקִים לְאָדוֹן לְכָל מִצְרָיִם

"Hurry and go up to my father and say to him, 'So said your son, Yosef: G–d has set me as a master to all Egypt'"

(*Bereishis* 45:9)

R' Baruch Ber Leibovitz's scrupulousness with regard to the mitzvah of *kibbud av v'em,* honoring one's father and mother, was a byword in his time.

R' Baruch Ber was *Rosh Mesivta* in the Kaminetz Yeshivah, and from time to time would deliver a *shiur* to the students. His father, R' Shmuel, himself a great Torah scholar, would come to hear these *shiurim*.

The hour of the *shiur* was approaching. The students sat expectantly, awaiting their Rebbe. The door opened, and R' Baruch Ber's figure appeared in the doorway. All the students rose respectfully to their feet. But R' Baruch Ber did not walk immediately to his appointed spot. He turned first to his father, and greeted him warmly. Then he added humbly, "Father, please permit me to deliver my *shiur* to the students!"

R' Shmuel smiled and nodded his head. Only then, after receiving his father's permission, did R' Baruch Ber walk up to the front of the room and begin his *shiur.*

The students listened attentively to every word, lost in a world of Torah. Even after R' Baruch Ber had finished speaking the group sat silently, still in the grip of the things they had heard. It was only when R' Baruch Ber stood up that the students rose, too, and waited with reverence for him to leave the room.

But R' Baruch Ber was in no hurry to leave. He went first to his father, and asked, "Father, did I deliver the *shiur* well?"

Intently, R' Baruch Ber listened to R' Shmuel's comments. Following the interplay between father and son, the listening students learned a marvelous and valuable lesson in *kibbud av v'em.*

Picking Up the Thread

וַיְדַבְּרוּ אֵלָיו אֵת כָּל דִּבְרֵי יוֹסֵף אֲשֶׁר דִּבֶּר אֲלֵהֶם
וַיַּרְא אֶת הָעֲגָלוֹת אֲשֶׁר שָׁלַח יוֹסֵף

And they related to him all the words of Yosef that he had spoken to them, and he saw the wagons that Yosef had sent

(*Bereishis* 45:27)

[Yosef] gave [his brothers] a sign, what [topic of study] he was involved in when he separated from [Yaakov], in the passage of the eglah arufah (decapitated calf). And this is why it says, "And he saw the wagons that Yosef had sent" — and it does not say, "that Pharaoh had sent." (Rashi)

On his fifth trip to Eretz Yisrael, R' Avraham Mordechai, the Gerrer Rebbe, went to Jerusalem to see R' Yosef Tzvi Dushinsky. The two sat together learning, exchanging their original thoughts. R' Avraham Mordechai mentioned a certain subject that the Chasam Sofer cited in his commentary on *Maseches Kiddushin,* and they spent a great deal of time discussing it. At last, they parted and the Gerrer Rebbe returned to his inn.

Those closest to R' Dushinsky noticed that he wore a special expression and smile that day. When they asked him the reason, he said, "When the Rebbe began talking about the Chasam Sofer's commentary, I didn't know at first why he had specifically raised that subject. But as we spoke, I remembered that I had met the Rebbe at the Marinbad spa seven years ago, where each of us had gone for our health, and we discussed that very same topic. Today, he simply continued our conversation at the point where we had left off seven years ago. He has a wonderful memory."

❧

In his youth, R' Avraham Mordechai, the Gerrer Rebbe, learned with R' Gershon of Ostrov. At that time, R' Gershon made a remark about a certain explanation of the *Maharsha*.

Forty years later, R' Gershon came to Ger and visited the Rebbe. The Rebbe suddenly jumped up onto a stepladder that stood beside his bookcase, took down a certain *sefer*, and opened it, saying, "This is where I found the comment you made concerning the *Maharsha* when we last learned together."

The Pinnacle of Love

וְאֶת יְהוּדָה שָׁלַח לְפָנָיו אֶל יוֹסֵף לְהוֹרֹת לְפָנָיו גֹּשְׁנָה

He sent Yehudah before him to Yosef, to instruct ahead of him in Goshen

(*Bereishis* 46:28)

To establish for him a house of study from which instruction shall go forth. (Rashi)

A year and a half after the marriage of R' Aharon Kotler, who later became the founder and *Rosh Yeshivah* of Beth Medrash Govoha in Lakewood, New Jersey, World War I broke out. The streets of his town were bombed at frequent intervals, and cannons spewed explosives in the streets.

Even in the midst of this nightmare, R' Aharon did not abandon his usual routine. He went quietly into a corner and prepared his *shiur*. When people asked how he was able to do this, he answered, "When you immerse your mind in Torah, you forget the rest of the world."

Later, during World War II, when Poland was caught in the

flames, all contact was lost with the outside world. The vital funds that supported the yeshivah were completely cut off. But R' Aharon continued to uphold his yeshivah with the sheer power of his faith — the faith that nourished his spirit all his life.

From the first day of the Russian conquest, the students became more and more diligent in their studies. Until the end of his life, R' Aharon would look back fondly on that period, which he labeled "days of desire" — because the study of Torah under such difficult conditions is considered the pinnacle of love for Torah.

Doing It Right

וַיֶּאְסֹר יוֹסֵף מֶרְכַּבְתּוֹ וַיַּעַל לִקְרַאת יִשְׂרָאֵל אָבִיו

Yosef harnessed his chariot and went up to meet Yisrael his father
(Bereishis 46:29)

He himself harnessed the horses to the chariot, to be quick for the honor of his father.
(Rashi)

R' David of Lelov went frequently to see his Rebbe, the Chozeh of Lublin. Each time he went, he made elaborate preparations in honor of his visit to his Rebbe.

On one occasion, R' David arrived in Lublin and heard that his mother was in town. He said to himself, "Here is a chance to do the mitzvah of *kibbud av v'em*. I'll go visit her!" He turned to go — and then stopped.

When he had left Lelov, he had intended to travel to Lublin only to be with his Rebbe, not knowing that his mother was there as well. Therefore, he had not made any special preparations in honor of his upcoming visit with his mother. "But such a great mitzvah requires special preparation. How can I perform such a great mitzvah without any prior preparation?"

R' David hired a wagon, returned to Lelov, and prepared for his meeting with his mother. Only when he felt that he had readied himself to perform the mitzvah properly did he return to Lublin, for the dual purpose of honoring his Rebbe and honoring his mother.

The Sigh That Brought Salvation

כִּי כָבֵד הָרָעָב מְאֹד

For the famine was very severe
(*Bereishis* 47:13)

One *Motza'ei Shabbos*, after *Havdalah*, the Ba'al Shem Tov instructed his driver to harness the horses and prepare for a trip. A short time later, he and his students were seated in the wagon and were on their way.

As was his habit, the Ba'al Shem Tov ordered the driver to leave the reins alone and allow the horses to run as they wished. The horses suddenly broke into a furious gallop. The hills were as nothing to them and the valleys were as plains. The horses carried the wagon and its passengers a tremendous distance.

After a while, the wagon stopped in front of a small house in a village. A humble Jew came out and invited them into his modest home. He explained to his guests that it had been a long time since he had had the chance to fulfill the mitzvah of *hachnasas orchim,* as a difficult winter had made travelers to that village a rarity. He was now overjoyed to have the opportunity to perform the mitzvah.

The Ba'al Shem Tov asked the man to prepare tea with hot milk for them all, and the man obeyed with pleasure. The *chassidim* ate and drank and rested from their travels. Then their host began a conversation with them.

"Where are you from?" he asked.

"From Mezibozh."

"Do you know the great *tzaddik,* R' Yisrael Ba'al Shem Tov?" the man asked eagerly.

Before any of the others could answer, the Ba'al Shem Tov asked not to be bothered with questions, and requested that a place be prepared where they could sleep.

For five days the Ba'al Shem Tov and his disciples remained in that humble house. During that time, they ate and drank and wanted for nothing. Their host sacrificed himself and everything he owned so that his guests might not lack any comfort. He took food from his own children's mouths as well as from his and his wife's, and gave it all to the guests.

Both he and his wife were ecstatic at this opportunity to fulfill the mitzvah of *hachnasas orchim*. When five days were over, the *chassidim* traveled back the way they had come, and the man accompanied them to the outskirts of the village. As they parted, he asked them to mention his name to the great *tzaddik,* R' Yisrael Ba'al Shem Tov, and ask for a blessing that he might merit being a good and G-d-fearing Jew.

"I am the man you are seeking," the Ba'al Shem Tov said quietly. "In time, you will understand the reason why we came to you."

The man stood rooted to the spot in wonder. The great and holy Ba'al Shem Tov had traveled especially to be with him! But before he had recovered his wits, the wagon and its passengers had disappeared down the road.

On his return home, the man found his children crying. His wife told him that there was no food in the house and the children were hungry.

The guests had not only eaten everything there was in the house, but the family had been forced to sell off certain household items in order to satisfy all their guests' requests and needs. Now they had left, and the house was empty.

The man looked at his weeping children and at his unhappy wife, and burst into bitter tears of his own. "*Ribbono Shel Olam!*" he cried. "Master of the Universe! Why must my children suffer hunger pangs? How are they guilty?"

He was still lost in these sorrowful thoughts when there was a knock at the door. The man opened it and an elderly gentile, a village resident, entered. His name was Ivan, and he would occasionally stop in at the man's house to drink a glass of whiskey with him. Before the man could tell Ivan that he had nothing in the house to eat or drink, Ivan spoke up. He said that he had come for a much more important purpose than a drink this time. Into the Jew's ear he whispered that he had a secret to tell him.

"Listen," said Ivan. "I am old, weak, and sick. I live with my daughter and son-in-law, but I don't get along with them. So listen well to what I have to say.

"I will come live in your house. I don't need much, but your reward for taking me in as a guest will benefit you greatly. I possess great treasure — tens of thousands of gold coins. You can go right now and take as much as you want. After my death, the entire treasure will be yours, and yours alone!"

Sensing that his words were being received with skepticism, Ivan led the Jew to his hiding place in the nearby forest. He dug beneath a large tree and pulled out a bag filled with gold coins. "Let's take it all home," Ivan suggested. "No one has to know about it."

Great joy filled the Jew's home. The entire family rejoiced in the miracle that had occurred to them, and from that day on they lacked for nothing.

The elderly gentile lived in the Jew's home for just a few weeks. One day he went to visit his daughter, and suddenly died there. The treasure came into the Jew's hands in its entirety. He began to distribute large amounts for charity, and for the needs of travelers and guests in particular. With the passage of time, the Jew became very wealthy and his name spread far afield.

One day, the man remembered the Ba'al Shem Tov's visit. He decided that the time had come to travel to see the *tzaddik* and to bask in his light. Upon entering the Ba'al Shem Tov's room, he was warmly welcomed and questioned closely about his welfare and that of his family.

His disciples were surprised at the way the Ba'al Shem Tov treated the stranger. The Ba'al Shem Tov turned to them and asked, "Don't you remember? We visited this man's house and stayed with him for five days. In the course of that time we ate his last crust of bread. Listen now, and I will reveal to you the reason why we traveled to that particular village and that particular Jew.

"Heaven had decreed that this man become very wealthy, in the merit of the mitzvah of *hachnasas orchim* that he performed with great aplomb. But he was a man who was satisfied with little and never *davened* for a better livelihood. There was a real danger that the blessing would not reach him, and that he would remain a poor man until the end of his life.

"When we visited him for those five days, we did not leave him anything. His children were crying with hunger. Then, and only then, did he sigh from the depths of his soul and cry out to his Creator to ask for money. Only then was the blessing able to work in his favor. Hashem sent him the gentile with the treasure, and he became a very wealthy man indeed!"

Vayigash

An Extraordinary Welcome

וְאֶת הָעָם הֶעֱבִיר אֹתוֹ לֶעָרִים מִקְצֵה גְבוּל מִצְרַיִם וְעַד קָצֵהוּ

As for the nation, he transferred it by cities, from one end of Egypt's borders to its other end.
(Bereishis 47:21)

[This verse] informs you of Yosef's praise, that he intended to remove disgrace from upon his brothers, so that [the Egyptians] should not call [his brothers] exiles [for after their resettlement, the Egyptians, too, were exiles].

(Rashi)

Apart from his greatness in Torah, R' Naftali Trop was known far and wide for his love of his fellow man, which expressed itself particularly in the way he performed the mitzvah of *hachnasas orchim*.

A certain Jew had the reputation of being a thief, and people shunned him. But when he chanced to be in Radin and encountered R' Naftali Trop, R' Naftali greeted him pleasantly and invited him to eat at his table. He also offered a bed for the night, and spared no effort to make his guest's stay an enjoyable one.

Those close to R' Naftali were taken aback. "What has the *Rosh Yeshivah* to do with a man whose actions are so dubious?"

R' Naftali replied, "A thief is required to pay double the value of what he has stolen. If he slaughters or sells a stolen ox or sheep, he must pay four or five times its value. And if he has no money, he himself is sold to pay for his thievery. But where does it say that one is exempt from fulfilling the mitzvah of *hachnasas orchim*? Is that man not a Jew? Did Avraham *Avinu* not fulfill this mitzvah even with Arabs? It is true that letting such a man into one's home endangers one's property, for the thief might steal it. One must be watchful all the time that such a guest is in his home. But there is nothing that exempts one from doing the mitzvah."

∞

It was a wintry Sukkos in Vilna. R' Chaim Ozer sent his distinguished guest out to his *sukkah* in the yard with an apology: "I'm afraid I am forced to stay in the house, as I am ill and unfortunately exempt from the mitzvah of *sukkah*."

The guest went out to eat in R' Chaim Ozer's *sukkah* while his host remained behind in the house. Suddenly, R' Chaim Ozer appeared in the *sukkah* doorway. He offered the following explanation: "It's true that I am sick and suffering. But I have just realized that this exempts me only from the mitzvah of eating in the *sukkah* — but not from the mitzvah of *hachnasas orchim*! Even Avraham *Avinu* did not refrain from serving his guests when he was sick and in pain."

※

The home of R' Tzvi Chanoch Levine, Rabbi of Bendin, was always open to guests to the point that it stopped being a private residence at all. The Rabbi was elated by every guest. Every person who walked into R' Tzvi's house felt as though he were the Rabbi's best friend in the world.

Every Shabbos, R' Tzvi brought numerous guests to dine at his table. The more Rebbetzin Fayga, daughter of the Sefas Emes, cooked and prepared for Shabbos, the greater grew the number of guests. It was hard to keep up.

Once, a man entered R' Tzvi's house. The Rabbi welcomed him with honor usually reserved for kings. Then he went to his wife and said, "Please bring some refreshments — a special guest has arrived!"

Rebbetzin Fayga brought out cakes and other tempting foods in honor of her husband's important guest. After the man had gone, she asked R' Tzvi, "So, who was that man?"

"I don't know," her husband responded frankly, spreading his hands. "He was a guest!"

פרשת ויחי

Parashas Vayechi

Time Is Precious

וַיִּקְרְבוּ יְמֵי יִשְׂרָאֵל לָמוּת
The time approached for Yisrael to die
(*Bereishis* 47:29)

    The Chofetz Chaim once entered a printer's shop and engaged the printer's apprentice in conversation. The boy told him that he had apprenticed himself to the printer for a period of five years, in return for his meals and a very meager salary. He was only 15 years old, and hoped to be an expert in the field by the time he was 20. He would then marry and be able to provide for his family.

    When he returned to the place where he was staying, the Chofetz Chaim said to his companions, "A young printer's apprentice aroused me to *teshuvah* today. He told me that he is prepared to devote five years of his life, between the ages of 15 and 20, so that afterwards he will be able to enjoy a comfortable life. How long does a man live? Seventy years. That apprentice is ready to sacrifice five years in order to enjoy fifty more in comfort.

    "If we think, we will realize that a person is sent into this world for just a short time, in order to earn his place in the World to Come. The next world is eternal, with no limit or end. This is more than many millions of years. In order to earn his place in that world, a man was given only seventy years. Seventy years to prepare for eternity. Such an investment is less than nothing, compared to five years preparing for fifty. This gives us some idea of how precious time is."

Destined for Greatness

וְגַם הוּא יִגְדָּל וְאוּלָם אָחִיו הַקָּטֹן יִגְדַּל מִמֶּנּוּ

"And he too will become great; however, his younger brother shall become greater than he"

(*Bereishis* 48:19)

The Ba'al Shem Tov was only 5 years old when his parents died. His father, R' Eliezer, left the following instructions for his son: "Yisraelik, don't be afraid of anything but *Hakadosh Baruch Hu*. Love every Jew with all your heart and soul, without distinguishing who and what he is."

The boy used to enjoy walking in the fields and spending time alone in the forest outside the city. Sometimes he even slept there. Once, he heard the sound of someone praying in the forest. He followed the voice and found a Jew wrapped in *tallis* and *tefillin*, *davening* with fervor and then reciting *Tehillim* with great devotion. The boy was convinced that this was one of the world's 36 hidden *tzaddikim*.

When the man had folded up his *tallis* and *tefillin* and replaced them in his bag, about to leave, the boy stepped out of his hiding place.

"How is it that a young boy is wandering alone in the woods?" the man asked.

"I love the fields and woods," the boy replied, "because there are no arrogant or false people here."

When the man learned that the boy was R' Eliezer's son, he took a *Gemara Pesachim* out of his bag and began learning with him. From that day on, young Yisrael clung to the man, traveling with him from town to town and from village to village. Together they traveled and learned for three years. Then the man left him to the care of a great and pious Torah scholar by the name of R' Meir, who taught Yisrael for four more years. R' Meir, too, was a hidden *tzaddik*, appearing to his fellow townspeople as a simple working man.

Once he learned of this secret group of hidden *tzaddikim* who traveled from place to place, R' Yisrael joined their ranks, fulfilling his own mission. By the age of 17 he already knew Kabbalah and *davened* with the Ari's *nusach*. At 18, he suggested a new mission for these hidden *tzaddikim*: to teach as they traveled, lifting the spirits of the masses and educating them in Torah and fear of Heaven. In this way, the boy grew in stature until he became the great Ba'al Shem Tov, a light upon all of his people.

Prayers in Place of Swords

אֲשֶׁר לָקַחְתִּי מִיַּד הָאֱמֹרִי בְּחַרְבִּי וּבְקַשְׁתִּי

"Which I took from the hand of the Emorite with my sword and with my bow."

(*Bereishis* 48:22)

" 'With my sword and with my bow' — this means my wisdom and my prayer." (*Rashi*)

R' Akiva Eiger, Rav of Posen, would visit all the sick people in his town. One day, he went to see a man who was suffering from a very rare disease. R' Akiva learned that the king's personal physician was in town, and hurried to summon him to examine the sick man.

"Why have you called me?" the doctor asked R' Akiva Eiger, after examining the patient. "Don't you know that this disease has no cure?"

R' Akiva Eiger answered this question with one of his own. "If it were the king himself who had this disease, would you also despair of helping him?"

The physician thought a moment, then said, "In fact, the king did suffer once from this very same ailment. I told him then that there was little help. There was only one medicine that could help, and this was very difficult to find. In a distant land lives a very rare bird, that is very hard to trap. If the patient were to eat the flesh of this bird, he would be cured.

"The king, with servants, armies, and ships at his disposal, sent a troop of soldiers to that distant land. They spread throughout the land, tracked down one of the rare birds, and managed to trap it. They brought it back to the king, who ate it and was indeed cured of his disease. But how is a simple person to get hold of such a bird?"

R' Akiva Eiger went home and began to pray to Hashem. "Master of the Universe, Your sons are also kings, and the sons of

Vayechi / 237

238 / STORIES MY GRANDFATHER TOLD ME

kings! And now, one of Your sons needs help. He needs that rare bird. Send her to us."

Not much time had passed, when there was suddenly a rapping at the window. A bird was there. R' Akiva Eiger gave orders that it be caught and cooked, and the sick man was fed its flesh. Only the wings, on R' Akiva Eiger's instructions, remained in his own home.

And, indeed, after eating of the bird the patient recovered completely from his illness!

When R' Akiva heard that the king's physician was once again in his town, he sent him the bird's wings. Seeing them, the doctor exclaimed, "Only a Jew could accomplish such a thing!"

Total Concentration

אֲשֶׁר לָקַחְתִּי מִיַּד הָאֱמֹרִי בְּחַרְבִּי וּבְקַשְׁתִּי

"Which I took from the hand of the Emorite with my sword and with my bow."

(Bereishis 48:22)

" 'With my sword and with my bow' — this means my wisdom and my prayer." (Rashi)

The *Chevrah Kaddisha* (Burial Society) in the town of Lvov had a notebook in which they jotted down significant facts about the bodies they handled. In describing the body of the Turei Zahav (the *Taz*), they mentioned that he was buried in a very torn *tallis*. This *tallis* was old and worn, and he had wrapped himself in it to *daven* for many long years.

In fact, when the women of the town had seen their Rav standing and *davening* in such an old, torn *tallis*, they had decided to collect money and buy him a brand-new one. They bought a beautiful *tallis* and presented it to the *Taz*.

The *Taz* looked at the gift, and then said to the women, "Thank you very much for your goodness and your generosity, but I have no desire to wear a new *tallis*. This old one will bear witness for me in the World to Come. It will testify that I never entertained a stray thought during *Shemoneh Esrei*."

R' Aharon of Karlin once related to his *kallah,* who was the granddaughter of the Maggid of Koznitz, that the Maggid was so weak that he had to be carried to shul for *davening.* But when they reached the verse, *"Shiru la'Hashem shir chadash"* ("Sing a new song unto Hashem"), the Maggid lifted the corners of his coat and danced with all his might in honor of his Creator.

Sparing No Effort

אֲשֶׁר לָקַחְתִּי מִיַּד הָאֱמֹרִי בְּחַרְבִּי וּבְקַשְׁתִּי

"Which I took from the hand of the Emorite with my sword and with my bow."
(*Bereishis* 48:22)
" 'With my sword and with my bow' — this means my wisdom and my prayer." (*Rashi*)

A certain Torah scholar tells the following story. Years ago, he met R' Yechezkel Sarna, *Rosh Yeshivah* of Chevron who had already reached an advanced age, walking late one night with the aid of his cane. R' Yechezkel was walking in the direction of the Zichron Moshe shul to *daven Ma'ariv.* Concern overwhelmed the scholar at the sight of the elderly *Rosh Yeshivah* walking with the last vestiges of his strength.

"It is questionable whether the Rav will find a *minyan* now," he ventured.

"Even for a questionable situation it is worthwhile making the effort!" R' Yechezkel replied.

In retelling this incident, the man would always add afterwards, "Ever since, any time that it is difficult for me to come to shul to *daven* with a *minyan,* I see the image of R' Yechezkel in front of me, dragging himself up the street to try to find a *minyan* for *davening,* even though the chances of finding one were slim."

R' Aharon Cohen was another *Rosh Yeshivah* of Chevron. Once, when he was ill, he traveled to the seaside town of Bat Yam. When he awoke in the morning, he saw that it was already too late to join the town's regular *minyan* for *Shacharis*. Though sick and weak, R' Aharon got up and traveled to the nearby city of Tel Aviv, certain that in such a large city he would be sure to find a *minyan*.

We Always Need Help

לִישׁוּעָתְךָ קִוִּיתִי ד׳

"For Your salvation do I long, Hashem!"
(*Bereishis* 49:18)

The Ba'al Shem Tov once sent two of his disciples to a distant place to fetch wine for Pesach. The students guarded the wine scrupulously. They supervised the grapes during harvesting, stood over the tramplers in the vats, and protected the wine from every harm on the road home, including keeping it away from non-Jews, lest the wine become forbidden.

But one day, to their dismay, a gentile walked into their inn and touched the wine. On their arrival, the brokenhearted students told the Ba'al Shem Tov what had occurred.

The Ba'al Shem Tov consoled them, saying, "You did everything you could to guard the wine. You invested so much effort in guarding it that you left no room for Hashem to help you protect it. As much as a person looks after himself, he still stands in need of Hashem's help. Even when we make our greatest efforts, we still require Heaven's mercy."

An Important Mitzvah

קִבְרוּ אֹתִי אֶל אֲבֹתָי
"Bury me with my fathers"
(*Bereishis* 49:29)

In the year 5660 [1900], a *talmid chacham* passed away in Jerusalem. The funeral took place on the eve of the seventh day of Pesach, and R' Yosef Chaim Sonnenfeld was present to accompany the departed to the Mount of Olives cemetery.

As the funeral procession passed through the Dung Gate, it suddenly encountered the Arabic "Nebi Moussa" procession which was taking place at the same time. A crowd of Arabs, 30,000 strong, was coming from the direction of Jericho.

This was a period when Moslems regularly acted with violence toward the Jews. If a "Nebi Moussa" day ended without Jewish blood being spilled, the citizens of Jerusalem were overjoyed.

The funeral group knew that if they did not hurry, the road to the Mount of Olives would be closed to them, delaying the burial. They decided at once that the elderly among them would return to the city, while the younger men, together with the members of the *Chevrah Kaddisha* (Burial Society), would carry the coffin on their shoulders and run to the cemetery.

One of these men approached R' Yosef Chaim and respectfully asked that he return to the city, because there was great need of haste to reach the Mount of Olives before the throng of Arabs arrived. R' Yosef Chaim did not reply, but only quickened his pace to keep up with the younger men.

The funeral procession had not yet arrived at their destination when thousands of Moslems approached, shouting wild cries. At their head marched Sheikh Neimer Effendi. A deadly fear descended on the Jews. They knew very well how such a meeting might end.

Then, to the astonishment of all, R' Yosef Chaim Sonnenfeld suddenly straightened up, climbed onto a nearby wall, and raised his hands to the Sheikh, asking him to stop his mob. With bated breath, the small group of Jews watched to see what would happen. With wonder, they saw the Arab procession come to a halt. Sheikh Effendi approached R' Yosef Chaim and said that because he respected him, he would wait until the funeral procession had passed.

R' Yosef Chaim thanked him, and continued with the other Jews to the Mount of Olives.

～～～

R' Noach Yitzchak Diskin, younger brother of the *gaon* of Brisk, R' Yehoshua Leib Diskin, was headed for the old cemetery in Lomza. The authorities had closed the cemetery to further burial because of severe overcrowding, and since then the Jews had been using a new burying ground.

R' Noach Yitzchak entered the structure in which his father, R' Binyamin Diskin, was buried, and found that one of its walls was crumbling. R' Noach Yitzchak sent off a letter to his older brother asking, among other things, if he should have the wall repaired. To his surprise, R' Yehoshua Leib wrote back responding to all the other matters that his brother had asked about, but regarding the broken wall he made no reply at all.

"Perhaps my brother forgot to answer that question," R' Noach Yitzchak thought, and hurried to send a second letter to his brother in Jerusalem. But this time, too, R' Yehoshua Leib ignored the question.

Years passed. The crumbling wall was not repaired, but it stayed upright. Then, one day, the town of Lomza received bitter news: R' Noach Yitzchak had passed away. Grieving for their loss, the townspeople gathered to accompany R' Noach Yitzchak to his final resting place.

Suddenly, a cemetery watchman came running to the *Chevrah Kaddisha*. "During the night, the wall next to R' Binyamin Diskin's grave fell over. Now there's room for another grave right beside his!"

"Really?" The listeners were astounded. At once, men of influence hurried over to speak to the town's governing authority, to convince him to permit R' Noach Yitzchak to be buried alongside his father.

"But no one has been buried in that cemetery for 40 years!" the governor protested. However, when he heard about the wall that had crumbled during the night, making room for the son to be buried next to his father, he issued a special permit to allow the burial to go forward.

Only then did the people of Lomza realize why R' Yehoshua Leib had neglected to answer his brother's question about the repair of that cemetery wall. Now they understood the secret behind his silence.

A Full Pardon

וַיֹּאמֶר אֲלֵהֶם יוֹסֵף אַל תִּירָאוּ כִּי הֲתַחַת אֱלֹקִים אָנִי.
וְאַתֶּם חֲשַׁבְתֶּם עָלַי רָעָה אֱלֹקִים חֲשָׁבָהּ לְטֹבָה

*But Yosef said to them, "Fear not, for am I instead of G-d?
Although you intended me harm, G-d intended it for good."*

(*Bereishis* 50:19-20)

When R' Yosef Dov HaLevi Soloveitchik, author of the *Beis HaLevi*, was a young man, he wanted very badly to meet the *gaon* of his generation, R' Shlomo Kluger, the Rav of Brody in Galicia. The trip from Lithuania to Galicia was very expensive, and R' Yosef Dov had no money. He went over to a man who was a wagon driver in Galicia, and offered himself as an apprentice. On the road, the wagon driver grew infuriated at his inexperienced apprentice. He berated R' Yosef Dov and even beat him.

On their arrival in Brody, R' Yosef Dov went directly to the home of R' Shlomo Kluger, who received him graciously and discussed Torah topics with him. R' Shlomo was struck with the Lithuanian youngster's keen grasp and understanding, and invited him to lecture in the town's largest shul.

The townspeople gathered to hear the young visitor's lecture. Among them was the wagon driver. When he saw who the speaker was, a shadow covered his face. "He is a *gaon*, and I abused and beat him!"

When R' Yosef Dov finished his lecture, the wagon driver approached him shamefacedly, to beg his forgiveness. R' Yosef Dov comforted him, saying, "If you had beat me for not knowing how to learn Torah, you would have done something wrong. But you beat me only because I did not know how to care for horses and a wagon. And you were absolutely right! I don't know the first thing about them!"

Returning Good in Place of Bad

וְאַתֶּם חֲשַׁבְתֶּם עָלַי רָעָה אֱלֹקִים חֲשָׁבָהּ לְטֹבָה
"Although you intended me harm, G-d intended it for good"
(*Bereishis* 50:20)

One day, R' Meir Alter, the oldest son of the Imrei Emes of Ger, emerged from his father's room shaken and angry. He met a friend, and told him what had happened.

"A man used to come here from time to time, and my father always received him warmly, with special tokens of affection. I never understood why my father took such pains to draw such a simple and unlearned man close to him that way.

"Today, I found out why.

"The man was wicked. He used to hate and persecute my father, though he pretended to be interested in his welfare. Once, he decided to spread evil gossip about my father, and wrote a letter denouncing him to the royal palace in Petersburg. At the same time, he sent a second letter to my father, a letter filled with words of friendship. If the first letter had reached its destination, my father would have been carted off to prison in chains. But Heaven watched over my father; the letters were switched. The letter of denunciation reached my father instead.

"Many years have passed since then. The man has continued to come to our house as he always did, without any shame. And my father, who prefers to return good for bad, did not reject him or say a word to him about the subject. In fact, the opposite is true: My father drew him close and treated him as a special friend.

"I just saw the letter of denunciation and learned the whole story. That's why I'm so furious!"

This volume is part of
THE ARTSCROLL SERIES®
an ongoing project of
translations, commentaries and expositions
on Scripture, Mishnah, Talmud, Halachah,
liturgy, history, the classic Rabbinic writings,
biographies and thought.

For a brochure of current publications
visit your local Hebrew bookseller
or contact the publisher:

Mesorah Publications, ltd

4401 Second Avenue
Brooklyn, New York 11232
(718) 921-9000
www.artscroll.com